He said, Sidhe said. . . .

Now, having heard *husband*, I hadn't paid a lot of attention to the rest of what the blonde chick had said. I mean, I was cool, totally dignified, but a little stunned, you know? I couldn't think of anything to say until we were alone again and the babe was trying to explain about how they were separated and I didn't have anything to worry about.

"He's the king?"

"Yes."

"And that would make you . . . ?"

"The queen."

Of the fairies as it turns out. No, not those kinds of fairies. Real fairies. Like in fairy tales. We got dressed and she led me out onto his balcony tree-branch thing and well, it was pretty damned clear I wasn't in Kansas anymore if you know what I mean.

I just did the Queen of the Fairies. Prime!

—from "He Said, Sidhe Said" by Tanya Huff

Faerie Tales

EDITED BY

Martin H. Greenberg
and
Russell Davis

DAW BOOKS, INC.
DONALD A. WOLLHEIM, FOUNDER
375 Hudson Street, New York, NY 10014

ELIZABETH R. WOLLHEIM
SHEILA E. GILBERT
PUBLISHERS
www.dawbooks.com

DAW TRADEMARK REGISTERED
U.S. PAT. OFF. AND FOREIGN COUNTRIES
—MARCA REGISTRADA
HECHO EN U.S.A.

PRINTED IN THE U.S.A.

ACKNOWLEDGMENTS

CONTENTS

Introduction

Russell Davis

I love the idea of *faerie*. Another world, not all that far from ours, where elves and pixies dance among dryad groves, and occasionally venture into our world to do deeds mischievous or heroic. It's not just the magic of it all that appeals (though the magic part is very cool), but the sense of something extraworldly. Something like us, but not quite us: magical yet fallible.

Theme anthologies, at least for me, have always been a bit like I imagine the land of faerie: a potpourri of places, races, and ideas that make a unique tapestry. I am continually surprised by the ingenuity of the authors and the stories they tell—sometimes what I expect, more often not. And that is what makes editing one of these such fun. Even when stories sometimes deal with the same basic premise (here, there are at least two tales that deal with a stolen child), seeing how each author makes it his or her own is really quite magical.

For this anthology, the possibilities were almost limitless: any story dealing with creatures from the land of faerie, the land itself, interactions with, so on and so forth. Yet many of the authors focused on children and childhood—perhaps because so many of us associate the world of faerie with our youth, and perhaps with youth in general. A world of magic, where people live forever and all things are possible if you wish for it hard enough.

Come to think of it, it sounds pretty wonderful even as an adult.

And for those of you wishing to escape to that place of magic, or yearning to hear tales of what comes from trifling with the creatures of faerie, the stories here will not disappoint.

Charles de Lint offers a love story of a temporary sort in "Sweet Forget-Me-Not," while Tim Waggoner tells a story of time and trees in "The September People."

In "Yellow Tide Foam," Sarah Hoyt's characters discover that the side effects of some drugs quite literally take them away, while Tanya Huff checks in with a hilarious tale of skateboards in "He Said, Sidhe Said."

Wen Spencer's "Wyvern" is an action-filled story about the human world and the world of faerie colliding within the point of view of two very different individuals, and Elizabeth Anne Scarborough offers a musical story in "The Filial Fiddler."

These, and the other stories here, like Michelle West's "The Stolen Child" or Adam Stemple's "A Piece of Flesh," give us glimpses into the world of faerie or our own, share with us how different we are . . . and how much alike.

I can't speak for the authors, but I suspect that writing about the land and people of faerie fills in them a need to engage that magic for a brief moment and share it with others. Is it possible that the magic we long for from that otherworld is accessible to us here? I don't really know, but if we wish for it hard enough . . .

If you turn the page, I guess you'll find out, won't you?

SWEET FORGET-ME-NOT

Charles de Lint

Charles de Lint is a full-time writer and musician who presently makes his home in Ottawa,
Canada, with his wife MaryAnn Harris, an artist
and musician. His most recent books are *Spirits
in the Wires* and *A Circle of Cats,* a picture
book illustrated by Charles Vess. Other recent
publications include the collections *Waifs &
Strays* and *Tapping the Dream Tree* and the
trade paperback edition of *The Onion Girl.* For
more information about his work, visit his Web
site at http://www.charlesdelint.com.

"**Y**ou don't want to get involved with the likes of
them."

I turned to see who'd spoken, feeling a little nervous
because I was skipping school, but it was only Ernie,
the old guy who did odd jobs around the neighborhood. He had a little apartment in back of the Seafair
Theatre, but I guess he didn't spend much time there
because you'd see him out in the streets at all hours
of the day and night.

I've heard my parents tut-tutting about him, the way

lots of people in the neighborhood do. Everybody seems to think it's a shame that a person can live their life the way he does, day to day, with no ambition. But I don't see a lack of ambition as that bad a personality trait. I mean, what if you don't have this drive to succeed at something? Are you supposed to pretend you do, just to fit in?

My parents would say yes. That's if they could even understand the question.

"Involved with who?" I asked.

I could hear my mom correcting my grammar in my head. Being an immigrant, she was very particular about how we use the language of her adopted country. I know she means well, but it gets old.

"Don't play the fool with me, boy," Ernie said. "I'm talking about that gaggle of girls you've been staring at for the last ten minutes."

"You can see them?"

"Do I look blind?"

I shook my head. "But nobody else seems to notice them."

"That's because most people *are* blind."

They'd have to be.

It was the color of them that first attracted my attention, and I don't just mean their clothing or their race. There seemed to be around six of them, but I kept losing count. Their hair was a wild tangle of curls ranging in color from a rich mauve to shocking pink. The ones with loose pants had tight tops, the ones with baggy shirts wore tights under them, and they all had clunky shoes that didn't seem to cause them the least bit of a problem as they danced and pirouetted about, as light on their feet as ballerinas. The color of their clothes was as wild as their hair—bright yellows, reds, pinks, and greens—and there wasn't much to them. They were just a gang of tall, skinny girls with narrow features and the same Mediterranean cast to their skin that I have.

"So what are they doing?" I asked as we watched them dance about.

They were singing something, too, but I couldn't make out the words. I could tell it had a beat, though. A little hip-hop, a little rhyming set to a finger-snapping beat.

"What do you think?" Ernie said. "They're having fun."

"I thought maybe they were stoned."

He laughed. "They don't need stimulants to have fun."

Well, they looked totally blissed-out to me, but what did I know? I still couldn't figure out how they could be having such a grand time, dancing and goofing around the way they were—and the way they looked—but nobody seemed to notice. I know people get jaded, but you'd think *somebody* would turn and have a look as they walked by the alley where the girls were having their fun, if only to shake their heads and then go on.

But there was only me, turned the wrong way around on a bus stop bench and getting a crick in my neck. And now Ernie.

"Why did you say I shouldn't get involved with them?" I asked.

"Because they only stay around long enough to break your heart."

"What's that supposed to mean?"

"They're gemmin," Ernie said. "Little mobile histories of a place. Kind of like fairies, if you think of them as the spirits of a place."

"Yeah, right."

He shrugged. "You asked, so I'm telling you."

"Fairies."

"Except they're called gemmin. They soak up stories and memories, and then one day they're all full up and off they go."

I couldn't believe this stupid story of his, but I couldn't help wanting to know more at the same time. Because there was the plain fact that *no one* seemed to notice them but us.

"So where do they go?" I asked.

"I don't know. I just know they go and they don't come back. Not the same ones, anyway."

I gave him a look. "What's that supposed to mean?"

"You're pretty full of questions, boy. Don't you have someplace better to be, like school?"

"I don't like school."

"Yeah, well, I'm with you on that." He shakes his head. "When I think of all the crap they expect you to remember—like it's ever going to be any use unless you become a brain surgeon or an accountant."

"No, I don't mind learning," I said. "I kind of like that part of it."

"Sure," he said. "If it's something you *want* to learn, right? But you can get that out of a library."

I shook my head. "No, I find it all pretty interesting."

He shook his head like he thought *I* was the one who was weird. He's not alone. Can you say nerd? That's me.

"Then what's the problem?" he asked.

"I just don't . . . you know, get along with the other kids much."

He nodded. "You telling them stuff they don't want to hear?"

"It's more like them telling me."

He'd been standing beside me on the sidewalk, but now he took a seat on the bench.

"What's your name?" he asked.

"Ahmad Nasrallah."

"Well, what are they ragging you about? You look like a nice, normal kid."

"No, I look like a terrorist."

He studied me for a long moment, then gave me another nod, a slow one this time.

"Because of the color of your skin," he said.

"Yeah. And my name. But my family's not from Afghanistan or Iraq or whatever. We're Lebanese. We're not even Muslims—although I guess my parents were before they emigrated. But I was born right here in this city."

"There's nothing wrong being Muslim," Ernie said. "There's bad apples in whatever way you want to group people—doesn't matter if it's religious, political, or social. The big mistake is generalizing."

"Doesn't stop them from doing it."

"Yeah, people are like that." He smiled. "And there's another generalization for you."

"So did you have trouble in school, too?" I asked.

"Oh, yeah. I was like a trouble magnet. And opening my mouth didn't help much either."

"So that's what you meant when you asked if I was telling people things they don't want to hear."

He nodded. "I had me a big mouth, no question. But the real problem was I couldn't stop talking about . . . them."

He didn't look at the gemmin, but I knew who he meant.

I couldn't imagine telling anybody at school about them. Why would I give the kids more ammunition?

"Why'd you do it?" I asked. "You had to know they'd make fun of you."

He shrugged. "It started in grade school, when I didn't know any better and the teasing just followed me through the years—long after I'd stopped talking about it. But the thing is, if anybody asked me straight out, I couldn't lie. Not because of who was asking, but because I thought lying would diminish the gemmin." He gave me a sad smile. "Like in *Peter Pan*, you know?"

I shook my head.

"Every time a kid says they don't believe in fairies, another one of them dies."

"Is that true?"

"I don't think so now. But it seemed possible back then. I didn't realize that they weren't dying. It's hard to see from here, but their eyes are the most amazing sapphire blue that turns to violet as they get filled up with the little histories around them. And once they do fill up, they leave."

I thought about that, then asked, "What did you mean about the same ones not coming back? Who does come back?"

"Coming back's not exactly the right way to describe it. You see those bits of color that seemed to spin off them sometimes, when they're dancing really hard?"

I nodded. "I thought they were ribbons or confetti or something."

"I don't know what they are either. But if you watch one long enough, you'll see it kind of disappears into the ground. I don't know what happens underground, out of our sight, but something does. Either a piece of that color incubates down there, or a bunch of them gather together, but eventually, when the ones we're looking at are gone, some new gemmin will come sprouting up."

He smiled, a faraway look in his eyes.

"They're just like the fairies I remember in the stories I read as a kid," he went on after a moment. "When they're new, I mean. Tiny, perfect little creatures."

"And then they grow up to be like these?"

The ones we were looking at seemed to be in their early to mid-teens, around my age, which was still fifteen. I wouldn't turn sixteen until next month. Unlike a lot of the girls in school who were already all curves and breasts, the gemmin were skinny, flat-chested, and almost hipless. They could almost be boys, except you knew from their faces that they were girls. And though they didn't have a lot of shape to them, they were still hot, like you'd see in some magazine.

I imagined kissing one of them and felt my neck and face get warm.

"They're really . . . sexy, aren't they?" I found myself saying.

Ernie laughed. "Not to me. I just see a bunch of cute kids. But I remember I felt different when I was your age."

"You're not that old."

But then I had to wonder how old he was. I figured he had to be at least forty, which was older than I could ever imagine being. Your life'd pretty much be over by then. I just had to look at my parents and their friends. They never seemed to have any fun, except every once in a while at a wedding or something, when they'd get a little goofy after having too much wine.

"I'm old enough to be their father," Ernie said. He said it in a certain tone of voice that made me think, for a moment, that he was going to rub my head, the way Uncle Joe does. "I don't rob cradles, Ahmad."

Whatever.

"So do they live here?" I asked. "In this alley?"

Ernie shook his head. "You'll see them all over the city—different little groups of them—but this bunch usually comes back here. They seem to have laid claim to our neighborhood, and that Dodge in particular."

He was talking about the junked station wagon that had been abandoned at the back of the alley. You see useless cars like that all the time around this part of town. They'll be in an empty lot or behind some building for a few months, slowly getting stripped of usable parts. Eventually somebody in one of the neighboring buildings gets the city to have it towed away.

"I've lived here all my life," I said, "so how come I've never seen them before?"

"Maybe you never really needed to."

"What's that supposed to mean?"

He shrugged. "How were you feeling when you first sat down on this bench?"

"I was fine."

"No, really. You told me you were skipping school. That the kids there had been ragging on you."

"Okay. So maybe I was a little pissed off."

"And sad? Or at least feeling hurt?"

"Yeah, whatever."

I didn't know where this was going, but it was making me uncomfortable to talk about it.

"And how do you feel now?" he asked.

"I told you, I feel fine."

"Maybe even a little happy?"

Then I realized what he was getting at. If I was going to be honest, I felt a *lot* better now than when I'd first gotten here. Before I'd noticed the gemmin and sat down, I'd been fantasizing about how I could get back at Joey Draves and the Ross brothers—the ones that were riding me the hardest. They weren't alone, but the other kids that gave me a rough time were just echoing Joey and his gang. Trying to show how they were cool, too. It didn't seem to help them much, but they didn't stop either. The only way it'd ever stop was if Joey and the Ross brothers laid off, and that wasn't going to happen any time soon. It was like I'd become a pet project for them.

But the funny thing was, while the fantasy of getting back at them was still a going concern—sitting there somewhere in my head where the stuff you can't get away from does—right now I couldn't really muster up a whole lot of anger towards them.

"Yeah, I guess," I told Ernie. I wasn't looking at him as I spoke, but at the gemmin. It was hard *not* to look at them. "I feel pretty good, actually."

"I've noticed that over the years," Ernie said. "The people who do seem to become aware of them are the ones that need a little help with the load they're carrying. It doesn't seem to work for everybody who's feeling bad. I've seen depressed people walk right through a crowd of gemmin and never notice them. But when people do, it's usually when they're feeling low."

"And then they start feeling better," I said. "Like magic."

Ernie laughed. "Hell, they *are* magic. But it's not some kind of cure-all. It's more like they give you a respite. A bit of time to regroup and take stock of the big picture, you know?"

I looked at him and shook my head.

"No matter how good a reason a person's got for

feeling bad," he said, "a change of perspective is sometimes all you need to get back on track again."

"And that's what they're for?" I asked.

He laughed again. "Not likely. I think the feeling good part is just a side effect of being around them. You know, you take in the pure joy that they seem to find in life and you can't help but feeling a little better yourself. But they're not here for us. They just *are*."

"They're something, all right."

"So sometimes," Ernie went on, "when I run across a person who seems to be feeling pretty down, I try to steer them to wherever the nearest gemmin are hanging out—just in case it can help, you know?"

So he did have an ambition—it was just a weird and useless one that you couldn't talk to anyone about, except another loser like me.

"How'd you figure out all of this stuff?" I asked.

"They told me."

I turned to look at the gemmin, still fooling around in the alley. Singing and dancing. I wondered what they'd tell me if I could get up the nerve to talk to them.

"They like meeting people," Ernie said, as though he was reading my mind. Maybe he was just reading my face. "They like making friends. The trouble is—"

I remembered what he'd said before, and finished it for him: "They end up breaking your heart."

"That pretty much sums it up."

There was a look in his eyes that I'd never seen before and I knew that when he talked about a broken heart it had nothing to do with what you hear in the songs on the Top 40. It wasn't even like when Sandy Lohnes broke up with me last spring because she didn't want to be going steady with somebody whose relatives were probably all terrorists. It wasn't anything she ever said, and I didn't think she actually believed it herself, but we both knew that was the reason all the same. It was what people were saying to her—the black cloud hanging over me starting to include her as well.

I carried a lot of anger around when she dumped me. Sadness, too, but it was nothing like what I saw in Ernie's eyes.

"I think I have to go talk to them anyway," I said.

Ernie nodded. "Yeah. I figured as much."

I wanted to explain it to him, but he got up then and gave me a little salute, index finger tipping away from his brow, and headed off down the sidewalk. It was just as well. I wouldn't have been able to find the words anyway.

It took me a while to get up my nerve, but finally I pushed myself up from the bench. I shoved my hands deep in the pockets of my cargo pants and kind of shuffled over until I could lean up against the wall, close enough to hear what they were singing. Turned out the words weren't in English. Maybe they couldn't speak English and I wasn't about to try Lebanese.

They noticed me, the way girls notice guys on a street corner, or at the mall, sort of not looking at you, but you can tell they're checking you out. They didn't seem to think I was a total loser—I guess they hadn't been talking to Joey Draves—but I was starting to feel like one anyway. They were just so . . . special. And I'm not, except to my mom and dad. And most of the time to my sister—when I wasn't bugging her. Nothing major, just the usual kid brother stuff.

I was trying to think of a way to just do a quick

fade away when the one with the brightest pink hair and this big baggy yellow shirt came up and leaned against the wall beside me, mimicking the way I was standing. The others started to giggle and I thought, oh great. It's even going to happen to me here. But then she grinned and took my hands, pulling me over to where the others were still dancing.

I tried to hold back—I'm the definition of two left feet—but she was stronger than she looked.

"Come on," she said. "What are you so scared of?"

Everything, I wanted to tell her.

"I'm not so good," I told her instead. "You know, at dancing and stuff."

"Then I'll have to teach you."

"You don't want to do that."

"But I do. You can see us. That means you could be our friend and we like having friends."

"Yeah, but—"

"And friends have to dance together."

One of the other girls started making this kind of bass-y noise with her mouth, setting a beat. The others kept time with their feet, clunky shoes tapping the pavement. One of them chimed in with a kind of *shouka-shouka* counter rhythm and then the one holding my hands began to sway back and forth.

"Just find the rhythm," she said. "Move your hips. Like this."

She was skinny under that baggy shirt, but she was sexy as all get-out. No way I could do what she was doing—not and look good the way she did. But when I started to shake my head, she slipped behind me and put her hands on my hips, showing me how to find the beat.

"What's your name?" she asked.

Her voice was right in my ear and I could smell her

breath. It was sweet and spicy at the same time, nothing like any other girl's I'd ever been this close to before, which so far has only been three. And I never did kiss one of them—I mean, real kissing. We didn't touch tongues.

"I'm Troon," she said when I told her my name.

The other girls chorused strange words that I realized were their names:

"Shivy."

"Mita."

"Omal."

"Neenie."

"Alaween."

And never once lost the music they were making while they did it. Their names became part of the music. I heard my own in there, too, made even more exotic by the sound of their sweet, husky voices.

Troon let go of my hips and came around in front of me again, the others girls circling around as we danced. Or while they danced and I tried.

But I have to admit, while dancing's nothing I'd ever done in public, I'd tried it lots in my bedroom in front of the mirror. Mostly it was just me trying to figure out how not to make too big an ass of myself, just in case I ever got up the nerve to go to a school dance again. But I did it for fun, too. I'd even tried belly dancing.

My sister Suha took it up for a while because it seemed like an interesting way of doing aerobics with the added bonus of putting her in touch with a part of our cultural heritage. She said. I think it was just a way to put on a sexy show at weddings and stuff, but in a way that our parents couldn't say was improper.

So anyway, I tried a couple of those moves with the gemmin, and sure enough, they all squealed with laughter and I wished I could disappear into a crack in the pavement. But then I realized they were laughing with me, not at me, and they were all started trying to shake their tummies like I'd just done.

That afternoon ended up being the best fun I'd ever had. Troon was the one who'd first got me dancing with them, but the one who really seemed to take a shine to me was Neenie. She was a little shorter than the rest, which made her about my five-six, and had the most perfect sky-blue eyes I've ever seen. Her hair was a tangle of tiny mauve braids and she was wearing big red cargo pants and a tight little pinkish top that showed off her belly button.

And when I finally left to go home for supper, she's the one who came up and gave me a kiss.

"You'll come back, won't you?" she asked.

I was still feeling the press of her body against me and the kiss that was tingling on my lips, and I couldn't find my voice. So I just nodded.

Somebody saw me that afternoon, dancing in the alley with the gemmin, except they didn't see the gemmin, only me. Dancing by myself beside a junked out old station wagon.

I don't know who it was, but Joey got hold of the story and by noon it was all over the school. I guess it made a change from them calling me "Osama," or—the height of Joey's stupid repartee—"Al Kida," but I didn't feel any better.

We were out in the schoolyard and they were all in a loose circle around me. I just kept trying to walk away, but whatever part of the circle I approached closed tight as soon as I got near it. Then Joey said something about me dancing with some wet dream in my head and I lost it. And I understood what Ernie'd meant about having to tell the truth about the gemmin, because doing otherwise diminished even the idea of them. At least in my head.

I didn't say anything, but I took a swing at Joey. He ducked it easily and gave me a shove that knocked me off my feet. A moment later we were grappling— I was just trying to hold onto him so that he wouldn't be able to hit me—but then we got busted by Mr. Finn and sent to the principal's office.

Once we were there, Mr. Taggart started lecturing us about how they had zero tolerance for violence on school property. I wondered where the zero tolerance was when Joey and his buddies were ragging on me all the time, but I knew there was no point in bringing it up. That's the way it always goes. Guys like Joey *always* get away with it. Mr. Taggart probably agreed with Joey that I should just go back to Afghanistan even though I'd never even been there before.

To get him to shut up, I told Mr. Taggart that I'd started it.

That got me a three-day suspension and I knew my parents were going to kill me. Though maybe that was the least of my worries, since the last thing Joey said as we were walking down the hall—him on his way to class, me going home to face the music—was, "This isn't over, Osama."

And I knew it wasn't. I guess the best thing about the suspension was that I was going to have three days before he beat the crap out of me—actually, five, I realized, since today was a Tuesday. The worst thing was that I got grounded for two weeks. My parents were really disappointed in me and Dad was into a major lecture before Suha spoke up for me.

"You should be proud of him for standing up for himself," she said, not realizing that this time I'd been standing up for the gemmin. "You should hear the things they call us. Ahmad gets it way worse than me."

"What kind of things?" Dad asked.

I saw him deflate as Suha told him about the whole terrorist business that had been dogging us since 9/11 and realized that he'd probably been the brunt of some of that same crap himself. But then he straightened in his chair.

"Is this true?" he asked me.

I shrugged.

"First thing in the morning," he said, "I'm going to have a talk with that principal of yours."

"Dad, no!" Suha and I cried at the same time.

It took us a while to convince him that talking to the principal would only make things worse, but finally, he nodded his reluctant agreement.

"Still, fighting's not the answer," he told me. "I want you to remember that."

"I will," I said, wondering what he'd have to say when I came back from school on Monday after Joey'd made good his threat.

"So you're still grounded. And no TV for a week. Suha will get your homework and I expect you to study here at home, just as if you were in school."

The studying part wasn't hard. I wasn't lying to Ernie when I told him that I like learning. But it's hard to do it on your own, all day long. The second day of my suspension I went out and sat on the fire escape that we use as a balcony and stared down the alleyway, wishing I could be with the gemmin. But I knew better than to try to sneak off. One of the neighbors would see me and they'd tell my parents and then who knew how long I'd be grounded.

So I sat there on the steps, feeling sorry for myself,

when I suddenly heard a bang on the metal steps behind me, like something big had just fallen onto them. I turned, my heart pounding because—don't ask me how he'd get there—I was sure it was Joey. Except it wasn't. It was Neenie. I don't know how she got there either, but the noise I'd heard was her jumping on the fire escape to get my attention.

"You didn't come see us," she said.

"I couldn't."

"But you said you would. I thought you liked me."

"I *do* like you. It's just . . ."

"Complicated," she finished for me and came to sit on the step me. "That's the trouble with being a people. *Everything's* complicated."

"It's not for you?"

"No, should it be?"

I shook my head. "No, I'm glad it's simple for you. I wish it was simple for me."

"Make it simple."

I smiled. "Easier said than done."

"Then say it at least."

It took me a moment, but then I realized she was asking me to tell her my problems. I remembered what Ernie had said, how the gemmin collected stories, so I thought, why not? She was probably the only person I could tell my troubles to who wouldn't have to feel the weight of them because they didn't touch her life.

When I was done she locked that perfect blue gaze of hers on mine. Then she leaned close and kissed me. Long. Tongue slipping into my mouth. When we came up for air I was feeling flushed and had to hold my legs together so that she wouldn't see the growing bulge in my pants.

Neenie licked her lips. "You taste good," she said.

"You do, too."

She did. All sweet and spicy, like her breath. I guess all the gemmin were like that. Must be their diet.

"I wish you felt better," she added.

Right now I felt like I was in heaven and I told her so.

She laughed. "Were you ever there?"

"No, but it's supposed to be a place where everything's perfect and that's how I feel right now."

"That's good. I feel heaveny, too."

I don't suppose anyone's ever had a stranger girlfriend—except Ernie, I guess. We spent that afternoon together, moving from the fire escape into my room. I played her some CDs, which she liked a lot, humming along and tapping her toes on the floor. I wondered if it was bothering Mrs. Robins downstairs, but she never came up to complain—and believe me, she would have.

So we listened to music and we necked and we talked and then necked some more. The afternoon went by in a blur. It took her a while to understand the concept of being grounded, but once she did, she promised she'd come back the next day. And she did. It was harder on the weekend because Suha was in and out of the apartment all day and my parents were home, but she snuck into my room at night and we lay on the bed whispering and kissing until we fell asleep. I never had to worry about anyone catching her in there with me in the morning because nobody but me could see her anyway.

Then came Monday and I had to go to school. Dad reminded me about not fighting and I reminded him that I understood. Mom's eyes were a little misty as she sent us off. She didn't know about Joey's threat, but I guess she didn't like the idea of her kids getting treated badly.

It wasn't so bad for Suha—maybe because she was a girl. She wasn't my idea of pretty—I mean, God, she was my sister—but I knew guys were always totally checking her out. And it helped that her boyfriend threatened to beat the crap out of Joey the first time he tried to do his little game on her.

But I didn't have anyone to stand up for me. The few friends I'd had before all of this started were as small or smaller than me. You couldn't miss us. We were the nerd squad that every school has, and while we all desperately wanted to be part of the cool crowd, we spent most of our time just trying to not be noticed. It was safer that way.

Joey waited until after school to make good on his threat.

Suha went off to the mall with some friends, so I had to walk home by myself. I was just as glad. There was no way to stop this from happening, so I'd rather she wasn't there when it did. Not just because I didn't want her to see me humiliated, but to keep her safe in case things got out of hand. She did ask me if I wanted company on the way home, but I told her no.

"I think he's just going to let it slide," I told her, and conveniently didn't mention the dark looks Joey'd been giving me all day. "He didn't even rag me at lunch."

"Okay. If you think you'll be all right."

"I'll be fine."

So I was alone when they herded me into the empty lot behind that strip of thrift stores and junk shops on Grasso Street. People kept saying condos were going up there, but they'd been saying that for years. I sure wished there were condos now, but I don't suppose it would have mattered. They'd just have gotten me in some alley instead.

Joey led the festivities, the way he always did. With him were Jack and Marty Ross. Phil Kluge. A couple of other guys. More than enough to really hurt me.

I'm useless in a fight—just look what happened last week—but I wasn't going to go down without a struggle. It's not that I was feeling brave. I was probably more scared than I've ever been. But I was mad, too.

They started shoving me back and forth between them. I took a swing at Marty, but he just grinned and pushed me away. And then I saw the last thing in the world I wanted to see: the gemmin, giggling and laughing as they approached us from the far side of the lot.

"Go away!" I cried.

"Not likely, Osama," Joey said.

But I wasn't talking to him and his friends. I didn't want the gemmin getting hurt. I didn't want Neenie to see me get beat up. But then I remembered the gemmin were invisible to most people. So they wouldn't get hurt. They'd just see me humiliated.

Well, they wouldn't see me go down without a fight.

I charged Joey, but he stepped aside and stuck out his foot. And down I went.

"You want to lick my shoe, raghead?" Joey asked.

Before I could get up, they all moved in, ready to kick the crap out of me. But suddenly the gemmin were among them.

The thing I hadn't considered was that just because they were invisible to most people didn't mean they weren't there. Neenie bent down behind Joey and Mita gave him a shove. Down *he* went. Troon had a stick in her hand and she whacked it so hard against Phil's knee that the stick broke. Phil went down, too.

So did the Ross brothers and the other two guys as Omal and the other girls went after them. And once they were all down, the gemmin kicked them with their clunky shoes. In the side. On the arm and thigh and leg. Hurting them, but not damaging them. Not the way they'd have hurt me.

Shivy and Alaween ran over to me and pulled me to my feet.

"Time to go," Troon said.

And off we went.

That night when Neenie and I sat together on the fire escape, I wondered aloud if my escape was going to make things better or worse. Better would be if they'd all just ignore me and leave me alone. Worse would be if they got me some place where I wasn't about to be rescued and they really went to town.

"They won't bother you," Neenie said. "We told them you were haunted and they had to leave you alone."

"I thought most people couldn't see you."

"They can't. Only the special people like you can do it on your own. But we can be seen if want to be. And we can be heard. We went back and found them in their homes and whispered into their ears." She grinned. "I gave the meanest one a good whack on the back of the head when he wouldn't listen."

"So you guys aren't all fun and dancing," I said.

"Oh, yes, we are."

"But . . ."

She laughed. "We can be fierce, too."

"Lucky for me."

"No," she said, snuggling closer. "Lucky for me. I can't have my boyfriend too bruised to hold me."

I put my other arm around her and pulled her tightly against me.

"Or his lips to sore to kiss me," she added.

So I showed her that wasn't the case at all.

I guess she was right. I went to school the next day feeling about as nervous as I've ever felt, but Joey and his friends wouldn't even look at me, except when they thought I wouldn't notice, and then I saw something in their faces that I'd only ever seen on the faces of their victims: fear.

I'd like to say everything was perfect from there on out, but I guess life just doesn't work that way.

October turned into November and it started to get colder, especially at night. I worried about Neenie and the other gemmin, nesting in their junked car at night, but she assured me that the cold didn't bother them.

"Don't be such a worrywart," she told me. "We're not like you, scared of the cold."

But for all the strange way they lived and the fact that they were invisible to the world at large, it was hard to think of them as not like me.

Neenie gave me a potted flower for my birthday— a little blue forget-me-not. I don't know where she got it at that time of year.

"It's so you'll think of me," she said.

"I'm *always* thinking about you."

"You're so sweet."

November became December.

Around the middle of the month, Neenie and I were walking up Flood Street after school, when she paused by the Chinese grocery store to eavesdrop on a conversation between Mrs. Li and one of her customers. I kept walking, waiting for Neenie a little further down the block. Being invisible, she could get away standing beside them while they talked, but I sure couldn't.

When she joined me, tucking her hand in my arm, she lifted her face for a kiss. I was happy to oblige, but then I realized that something had changed about her. It had happened so gradually that I'd never noticed. Those blue-blue eyes of hers were almost violet now and I remembered what Ernie had told me, all those months ago.

Something tightened uncomfortably, deep in my chest.

"You . . . are you going away?" I asked.

"I have to go away," she said. "That's what we do. We're here and then we go away. You do, too."

"But . . ."

"I know. You're here walking around ever so much longer than we are. But it's still the same."

"You . . . die?

She frowned, still looking so pretty. "If you mean, do we move from one world to another, then yes. We do. But we don't think of it like that at all. It's just a part of the whole long story of our lives."

"How . . . how long do we have?"

"We're leaving when the days start to get longer again."

She meant the winter solstice. It was less than two weeks away.

I thought knowing this would change everything, and I did brood about it when we weren't together, but it's impossible to have a heavy heart when you're actually around the gemmin. Ernie was right about that, too.

On the night of the winter solstice, there came a tapping on my window and I looked up to see Neenie's face at my window. I don't know how she got up to a third floor window, but I hurried over to open it and let her in. A gust of cold wind rushed inside and made me shiver. Neenie leaned in, resting her elbows on the sill.

"We're going," she said. "Come meet me on the roof."

Then she did this sort of Spider-Man swing and went monkeying up the side of my building. I didn't hesitate. I put on a coat and shoes and snuck out of the apartment, heading for the stairs.

I thought we'd said good-bye this afternoon when I saw the group of them in the alley by their car. The parting hadn't been hard—my sadness pushed away by their presence—but I'd spent the evening feeling bleaker and bleaker before she showed up at my window.

She was waiting for me on the roof, standing out of the wind beside the little structure that's up there enclosing the top of the stairs. I shivered in the wind as I stepped out the door and joined her, knowing she'd picked this spot for my sake, not hers. She was still just wearing her baggy pants and that little shirt that showed her stomach. The only tracks in the snow leading to where we stood were mine.

"There's something wrong inside me," she said. "I don't know what it is. It feels big and heavy and sometimes it makes it hard to breathe." She lifted her hand to her eyes. "And tears keep wanting to leak out of my eyes."

I knew exactly what she meant. I'd been feeling that way all night.

"Is this what sadness feels like?" she asked.

"That's what it feels like for me."

"It's funny. I've heard about it in a lot of the stories I've collected, but I never knew what it felt like before." She sighed. "It's so heavy."

"I know."

I put my arms around her and held her close. I'd been trying to not cry all night myself.

"It's weighing me down," she said into my shoulder, her sweet, spicy breath lifting to my nose. "It's so heavy that I don't think I can go."

I felt my heart lift. But then she added:

"The others will have to go on without me."

"But . . ."

I couldn't imagine her on her own. The gemmin were such a close-knit group. Neenie and I had spent a lot of time together, but most of the time we were with the others. I think they needed to be together because I'd noticed that when Neenie and I spent too long a time away from the others, Neenie would start to get quieter and quieter. No less sweet, no less loving. But a stillness would gather around her that became poignant and unfamiliar.

"Troon said you could help me," she said. She lifted her face to look into my eyes. "Is it true? Can you help me feel not so heavy?"

I didn't want to, but I knew what I had to do. I had to let her go.

"I love you, Neenie," I told her. "And I'll always remember you. But you have to go."

"Do you want me to go?"

I shook my head. "But you have to. It's . . ." I had to swallow. "What you do."

"It is, isn't it?" she said in a small voice.

When she looked up, those violet eyes of hers were

shiny with tears, reflecting the streetlights from below. I nodded.

"And you really love me, like people do?"

"I do."

"And you'll really remember me forever and ever and always?"

"I really will."

She gave me a small smile. "I still feel sad."

"Yeah, me, too. But . . . I feel glad, too. I would never want to have missed out meeting you and knowing you and loving you. You're the best thing that ever happened to me."

"But now I'm going. Doesn't that take away from the happiness?"

I shook my head. "Nothing can take that away."

We held each other for a long moment, the wind rushing across the roof, but not touching us. Then I felt a presence. I turned and the others were there. Troon and Alaween. Mita and Omal and Shivy.

Troon walked up to me and kissed me on the brow.

"Thank you," Troon said. "We would have missed her so terribly. And she . . . she would have . . ."

"I know," I said.

One by one the others came up and gave me a kiss and a hug. And then there was just my Neenie.

"You think of me, too," I told her.

"Oh, I couldn't not," she said. "You're the biggest part of all the stories I carry inside me."

Then she kissed me, too, long and hard and sweet.

And they were gone.

I stood there, staring across the city, alone except for the wind, then I went back downstairs to my bedroom.

Ernie was wrong, I thought, as I sat at my desk.

They don't break your heart. They fill it up and the memory of that never goes away. Not unless you let it.

I took out a pad and a pen and I started to write.

I went to Ernie's apartment on Boxing Day. I brought him a wrapped-up box with some of Mom's baklava in it and his face lit up with pleasure when he took off the wrapping and opened the box.

"I can't remember the last time somebody gave me a Christmas present," he said.

He took me into his kitchen and made us some tea. We talked a while, about the neighborhood. Like him, I'd learned to pay attention to all the small stories that ebbed and flowed through its blocks—something we'd learned from the gemmin. It was just a natural part of our lives now.

"They're gone again," he said after awhile.

I nodded. "They left on the solstice."

"Any regrets?"

"Not one. No, maybe one. That I couldn't go with them."

"Yeah, I know that feeling." He hesitated for a moment, then leaned forward across the kitchen table. "Don't end up like me, Ahmad. Don't let this define your life. The neighborhood doesn't need another guy like me."

"Not even when you're gone?"

"Hey, I'm not that old."

"I know." I looked down at my tea, then back at him. "Just before Christmas break my English teacher gave me this flyer . . . about a workshop that's going to be at the library in the new year."

"What kind of workshop?"

"For people who want to be writers. It's being given by this local writer named Christy Riddell, so I took out a couple of his books from the library, and you know what? He's got a story in one of them about the gemmin. He didn't see them, but a friend of his did and he wrote about it."

"So you're going to be a writer?"

"I don't know. I'm going to try. My parents'll hate the idea. They're pretty set on me being a doctor or a lawyer. Somebody important."

"Maybe they'll surprise you."

"Maybe."

"Are you going to write about the gemmin?"

"I'm going to write about all the things that people don't pay attention to."

Ernie smiled. "So am I going to be in the story?"

"Yeah, but don't worry. I'll change your name."

"Don't," he said. "I'd be proud to be in your story. Only . . ."

"Only what?" I asked when his voice trailed off.

"Could you mention Mixie?"

"Was she the one you fell in love with?"

He nodded. "They're all dear to me—from the first ones I met to every new bunch that comes along. But I think you only ever get that one special connection."

"I'll mention her," I told him.

And I did.

THE SEPTEMBER PEOPLE

Tim Waggoner

Tim Waggoner has published more than fifty stories of fantasy and horror. His most current stories can be found in the anthologies *Civil War Fantastic, Single White Vampire Seeks Same,* and *Bruce Coville's UFOs.* His first novel, *The Harmony Society,* has been published by Prime Books, and he is currently working on projects for both White Wolf and Wizards of the Coast. He teaches creative writing at Sinclair Community College in Dayton, Ohio.

That's it—that's the trail.

It had been . . . Maggie thought for a moment . . . seventy-four years and change since she'd last seen it, but although she'd lost many memories to the eternally hungry beast called Old Age, her memory of the trail—its location, the surrounding vegetation, even the color of the dirt—was as sharp and clear as ever.

It should've changed after all this time, she thought. The trees should be larger, the trail overwhelmed by decades of unrestrained plant growth. But it looked exactly the same as it had when she'd first seen it at the now impossibly distant age of nine. A bittersweet smiled played across her lips. Had she ever been so young?

A stern adult voice, a voice that had lectured countless uninterested college students over the years, spoke up.

It's a different trail. You only think it's the same one because that's what you want to think. What you need *to think.*

So? Even if it was an old woman's delusion, what of it? A delusion was better than nothing. Besides, wasn't this the way it worked in the stories? The pathway to Otherness always remained eternal and unchanged. It was the way of such things.

You're insane.

Maggie smiled. Maybe, but she also felt alive, more so than she had in years. She had a place to go, a destination to reach, and—far more importantly—questions to ask. Delusional or not, she had a *purpose*.

She started toward the trail, ignoring the less-than-gentle protests of the arthritis in her knees and hip. Her journey, perhaps the last she would ever undertake in this world, had begun. She was going to see if she could find them again.

The September People.

* * *

From the preface to Legends and Folklore of the Ohio Valley, *by Margaret C. Dessick, PhD.*

Many of the same myth-structures that predominate in Europe and elsewhere can be found—albeit in somewhat altered form—in Southwest Ohio, the region also known as the Ohio Valley. For example, the Native Americans who once inhabited this area told stories of the Untchatak, little people whom they believed could cross over from their world to ours through the flames of a untended campfire. Much later, German settlers enthralled their children with tales of the mischievous die Katze, a sprite who roamed the countryside in the form of a black cat, searching for unwary people on whom he could play tricks.

There are many more such examples to be found in the following pages. But all talk of Jungian archetypes aside, these scraps of tall tales, half-remembered dreams, and personified wishes suggest an inescapable— if fanciful—conclusion. In the end, there is truly no difference between the world as our senses perceive it and the world as our hearts would have it. All is Faerie.

*　　　*　　　*

Maggie struggled up the trail's incline. It was steeper here than she remembered, and also she was a wee bit older than nine now. She had to grab hold of the underbrush from time to time to help maintain her footing.

Should've worn hiking boots instead of tennies. And brought a cane.

She was fit for her age—walked every day, swam twice a week at the rec center—but despite this she was already winded, and, though she tried not to think too much about it, she was worried about falling. She'd been taking medicine since she was sixty to fend off osteoporosis, but even so, a fall out here could very well snap a bone or two, maybe even a hip, incapacitating her. She hadn't brought a cell phone (didn't own one), and she didn't have one of those medical alert devices (too demeaning). If she became immobilized, it was quite possible that she'd die of exposure before someone could find her.

It was mid-September, but the heavy, humid air felt

more like August. Perspiration coated her brow, trickled down her face and neck, ran along her spine to pool at the small of her back. She'd worn a pair of gray sweats, the kind she used for walking, thinking it might be a bit chilly in the woods this time of year. Now she wished she'd worn something cooler. The sound of her pulse thrumming in her ears seemed at once too loud and too weak, and her knees felt watery, as if they might give out on her with each step she took. She knew that if she stopped and held up her hands to examine them, she'd see they were shaking. She wouldn't have been surprised if she had a heart attack or stroke any minute. Maybe both.

Stop it, she scolded herself. *You're only as old as you feel.*

Dry dirt slid out from under her right shoe, and she had to grab a branch to keep from falling. Whatever the plant was (botany was definitely not her field), the branch was covered with thorns, and she hissed as they bit into the flesh of her palm.

If that's so, then I must be two hundred. At least.

She forced herself to hold on until she was confident she'd regained her balance, then she let go of the branch. She looked at the red beads welling forth from the tiny wounds in her hand, and the scholar in her couldn't resist making a mental comparison to stigmata.

She wiped the blood on her leg, half smiling and half grimacing.

I don't think I quite qualify for martyr status just yet. Maybe when this is all over.

Assuming she survived . . . that she *wanted* to survive. And wasn't that a nasty little thought that was better off being left unexamined for the time being?

Doing her best to ignore the throbbing in her hand,

Maggie continued on the trail. She tried to swallow, but it felt as if her throat was caked with desert sand and pyramid dust.

And you forgot to bring any water.

She shook her head. How many students had she scolded over the years for being unprepared? If they could see her now, they'd laugh their collective ass off, and rightly so. She should've done more to prepare for the journey, but there was no going back now—in so many ways.

A deep breath, an encouraging nod to herself, and she continued along the trail.

*   *   *

Wind whispers secrets to the trees, and in turn, branches sway and leaves rustle one against the other. Vibrant reds, rich browns, soothing yellows . . . Hard to believe these striking hues are the colors of time passing, one season giving way to another.

The colors of death.

*   *   *

Deep in the wood—deep in a way beyond mere distance, beyond the size and number of trees, deep beyond the limits of human language and thought. Deep beyond Deep.

They sense the presence of a newcomer entering the wood. No, not *new,* they realize. This one has been here before, mere moments or perhaps countless ages ago, as near as they can reckon with their slippery and imperfect sense of how time—whatever exactly that might be—passes outside.

She is . . . a wordless concept here, one that can most closely be rendered as not-as-she-was-before. (A particularly difficult concept to grasp for those who inhale forever and exhale eternity with every breath.)

And here . . . another concept, this one crudely

translated as inner-fire-has-dimmed-to-a-dangerously-low-point-and-may-soon-go-out. (An even more difficult notion for them. Beginnings they understand well enough, but endings?)

She seeks us.

Yes.

Will she find us?

Perhaps.

She did before.

Yes.

But this time?

Perhaps.

And so they wait for the next few seconds—or the next ten thousand years—to pass.

Whichever.

* * *

Freckle-Face, Freckle-Face, dots and spots all over the place!

Maggie ran across the field, red hair trailing behind her like rust-colored flame. Tears poured from her eyes, making her vision watery-blurry. Her breath came in ragged, hitching sobs, and snot trailed down her nose and over her lips, but she didn't care. All she cared about was running, running, running.

Nice dress, Freckle-Face! Did it used to be a potato sack?

What do you mean, "used to"? Look at how lumpy she is!

Freckle-Face-Potato-Belly!

Laughter then, so much laughter.

Maggie tried to shut out the memory of her classmates' taunts, but her mind refused to obey; it kept playing them over and over, like a phonograph record with a scratch in it. Not that she'd ever listened to one herself, but she'd heard tell of them from some of the other kids. Kids whose families had more money than hers.

Hey, Potato-Belly, what color's your hair?

It's red! she'd said defiantly, fighting tears and losing.

No, I mean what color is it when it's clean?

More laughter.

Dirty-Hair-Freckle-Face-Potato-Belly!

The laughter and insults followed her as she ran, echoing in her ears long after the school yard was behind her.

There's always one, the child who serves as a sin-eater for the others, a psychological dumping ground for all their insecurities and self-loathing. A child who, by becoming a pariah, helps the others belong, if nowhere else, then at least to the group of those who Aren't Pariah. In Locust Falls, Maggie Steadman was that child.

Perhaps it was because her family was poor. Her father (when he was sober) worked as a hired hand for some of the farmers in the county, but what money he brought home usually went to pay for liquor, leaving little left over for food, let alone luxuries like new dresses or shoes for his only daughter. Her three older brothers had taken to stealing to help put food on the table—some eggs here, a handful of vegetables there, and last Christmas, a whole pig from the Jensens' farm.

Perhaps it was because of her mother. A frail, ivory-skinned woman who rarely talked above a whisper, didn't like to leave the house, and never, ever smiled, at least not that Maggie had ever seen. Her mother would sometimes spend most of the day sitting in a old rocking chair by the front window—not rocking, just sitting—and looking out at the world with a blank expression on her face. Maggie was never sure if she really saw what she was looking at, saw something that existed entirely within her mind, or saw nothing at all. Some of the townsfolk said that Mrs. Steadman was feeble-minded, that she'd always been that way, but it'd gotten worse over the years. Others (more than a bit feeble-minded themselves) said that she was a witch-woman who sat before her window, waiting to cast the evil eye on anyone foolish enough to pass within her sight.

Perhaps there was no reason at all why Maggie had been chosen by the other children to be their whipping girl, any more than there's a reason lightning chooses to strike one spot and not another. She just *was*.

But the worst of it wasn't the teasing or the mocking tones in their voices, the sneering smiles or the cruelty mixed with dark delight that shone in their eyes . . . the worst thing was that Maggie was beginning to believe them, beginning to believe that she *was* a dirty-hair-freckle-face-potato-belly. That she *deserved* every nasty thing they said about her—deserved it all and much, much more.

She became aware of browns, reds, oranges, and yellows whipping past her, and she realized that she had entered the woods, though she had no memory of doing so. The trail she ran down was narrow, hardly a trail at all, really, and a corner of her mind realized that she had never been here before, that she didn't know where she was, that it might be a good idea to stop, turn around, and make her way back to the beginning of the trail before she got herself good and lost.

But she didn't. After all, she was just a dirty-hair-freckle-face-potato-belly, and she deserved to be lost. Lost and forgotten. Besides, in the woods there were no sneers, no hard-edged laughter. Just trees and leaves and wind and bushes and the moist brown-black earth beneath her running feet.

She felt a sudden release, like a knot in her chest had worked itself loose. She was alone in the silence—alone and free.

Her ragged sobbing gave way to a joyous laugh, and she decided then and there that she was going to keep on running down this trail, no matter where it took her, keep on running forever if she could. Running and running and running and running . . .

*   *   *

From Chapter Six of Legends and Folklore of the Ohio Valley.

The Quest is perhaps the most enduring and universal of mythic narrative structures, and with good reason. It scarcely matters what the hero is questing for—a magic sword, an enchanted amulet, long-forgotten knowledge—the point of the journey isn't the attainment of a goal so much as it is the search itself. A quest gives the hero's life meaning and purpose. In fact, the quest is, in the end, nothing but a metaphor for the journey from cradle to grave that we all must take—from one dark unknown to another.

Ultimately, the beginning and ending points of this twisting, turning path are the same; it's what we do along the way that defines who and what we are.

*   *   *

Maggie's hip throbbed in time with her pulse, her knees ached (in her mind she saw the Tin Man's face, his rusted lips barely moving as he gritted out, *Oil . . . can!*), her chest felt like it was wrapped in bands of sheet metal, and her breath came in ragged panting gasps.

"Perhaps . . . this wasn't . . . one of my more . . . brilliant ideas."

She was drenched in sweat now, her clothes wet and heavy with it. In addition to the pinprick wounds on her hand from the thorny branch she'd grabbed, she now had a half dozen scrapes and cuts on the backs of her hands, wrists, face, and neck. It was almost as if the trees and brush were giving her little stinging warnings, telling her to turn back before something much worse happened to her.

She laughed, though there wasn't much sound to it since she couldn't spare the breath. *Too much imagination—that's always been your problem, girl.* Her father's voice, with a hint of drunken slur. The memory killed her laughter, made her aches and pains seem to hurt all the more.

Not my problem, she answered. *My salvation.*

She had no clear notion of how long she'd been on the trail. It seemed like hours, but surely was much less. Though it had been well before sundown when she'd entered the woods, the light appeared to be growing dimmer the farther she penetrated. Her imagination again. This portion of the forest was older, the trees and undergrowth thicker, that's all.

Maybe the light's not welcome here, she thought, and instantly wished she hadn't.

When she'd first started walking the trail, she'd been convinced it was the right one, the same she'd taken when she was nine, but she was no longer so certain. She thought the surroundings looked familiar, more, that they *felt* familiar, but while the girl she had once been might have had no doubts, the woman she had become in the intervening seven decades had far too many.

Is this what time does to us? she wondered. *Makes us timid and unsure when we're so close to the finish line that we should have nothing left to fear? Or to lose?*

There's always something to lose, she answered herself.

And how well she knew that. While her doctorate was in folklore and mythology, anyone who survived to reach her age also possessed a most thorough education in the ways of loss.

In the twilight of her life (not to be too overly poetic about it), Maggie supposed she hadn't suffered that many more losses than anyone else, but that didn't make them any easier to bear. The first was her husband Charles. (Oh, her parents went before him, but they didn't count. One expected one's parents to die eventually, and besides, it wasn't as if she had ever been close to them.) They'd met in graduate school. He was working on his doctorate in math—she couldn't imagine a field more diametrically opposed to her own—but he was light years away from the stereotype of the dry, dull mathematics professor. Charles was a warm, outgoing man with a delightfully wry sense of humor. They were married a week after they'd both successfully defended their dissertations.

He'd only been forty-six when he was hit by a sudden, massive heart attack. Given the advances in medical technology, today he might be saved. Hell, the way folks monitored their cholesterol and took statin-lowering drugs, heart attacks like Charles' might be avoided entirely.

She'd had lovers in the years since her husband's death, but none had ever truly taken Charles' place in her heart, and she never remarried.

The second major loss in Maggie's life was Chloe,

her only child, the last part of Charles remaining to her. From almost the first moment out of the womb, Chloe seemed determined not to follow in her parents' academic footsteps. She didn't like to read and was almost pathologically obsessed with television. In her teens, TV gave way to hair, clothes, and boys (not necessarily in that order), and homework was something to be avoided at all costs. Maggie had spent her daughter's adolescence worrying that she would get pregnant before she graduated high school, but a pair of cysts on her ovaries (benign, thank the gods) and the subsequent surgical removal of her uterus took care of that concern. Of course, it also meant that Maggie would never have grandchildren.

Chloe took a few courses at a community college (she refused to go to the university where her parents taught, despite the fact she could get free tuition as the daughter of faculty), but she never obtained a degree, and eventually ended up working as an office manager for a construction company. Maggie tried hard (*very* hard) to not be overly critical of Chloe's lifestyle choice, and for the most part, she succeeded.

Chloe married a nice, if somewhat colorless man who worked for the highway department, and, as near as Maggie could tell, she was happy enough. There was some talk of adopting children, but nothing ever came of it. And so the years passed.

Chloe had inherited her father's problem with cholesterol, however, and in addition, she picked up a smoking habit from her husband. A deadly combination—Chloe died of congestive heart failure at the relatively young age of forty-one, lasting four years fewer than her father.

Maggie had a civil relationship with her son-in-law, but that was all, and once Chloe was buried, she fell out of touch with him. So she continued teaching at the university, though with less enthusiasm than before, writing little and publishing less, marking time until retirement.

That was eleven years ago. Now the home Maggie had lived in with her husband and daughter belonged to another family, and she resided in an assisted living facility, which wasn't as bad as it sounded, though it wasn't all that great, either. The staff was friendly enough, as were the other residents. In particular, she'd grown close to another woman her age named Elizabeth (never Liz or Beth), who'd been a nurse and was always giving the staff medical advice whether they wanted it or not. Maggie admired her fiery spirit and no-nonsense attitude, and they became fast friends.

Last week, Maggie had found Elizabeth in her room, the door unlocked. She sat in front of her television set while on the screen a tabloid talk show host hurled thinly veiled insults at his guests. Not that Elizabeth could see or hear him anymore.

Like Maggie, Elizabeth was alone in the world, and the only people who attended her funeral service (her all-too-short and monstrously inadequate service) were other residents and staff of "The Home," as Elizabeth had always referred to it.

And then, this morning, for reasons Maggie wasn't entirely sure of herself, she put on her sweats and walking shoes, called a cab, and had the driver take her to Locust Falls. It was a forty-five minute trip from the university town where she'd lived for so long, but a far longer journey in emotional terms.

Now here she was, struggling along a forest path, like Red Riding Hood's grandmother who'd somehow gotten away from the wolf and, now that she'd completely screwed up the story she inhabited, had no idea what was going to happen next.

She thought of the advice Red's mother always gave her before she set out on her trip to Grandma's house one more time. *Remember now—don't stray from the path.*

Maggie smiled grimly as she fought to ignore her body's protests at being treated so poorly after so many years of faithful service.

Don't worry; I don't intend to.

*   *   *

She's closer now.

Yes.

Still so very far away, though.

Yes.

Her inner fire grows dimmer with each step she takes. We can barely see it now.

Perhaps we should . . . (This one struggled to articulate a concept that could best be translated as "intervene," but the idea was alien to beings that had kept themselves apart from the temporal world—the solid world, the so-very-limited, so-small world—since before the beginning of the beginning. This one failed to express the thought, but it hardly mattered, for the others would never have understood, could never have.)

We shall watch and wait then? (As if they had ever done anything else.)

Yes.

And so they did, but with increasing interest.

*   *   *

Maggie's tears had long since dried, and her sobbing, hitching breaths had given way to tired gulps for air. She no longer ran but walked along the trail, her feet heavy as lead blocks. Her feeling of liberation was gone, and in its place was a cold, jittery fear that gnawed at the inside of her belly. Even so, she didn't turn back. All that waited for her outside the wood were more hurtful words, big brothers who would just as soon torment her as ignore her, and a mother and father who were parents in name only. Besides, if anything happened to her in the forest (anything *bad*), she deserved it, didn't she? After all, she was nothing more than a dirty-hair-freckle-face-potato-belly—and they deserved everything that happened to them, and more.

Besides, even though the forest was creepy—it was darker than where she started, the trees closer together, taller, trunks and branches thicker, twistier, *wilder*—mixed in with her fear was a deliciously shivery feeling of anticipation, of adventure. Her parents had never read to her or told her stories: her father was usually too drunk, her mother too caught up in whatever unguessable thoughts moved behind her expressionless face. But Maggie's third grade teacher, Mrs. Weaver, would sometimes read the class stories, and though Maggie didn't have any books at home, there would occasionally be free time in the classroom, and then she could read stories on her own. Her favorites were tales of magic and mystery concerning children whisked away to magic lands where scarecrows and men made of metal came alive, brave kings and knights struggled to maintain their code of honor in the face of evil and temptation, and wiley youths managed to obtain mystic lamps or outsmart dimwitted giants by luck or pluck. Maggie would lose herself in these stories, these fabulous worlds that were so much better than the dull, gray one she inhabited. Worlds where enchantments waited around every street corner and poor, homely girls discovered they were really beautiful princesses all along.

This was like one of those stories—a sad, lonely girl walking through the woods, possibly lost, perhaps in danger, traveling down a trail that led ever deeper into the unknown. And then this girl would come across a doorway to another realm (an *invisible* one, of course), and sensing it, she would close her eyes, picture the door in her mind, and step through . . .

Maggie experienced a sudden feeling of vertigo, and her vision clouded, as if she were now looking at the world through ripples of murky water. She took three stumble-steps forward and nearly fell on her face, but she managed to keep her feet beneath her, and the sensation of dizziness was gone as quickly as it had come. And when it had passed, Maggie found herself . . . elsewhere.

It was still a forest—though more accurately a small semicircular clearing within one—but this was a Forest with a capital F. The trees were gigantic ancient things whose branches stretched so far upward it seemed they might very well support the sky itself. The smallest of their leaves were still larger than Maggie, and their colors were blazing reds, yellow, oranges, and browns, so bright that it appeared they were on fire. As beautiful as the leaves were, it hurt to look at them, and Maggie had to avert her gaze. Even though the Forest canopy blocked the sky, there was still more than enough light to see by—how could there not be with the leaves as bright as they were?—and Maggie saw three figures standing before her, figures she would've sworn (if anyone had been around to ask her) that hadn't been there a second before.

They were tall, taller even than her Uncle Homer

who was a hair's length away from seven feet, or so
everyone said. Thin (*willowy* would've been a more
appropriate descriptor in more ways than one, but it
was a word she was as yet unfamiliar with), garbed in
robes—at least, she thought they were robes; perhaps
they were something else entirely—that seemed to
have been woven from the lush, green tendrils of
plants. Their skin was brownish-gray, corrugated, crag-
ged, and crevassed, their fingers long, curving, and
stiff, like tiny branches. She looked for their feet and
saw none. Possibly they didn't have feet at all, for the
hems of their "robes" extended into the rich, brown-
black soil like roots.

Their foots are roots, she thought, and couldn't
help giggling.

Their heads were hairless ovals—although creatures
like these wouldn't have *hair,* would they? Maybe
moss or lichen, but they didn't have any of that, either.
No ears, at least not any Maggie could see, nor noses,
for that matter. Mouths, yes. Small round holes that
looked as if they'd been bored by insects or drilled by
woodpeckers. The tiny *O*s gave the creatures a comi-
cal aspect, as if they had been frozen in a state of
perpetual surprise. What sort of sounds could they
make with mouths like that? Did they whistle instead
of talk? Their eyes . . .

Maggie frowned. She didn't *see* any eyes—the bark-
skin where they should be was unbroken, featureless—
but she sensed gazes trained on her with interest . . .
many more than could be accounted for by the trio
of beings before her. Were there others hiding somewhere among the leaves and branches of the gigantic
trees, or did she only see three creatures because that
was all they were *allowing* her to see?

Maggie felt no fear any more, only joy such as she had never known. It was all she could do to keep herself from jumping up and down like a little kid, but she was nine, a big girl, and she managed to keep still—barely. Just being in their presence was a miracle, if for no other reason than it proved something both wonderful and profound to Maggie: dreams can come true. Maybe not all the time (maybe hardly ever), and maybe not always in the way you expect—in all her reading and imaginings, she'd never pictured creatures quite like these before—but they *did* come true, at least sometimes.

The middle one's head tilted slightly to the side, and Maggie felt a tingly-itchy sensation at the base of her skull, like a column of ants was marching just beneath the skin. A cascade of images poured through her mind—so many, so fast that she couldn't make sense of them. Black stars wheeling through an ivory sky, honey-colored rays of light that could be touched and shaped like clay, rainbows that smelled like cinnamon and thrummed like cicadas, crystalline fish with ruby eyes swimming languidly through solid rock . . . and on and on and on, pressure building until she thought her head might explode like a pumpkin hurled against concrete.

The same creature raised its right arm and stretched twig-fingers toward Maggie's forehead. At first she couldn't move, could only stand and watch as the brown-barked hand came closer until she could feel the barest touch of rough fingertips grazing her skin.

Terror surged through her and she screamed, the sound seeming not to issue from her throat but rather from the very air around them. Control of her body returned to her, and Maggie whirled around and fled before the creature's hand could make full contact. She ran blindly, madly, not knowing where she was going, not caring, just so long as it was *away*.

*　　*　　*

Minutes, hours, days, seconds, weeks, an eternity later, Maggie stopped running and collapsed to the trail, lungs burning as if they were on fire. She rolled onto her back, gulped air, and looked up at the autumn leaves blocking the sky: normal-size leaves on the branches of normal-sized trees. Somehow, she had found her way back from whatever strange part of the forest the tree-people inhabited. She was home—or close enough, anyway.

As she lay breathing, her terror slowly ebbed and was replaced by relief. She smiled, then giggled, then laughed out loud, hugging herself and rolling back and forth on the trail.

After a time, her laughter died down and she got to her feet, but her smile remained firmly in place. She started down the trail, half-walking and half-skipping. She knew she would never tell anyone about what she had seen this day in the forest; no one would believe her, they'd say it was only her imagination. But she knew better. She also knew something else now: magic was real—she had been touched by it. She also knew one more thing. No matter what anyone said, she wasn't a dirty-hair-freckle-face-potato-belly. She was *Maggie,* and she was special. She would find her way out of the forest to whatever waited beyond, and she would no longer be afraid.

She continued down the trail, whistling.

*　　*　　*

Maggie watched the ghost-image of the little girl flee. Though she'd known better, she'd attempted to catch the girl's attention—calling her name, waving her hand in front of her face—but the girl had been oblivious to the old woman's presence, which only made sense. After all, Maggie had seen no one but the three sylvan beings the first time she'd been here, so why should that little girl—the same girl Maggie had once been—see her now?

Tears in her eyes, Maggie turned to the three figures. She'd found them the same way she had the last time: one moment she was walking the trail (or in the case of her older self, *hobbling* the trail), and the next she was here—wherever precisely *here* was. No warning, no sense of transition at all. But then, that was the way of stories like this, wasn't it?

Wherever and whatever this place was (even though they stood in a clearing, the word *underhill* came to mind), Maggie knew one thing: time didn't mean anything here. What she'd just witnessed proved it.

The trio of beings turned their eyeless, corrugated faces toward her, and an image flashed through Maggie's mind: her nine-year-old face superimposed on that of her eighty-three-year-old self. With the image came a sense of puzzlement that could almost, but not quite, be verbalized as *Same/not same?*

"Yes, that was me." Maggie was surprised by how steady her voice was. She should be terrified—that she'd had a complete mental breakdown and was hallucinating, if nothing else—but she wasn't. She felt calm, if not exactly relaxed. "I'm older now. It's been seventy-four years since I last saw you."

No images this time, but the sense of puzzlement, of confusion, was stronger.

Perhaps these beings—*these Fey,* she thought, for lack of a better term—didn't have a spoken language. How could they with mouths shaped like that? So she tried to put the concept she was attempting to express into images. She thought of ticking clocks, of parents playing with their children, of the sun traveling from one horizon to the other, of seasons passing, one blending into the next and the next and the next without end.

From the Fey—the trinity (how appropriately mystic the number!) that she could see and the untold others she couldn't—Maggie sensed puzzlement again, this time mixed with amusement at her crude attempt at communication, much like a human might chuckle as a favorite but clumsy pet awkwardly attempted to perform a trick. She wasn't getting through.

She tried again, gesturing at the gigantic leaves overhead. "See the colors? Those are *autumn* leaves. Autumn is a time of change . . . leaves dying and falling away as winter approaches. How can you live in a place like this—where it's always fall—without understanding the concept of time passing?"

The Fey didn't move, didn't turn to face one another, but she had the sense that they were conferring nevertheless. More images in her mind, then: the leaves, the colors, and a strong feeling of permanence, of Always. The leaves were the way they were because they had been and ever would be that way.

Maggie knew then that it was hopeless. How could beings that were eternal ever fully understand the concept of *not*-eternal? Besides, that wasn't the reason she was here.

"I know that you don't understand that I'm old and nearing the end of my life. And you probably wouldn't understand how my first encounter with you affected me, since you can't understand the concept of change. But it *did* change me. I went from being a little girl who thought she was . . . well . . . nothing, to believing she was special. You see, I had a secret that I never told anyone—not even my husband or my own daughter. I had been *chosen*. I had found a doorway to a magic world, walked through it, met the strange and wonderful creatures that lived there, and then found my way back home. After that, it didn't matter what anyone else thought about me. *I* liked me, and that was more than enough. I had always been a good student, but I applied myself even more diligently to my studies, and somehow—perhaps because of my newfound confidence—the other children stopped teasing me, and I began to make friends. Everything wasn't perfect, of course. My father never stopped drinking and my mother never got better, but their problems no longer held me back.

"I was able to make a life for myself, a good one, and it was all because I met you. But there's one thing I never understood," she took a deep breath. "Why me?"

The Fey looked at her with their nonexistent eyes. A simple, easily understood message from them this time: ?

"Why did you choose me?"

?

"Why did you allow me to find the entrance to your world when I was a child? And why did you allow me to find it again today?"

No response this time.

"Don't misunderstand—I'm most grateful! But there has to be some *reason* . . ."

At first, the Fey did nothing, and Maggie began to fear that she hadn't gotten through to them, that she could never get through. But then, as when she was last here, the middle member of the trinity raised his/her/its arm and stretched the slim branches of its fingers toward her forehead. This time, she gritted her teeth, closed her hands into fists and stood her ground. Whatever was about to happen, she wouldn't turn away from it.

Wooden fingertips touched skin that had once been smooth and supple but was now sagging and wrinkled. Maggie felt a slight pressure on her forehead, and for a moment she was afraid the fingers would sprout fresh shoots that would pierce her skin, drill through her skull, and burrow their way into the soft, yielding pulp of her brain. But that didn't happen. The fingers just made contact, their touch cool and dry.

A word whispered through her mind then. Not an image, not a concept, but a clear, recognizable word—in English, no less.

No.

The fingers withdrew, and the arm lowered.

Maggie was stunned. "No? No *what?* No, you didn't choose me? No, there wasn't a reason? No, you won't answer me?"

The Fey stood unmoving, impassive. They might as well have been actual trees instead of treelike beings.

Maggie struggled to frame a better question, one that might elicit a more detailed response from them. But as she thought, she noticed that her vision was beginning to go gray around the edges. Fear surged through her—was she having a stroke? A heart attack? Had the stress of making this journey finally taken its toll on her octogenerian body? But then she realized that the problem didn't lie with her eyes but rather the world around her. The Fey, and the otherworldly realm they inhabited, were fading. It appeared her audience was over.

"Wait! Please, I have so many questions!" Beings of such power and wisdom could surely tell her all the things she so desperately needed to know. Why had her husband and daughter—and just this last week, her new friend Elizabeth—left her? Was there life beyond life? Would they all be together again in one version of heaven or another? Was there a plan to existence, a point, a *meaning?*

But the Fey and their world became more and more insubstantial, until they were little more than a ghostly afterimage. Maggie rushed forward, hoping to grab hold of one of them and by doing so, anchor it in reality and keep it from disappearing. But even if such a thing were possible, it was too late. She passed through the space where the middle Fey stood—had been standing—without resistance. The huge trees and their equally huge leaves were gone, replaced by normal-sized ones. She turned around to face where the Fey had stood. She looked down, saw her feet were on the forest trail and knew she was back in her own world.

Tears rolled down Maggie's face, and she felt a hollow pit of loss open up inside her. It wasn't fair! She had touched Otherness, not once, but *twice!* The first encounter had given her the strength to make a better life for herself, but all this one had done was confuse and upset her. It was a missed opportunity—there was so *much* she could've learned from the Fey, if only she had been able to make them understand!

This wasn't the way stories like this were supposed to turn out. The hero always completes the quest, maybe not easily and without cost, but at journey's end, the goal (a physical object, usually) is obtained. But that object is nothing more than a symbol for enlightenment. Arthur discovers that while the chivalrous ideal can never be reached, the important thing is to never stop trying. Dorothy learns that there's no place like home. Indiana Jones realizes that the material is far less important than the spiritual. But *her* quest, *her* story had no end. She had gained nothing, learned nothing. It was pointless. And if her quest had no point, what did that mean for her entire life?

As she stood there despairing, a single leaf spiraled to the ground to land on the precise spot where the middle Fey had stood.

Maggie looked at the leaf for a long moment, studying its golden color, ragged edges, and pattern of veins as if she were an ancient priest performing an augury. After a bit, she knelt, her knees grumbling, and picked up the leaf by its stem. She straightened, causing her back to complain this time, and held the leaf close to her face. She could see nothing special about it. As near as she could tell, it was just an ordinary leaf that had fallen from an ordinary tree in an ordinary forest.

Still, she couldn't help but smile. The leaf probably didn't mean anything, its falling nothing more than coincidence, but then again, it *might* mean something. The important thing, she supposed, was that it meant something to *her*.

And it did. What, precisely, she couldn't say just then, but she'd figure it out. Or she wouldn't. And that would be okay because it had to be okay. The only choice was whether to walk the trail or not, questions answered or not. Maggie chose to walk, carrying the leaf—and her questions—with her, for as long and as far as they would take her.

*   *   *

Gone.

Yes.

Strange . . .

From their vantage point in Elsewhere, they could see that, while the woman's inner fire was still dim, it was stronger that it had been before her arrival. They were at a loss to account for this.

But one of their number—the one who had touched the woman—raised his/her/its hand to examine it. There was an odd sensation in the fingertips, one their kind had no name for. Then, as he/she/it watched, small tendrils sprouted from the wood and new growth blossomed forth.

And as their world filled with green, a new concept formed among them, exciting and terrifying in equal measures.

Change.

*   *   *

As Maggie continued down the trail once more, she felt better, though she didn't know exactly why. Maybe it was simply because she'd been there and back again—again. She was surprised to find herself looking forward to going home and . . . well, doing what, she wasn't sure, but doing *something*.

She grinned. Who knew? Perhaps she'd begin another book.

*   *   *

From the Epilogue to Legends and Folklore of the Ohio Valley.

Years ago in an introductory mythology class, we were discussing one of the many gods-in-disguise-visit-mortals tales—this one a Roman story concerning Jupiter and Mercury. The two gods, posing as simple travelers, pay a call on a shepherd and his family. After enjoying the man's hospitality, Jupiter gives him a gift: a bowl of water that will never be empty. At this point, one of my students raised his hand and asked what would happen if the bowl was accidentally knocked over. If it truly could never be empty, would a tidal wave of water pour forth? And if the bowl wasn't righted, would water continue to come out until the entire world—perhaps even the universe itself—was flooded?

After praising the young man for asking such an imaginative question, I told him that the tale was a metaphor about the importance of showing kindness to strangers, and as a metaphor, logic couldn't, indeed shouldn't, be applied to it. Simply put, it didn't matter what would happen if the bowl were upended.

I could tell the student wasn't satisfied with my answer, but he didn't pursue the point further, and the class moved on. Later that night, however, I found myself once again pondering the young man's question and my somewhat inadequate response. So often we who have made it our life's work to study and interpret the fanciful say that these stories are attempts by people to understand the baffling and often disappointing world in which they find themselves living. But the truth of the matter is that these tales explain nothing. They provide no reliable advice—in the real world, kindness to strangers might just as easily go unrewarded, or worse, repaid with derision or even violence—and they certainly give no answers to the ultimate nature and meaning of existence, regardless of how much we wish they would.

What these stories do, though, is serve as Rorshach blots, or mirrors. We see what we want to in them, and what we see, in the end, isn't gods or magic bowls.

What we see is ourselves.

JUDGMENT

Kristine Kathryn Rusch

Kristine Kathryn Rusch is an award-winning mystery, romance, science fiction, and fantasy writer. She has written many novels under various names, including Kristine Grayson for romance and Kris Nelscott for mystery. Her novels have made the bestseller lists even in London, and have been published in fourteen countries and thirteen languages. Her awards range from the Ellery Queen Readers Choice Award to the John W. Campbell Award. She is the only person ever to have won a Hugo Award for editing and a Hugo Award for fiction. Her short work has been reprinted in seven *Year's Best* collections.

Tyrone stopped in front of the statue of Hans Sachs, which had somehow survived the bombings. The buildings around it had all been destroyed. No matter how hard Tyrone tried, he couldn't remember what they had been. The remains of a wall, two stories made of stone, suggested a church, but so many buildings in Nuremberg were made of stone that his impression was probably wrong.

The air smelled of dust, and beneath it, the faint

hint of rot. He clutched his camera as he sat on a pile of rubble, the debris loose beneath his feet.

He had known Sachs, although the man did not look like his statue. The statue portrayed a robust figure, draped in robes and wearing medieval garb. The curly hair was right, but the artist failed to capture the thick brown tangles, and the beard was too neat, too well-trimmed.

Sachs had been too busy to be tidy.

Sachs, *Die Meistersinger von Nürnberg*. Amazing that Tyrone had forgotten Sachs. Sachs, after all, had been the one to lure him away from the forests and hills of his own people, had somehow started his strange romance with humans, and led to this moment, four centuries and a thousand lifetimes later.

Tyrone couldn't even remember what he had called himself in those early years. It hadn't been his own name—the magical never let anyone discover their true name. It gave others too much power.

Now he was calling himself Tyrone Briggs, although most of the people he encountered insisted on calling him Ty, a habit he hated, but never decried. He tried not to complain about anything American. He had learned after the First World War that not even Americans were safe from the kind of unreasoning patriotic fervor that made a man with a slight accent and an aversion to being called Ty suspect.

But those days were long past, just like that war was long past. This one was finally past too, but only by a few months.

And he hadn't expected to find himself on his native soil for the first time in many years.

The statue had not been here for all of those centuries. Hans Sachs would have been surprised to see it.

Die Meistersinger von Nürnberg. Tyrone shook his head. How had he forgotten that moment, when he'd hidden in the trees, and watched Sachs fiddle with his lute, trying to find the right words to go with a new melody, one that captured the exact sound of the wind in the leaves?

Tyrone had thought it a new magic, even though his father—a slight man with ears so pointed they poked through his long black hair—claimed it was no magic at all.

You are fooled by something that is not there. Humans only appear to have depth. They are fickle and violent and terrifying creatures. They will be the death of you.

But they hadn't been the death of Tyrone. He had not become mortal, and they had not discovered him. He had passed for generations. So many generations, in fact, that Tyrone had come to think of Sachs not as the man he knew, but as the title character in Wagner's opera *Die Meistersinger,* the opera that had always been performed before the annual Nazi rallies held in Nuremberg, an opera he had always hated.

Tyrone shuddered, even though it was not that cold. The thin November sun filtered through the rubble, back-lighting the crumbling walls, peeking through the falling doorways.

Nuremberg had been a medieval city, with its ancient wall still intact. The castle, Kaiserburg, stood on a sandstone crag above the wall. When Tyrone had first come here, the castle had seemed a lone outpost, the guardian of the city. Over the centuries, it had become part of the city—a talisman, guarding the place.

Now it was a ghost, windows shattered, walls fallen,

an entire section gone. Tyrone had thought some human things timeless. This war, more than the last, had proven him wrong.

He clutched the camera, knowing he should photograph the devastation. That was what he was here for—he was supposed to photograph the trials, which would start in a few days, and he was supposed to photograph the city, which had suffered a devastating Allied attack, second only to the bombing of Dresden in loss of German civilian life.

It would cheer the Americans to see this—the good ol' U.S. of A. loved the destruction. It made them feel virtuous. Nuremberg had been the center of Nazism. The frightening newsreels of Adolf Hitler waving his small fist and shouting at the top of his scarred lungs at hundreds upon hundreds of jackbooted Nazis had come from here, from Zeppelin Field, which was not in the old city, but the new. Or what had been the new.

That's why the trials were being held here. To show the world that the Allies had won. To prove to the surviving Axis citizens that destruction awaited anyone who crossed the United States, Great Britain, and Russia. Or maybe not Russia. Not anymore.

That alliance had been one of convenience, already collapsing.

Tyrone sighed and stood. Human interactions. Human thoughts. He had abandoned his magic in this city, lifetimes ago and had embraced everything human. He last used his powers to round his ears and his eyes, to straighten his eyebrows and to dull his teeth. When he had done that, he had sacrificed his feral beauty—something that marked him as Other. But a spark of it remained. If he wanted to, he could attract a woman with a simple smile and the glimmer of an eye. He could make men—some men—remain at his side for life, ever loyal.

He could bewitch anyone he wanted for as long as he wanted.

But he hadn't done those things in centuries either.

The sunlight was fading. He stood, photographs untaken, the image of Hans Sachs—as he had been, not as he had been immortalized—burned into Tyrone's brain.

And the music, nearly forgotten, whispering, whispering—like a faraway wind through a pile of dead, dry leaves.

Tyrone had lived through two of what his people called cycles—near as he could figure two hundred years in human time—and had been betrothed to a woman with a far more savage beauty than his own. Her family's magic was legendary; their penchant for mischief even more so. The sagas he later learned from human troubadours—sagas of stolen infants, mistaken identities, and chilled souls—all came from her family, with its courage, and willingness to challenge the humans.

Tyrone had watched the humans long before his betrothal. At first, he thought them a dirty, loutish lot, and could not understand why his people insisted on coexisting with them.

He had been less than half a cycle when he asked his father why the People had not made humans into slaves. His father had studied him for a long time, as if he had asked a forbidden question, and then had said, *We have magic. They have strength.*

And no matter how much more Tyrone asked, he never got a more satisfactory answer than that.

His people lived in a half-world, a twist away from the world humans called real. The People built their own castles out of air, hiding them inside forests of tall, ancient trees, and believing the cities safe. Sometimes a youngling emerged from the forest, living among the humans as a rite of passage. If discovered, the youngling returned in shame, destined to be one of the Low Folk. If the deception had been successful, the youngling became one of the High Folk, the rulers, the aristocracy of the People, those who decided it all.

His betrothed's family always participated in the rite. She had, and seemed appalled when she learned that he had not. No one in his family had passed for human in several cycles.

Why take the risk, his father had asked, *when our family's place among the High Folk remains guaranteed thanks to the deceptions of our ancestors?*

Perhaps Tyrone had ventured out that day because of his betrothed's taunting. Sometimes he thought it nothing more than that. Then he remembered the suffocating feeling he had whenever he participated in the People's rituals, the knowledge that for twenty cycles, maybe more, he would do the same things, be bound to the same woman, and live on the same land.

There had to be more to life than magic classes in which he graduated to ever more elaborate spells, spells designed to create fancy palaces or beautiful clothing or marvelous pranks with which to entrance the humans. Most of the People loved these games, and found them endlessly fascinating. Some specialized in various parts of the magic—like his betrothed's family in Passing and Pranks, and his own in Light Weaving and the Architecture of Air.

But Tyrone's mind was restless—undisciplined, his

father said—and he wanted to use his magic in the old ways, outside the prescribed laws and rules.

He had tried that only once—a simple spell, changing leaf color before the fall—and his punishment had been severe. No magic for a dozen seasons, and then, when the ban was lifted, only supervised spells. He had been watched over as if he had slaughtered a unicorn, and even though the incident was five seasons in the past when he became betrothed, he had not forgotten it.

He doubted he ever would.

But other younglings felt dissatisfaction with the People. None had fled before. None had spent their entire lives among the humans.

Tyrone often thought his dissatisfaction a symptom of something more, of a part of him no one spoke of, a part only hinted at. For no one mentioned his mother, and the People were famed for seducing—and abandoning—human girls, only to steal their infants later.

Tyrone suspected that his restless "undisciplined" mind may have had another source, one his family was not willing to acknowledge—one that had given him a fascination with things human that the People could never ever understand.

The press corps had its own buildings near the Palace of Justice because the world wanted this trial reported. Tyrone had already met two newsreel photographers who planned to record the entire event on film. He felt almost redundant—a still photographer in a world that was starting to move.

At least he didn't have to put everything together like the print guys, who would be writing not just about the daily events, but trying to make some sense of the atrocities that would be brought as evidence.

Tyrone had seen none of that material, and he didn't want to see it, although he would have to as part of his job. He had been sent here as principal photographer for a major New York daily, thanks to his own stupidity and an argument he had had with his editor.

Tyrone had spent most of the war in the States—too old to fight (even in his human identity), and unwilling to tromp through Europe and Asia chasing stories with bombs exploding around him.

He had almost succeeded. He would have succeeded if he had kept his big mouth shut.

Instead, he had argued with a coworker, telling him that Hitler had not been a mustachioed buffoon as he was presented in the American papers, but a real threat. It had been clear, Tyrone had said, from the moment Hitler's first speeches had aired in the 1930s. Anyone with even a passing understanding of German and the German mind should have realized the danger that Hitler presented.

Of course, Tyrone's editor had overheard that and had expressed surprise that Tyrone knew German or the German mind. Then he remembered Tyrone's phony application, which claimed he was an American raised in Europe, and decided that what the paper needed was, quite simply, a fresh perspective on the war, from someone who hadn't experienced it.

No matter how many arguments Tyrone made, he couldn't prevent the trip to the city he sometimes like to imagine he had been born in, for it was the place when he became truly human, a city he hadn't returned to in hundreds of years.

He had been among the humans so long that it took until he reached the reporters wing in the compound around the Palace of Justice to realize that he could have argued with his boss or simply quit.

Instead, he had come to Nuremberg like a puppet, determined to find the photographs that best represented each day's trial highlight.

So far, he hadn't taken many. He hadn't even seen the prisoners—Göring, Hess, and all the rest—the admirals, and generals, and others that had been captured because Hitler had been too cowardly to face his enemies. Even if Tyrone had seen the prisoners, he wasn't sure if he would take their pictures.

Since he had come to Nuremberg, his interest in photography had faded.

That very first night, as he lay on the army issue cot, in a room so narrow that it felt like a cell, he had dreamed of his own past. Sneaking over the ancient wall, going to Sachs' cobbler's shop, and listening for the music, convinced that it was something more than even his people could do.

In the dream, Tyrone had spoken to Sachs, but in life, they had never had a conversation. Tyrone had merely listened to Sachs' music, and tried to learn, thinking music beyond him.

Later, he realized that Sachs would have helped him, that the *meistersingers* believed that their art was a trade, as simple as shoe-making, and that anyone could have trained in it.

But Tyrone had thought it magic, and had approached it as such, believing that innate ability counted for more than sheer drive and willingness. The People had no musical traditions—he didn't know what songs were until he had emerged from the forest, and he certainly hadn't understood instruments—so he had had nothing to build on.

Just as he had had nothing to build on when he had tried his hand at other human "magics": painting and sculpture and the creation of books. Over the generations, he had tried most of the human art forms, and they had all failed him.

Until photography. The combination of light and shadow, the ability to frame the world into single images, accented his family's real magic—their manipulation of light, their willingness to create buildings out of air.

In his dream, he had gone back to Sachs' cobbler shop with a camera, trying to photograph the music that had drawn him from the woods, but he had been unable to do so. Too much time had passed; he had learned too much—realized that Sachs, like most of the other *meistersingers,* had left no lasting legacy, not like Bach or Beethoven or Mozart. Their legacy had been composition and genius and true music. Sachs, while gifted, had followed the guidelines of his trade: he had rarely composed his own melodies, and his lyrics—his pride and joy—had been instructional stories, not cries from his heart.

Tyrone had awakened from that dream shaken and spent. The feelings that rose within him, the fear, the longing, the loneliness, seemed as real as they had all those years ago.

He blamed the dream on Nuremberg itself—on the distinctive sparkle of the Pegnitz River, on the shadow of Kaiserburg falling across the destroyed city of his past, on the stench of the unburied bodies still lying beneath the rubble—bringing to mind the first deaths he had seen, shortly after he had arrived in the city and learned that humans were not immortal.

The city brought out a disquiet in him, a disquiet he hadn't felt since he had first taken a camera in his hands seventy years before. The nearness of his past, combined with the feeling of violence still shuddering in the air, awakened a part of him that had been dormant too long.

The trial was not set to start for another day or two, and his only assignment was to photograph the city, give the readers a sense of the setting for what his editor called one of the most important moments in human history.

Other photographers were already getting shots of the ruins, of the hollow-faced children, of the women, heads bowed in defeat.

He wasn't interested in any of that.

Since he returned here, he was interested in only one thing.

Home.

Which was how he found himself, threading his way through Nuremberg, trying to compare the topology of his memory with the destruction before him. The cobblestone streets had been cleared so that army jeeps could make their way through, looking official and abnormally clean in the late fall sunlight.

Tyrone wore his favorite boots beneath khaki pants and a warm bomber jacket over all of it. His hair was tucked into a stocking cap and he had gloves in his pocket. He also brought a flask filled with water, three candy bars—as precious as gold here—and his camera.

The camera seemed like a drag on him; extra weight he thought of leaving behind more than once. But each time he set it down, he couldn't let go of it, and finally he put the strap around his neck, letting the camera hang, heavy and solid, against his chest.

Nuremberg seemed to go on forever. Once he passed the wall, he entered the new city, with its curving streets and burned homes. They had been made of wood, not stone, and the conflagration must have been horrible.

He saw no people here, no lost children, no sad women. Only the occasional shoe and scrawny dog, poking its face in the ruins. More than one of these half-wild dogs chewed on things they had found beneath the ashes; he did not stop to see what they were.

Instead, he walked and walked and walked, and knew he had never walked this far as a young man. He supposed he could have looked at a map—if he could find one—or asked one of the locals, if they would deign to talk to him.

But he did not. Instead, he followed the bend of the river, knowing it would take him to the outskirts of the city eventually.

It took half of the day to reach the edge of the city, half of the day and two of his three candy bars. There were only a few hours of light left when he stepped onto the bombed-out road and looked down the slight hill into the clearing beyond.

No trees. That was the first thing he noticed. No trees, and little growth. The brown earth had been churned up by vehicles and bomb craters and scavengers.

This was not the land of his memory. There were no forests, no birds, no green—only destruction as far as his eye could see.

For a long time, he stood on the slight rise, feeling his heart pound. The breath burned in his lungs—he wasn't used to walking any longer—and his muscles shook.

He hadn't expected to find the People, not when he had started on this trip, but he had thought he would catch a hint of them, a flash of light in the trees—the hint of a building against the clouds.

He hadn't expected to find them, but he had hoped he would, even imagined it: ducking into the trees, speaking the old words, having the world twist ever so slightly—and then he would be in the sky.

His father, a touch of silver in his thick dark hair, would praise him. *You have extended the family honor,* he would have said. *We will be among the High Folk for several more generations.*

And Tyrone would sit on the Throne of Success, telling all about his adventures, showing them the camera and explaining its ability to capture light, singing to them a bit of Brahms' "Lullaby," and attempting to explain the purpose of art.

Some wouldn't have believed him, of course. They would think that he hid during his tenure, that he had seen nothing, participated in nothing. They wouldn't know of the human women he had tried to love, the friends he could never quite get close to, the judgments he had formed about a life that would mean nothing inside those gossamer walls.

He would have gone back and once back, he would have to decide if he wanted to stay, decide if now he was ready to do the same things, be bound to the same woman, and live on the same land.

But, he realized now, it wasn't going to be that easy. He stood on the rise and stared at the destroyed land, knowing that he would never go home—at least not the home of his youth.

He had been wrong. He would not have lived in the same place for all of his cycles. He would have moved on, to somewhere else that humans hadn't invaded, a place that still had greenery, trees, and a bit of water.

Because his people had to have moved on. They had survived other human destructions—wars that

lasted decades, horrible diseases that sometimes transferred to the magical, terrible fires that destroyed all
of the surrounding countryside. But this time something had happened, something which made them find
new ground.

But they would be close, and he would find them.

Although he wouldn't find them on this day. He
had weeks now. Weeks of a trial that the humans
thought would make everything better. Just like the
previous war was the war to end all wars. Just like
the way Europe thought it was through with dictators
when Napoleon was banished to Elba.

Tyrone didn't know how long he was standing there
before he lifted his camera. He didn't know how long
he shot before he realized he was taking pictures.

Capturing the present in light and shadow, making
memories out of air.

By the time he returned to his small room, he had
a plan. He would talk to the locals, find out if there
were examples of pranks played in the last generation,
maybe even on the Nazis themselves.

There would be stories—there were always stories—
of a haunted wood, visions of light against darkness.
Stories of drunken men taken to buildings in the
clouds only to return years later. Stories of women
seduced by men of great beauty only to have the children of those unions stolen in the middle of the night.

He would find his people.

At least, he hoped he would.

Two weeks into the trial, he had gotten nowhere.
The locals would not talk to him, seeing him as the
enemy—one of the destroyers. They seemed to have
no concept of their own guilt—in believing in the filth

that Hitler had spoken—that brought this disaster upon themselves.

Photographs were not allowed during testimony and arguments, unless they were taken without flash from a great distance. So Tyrone rarely stayed for the entire day, preferring to photograph the justices as they gaveled the session to order, or the witnesses as they climbed into the box.

He specialized in candid shots—a young guard, smoking outside the Palace of Justice, a soldier standing at rigid attention against the doors leading into Room Number 600, a young boy staring at the curtained windows of the east wing, allowing no one to see inside.

His editor proclaimed himself pleased. *You have an artist's eye, Tyrone,* he had said during an expensive international call. *Keep doing what you're doing. No one else is getting this stuff.*

Everyone else was running in packs, trying to be journalists, when the work of journalists was long past.

Tyrone was walking the streets of Nuremberg, familiarizing himself with the city that the Allies once considered bulldozing before they fixed it up.

He finally found himself on Zeppelin Field. Bombs had cratered it, but the marble stands still remained. He could almost hear the roar of the crowd, feel the vibrations from a thousand jackboots hitting the earth in unison.

There was an electricity here, a sick and dangerous magic, one that lingered, like the scent of rot in the air.

It was December, and the light was fading early. Even at midday, there was a twilight sort of darkness to the city and no sense of merriment. Germans, who had loved the pagan holiday their priests had confiscated for Christ, were not celebrating this year.

They had nothing to celebrate, nothing at all.

Tyrone was wondering how he could photograph this, how he could catch not just the weeds and craters in the field that once held the flower of Nazi youth, but the sense of illness here, of a twisted and decaying ideology that had somehow captured an entire people.

And then he saw her, huddled in rags against one of the benches, watching him.

She was slender to the point of gauntness, her clothing in rags. Her hair, midnight black, was tangled over her face, but he didn't need to see it.

The magic sparkled off her like the aftermath of a flashbulb's light.

He did not try to photograph her. He knew it would be useless. At best, he would get a collection of rags. At worst, a ruined film with none of his pictures saved.

Instead, he let his camera hang around his neck as he walked toward her, slowly enough to let her flee if she felt she had to.

As he approached, she pushed her hair away from her face. Her savage beauty remained, perhaps even stronger now that no fat lined her bones.

"I thought it was you," she said, her voice huskier than he remembered. She spoke an old German, one he barely understood. "You look like them."

He could not remember her name, even though they had been betrothed. Like his own, he had not thought of it in centuries. And now she probably blocked it from his mind so that he would have no power over her.

He sat beside her, the marble cold through his wool pants. "I came looking for you," he said.

"Not me." She gave him a small smile, and he was grateful that it was small. He no longer had defenses against even the slightest magic. "You wanted to be the conquering hero, just like those you've emulated for so long."

He almost denied it, and then he remembered his fantasy—sitting on the Throne of Success, extending his family's honor, becoming one of the High Folk for all of eternity.

"It's like a disease, isn't it? Some kind of infection that gets passed from creature to creature. Now you have it." She shook her magnificent head, then gazed across the empty expanse of field. "And look where it got them."

He started when he realized that she thought he empathized with the Nazis. He wondered if she knew what was going on across town, how Hitler's henchmen were just beginning to find out there was no justification for their crimes.

Her eyes glittered as she watched him, and they made him even more uneasy. There was a great intelligence in them, but nothing else.

He had never loved her—the People did not speak of love, thinking it a human invention—but he had been bound to her, by tradition and fascination and a common heritage.

It all felt so long ago.

"My father?" Tyrone asked. "How do I find him?"

She looked down, smoothed her rags as if they were a gown made of silk. Then she shook her head.

"I can't find him?" Tyrone asked. "Because of what I've become?"

She shook her head again.

"He can't be dead." Tyrone's voice shook. "The People do not die."

"Did not die," she said. "But all things have an end."

She almost said his name then—his true name—but

she caught herself just in time. He could feel it, hovering between them, before it vanished.

"The People can't be dead," he said. "You're not."

She shrugged. "Dead, scattered, destroyed. Even we had no defense from fire that rains from the sky, burning the trees and sucking away the air. Some of us managed to escape, only to be discovered and taken . . . hideous places. Hideous."

She shuddered, lost in memory.

Then he heard his father's voice, as clear as if the man had been beside him. *We have magic. They have strength.*

Had his father foreseen this? The craters, the destruction, the rubble? Had his father known?

"Why did you reveal yourself to me?" Tyrone asked.

She brushed her hair away from her face again, and this time, her smile was soft. She put her hand on his cheek, and her skin was cold. Not the cold of a person who had sat too long in the December twilight, but the cold of marble, of something that had no life at all.

"Because," she said, "it is rare to get the chance to say good-bye."

And then she vanished, leaving only a swirl of air. He reached for her, knowing that she hadn't moved, but he could not find her. He recited the old words, but she did not come back.

He sat on the marble seats long into the growing dark. But the only ghosts that surrounded him marched in unison under what they believed to be a bright, sunlight sky. He could not banish them, and he could not photograph them.

Not that he really wanted to try.

* * *

He searched for the next two hundred days, while he listened to testimony about atrocities that shocked even his ancient spirit. He befriended a few locals, but heard only sad stories of beautiful people in rags, of lights exploding against the darkness as if hit with invisible grenades, of a sense of loss so deep that it seemed to come from the earth itself.

And finally, finally, the trial ended, and he was able to go home—although not the place he had meant by home all those months before. He was an American raised in Europe, a Europe that no longer existed, if it ever had. A Europe as misremembered as Hans Sachs had been, a *meistersinger* who may not have been a master singer at all.

Years later, Tyrone was going through his old photographs, looking at the best of the unpublished ones for a history book he had been hired to illustrate, when he found the shots he had taken that afternoon early in the trials, the afternoon he had walked to the edge of town with only three candy bars, a flask of water, and his camera.

Wisps of light appeared at the edge of the exposures, hints of turrets rising in the air. It took him a while, but he eventually located the negatives and made new prints.

The wisps were in every one.

The People were still there. They had seen him, sensed his thoughts, and had judged him unworthy.

So they had sent her, his betrothed, a woman whose family specialized in Passing and Pranks, to test him.

She had fooled the human, just like her family had done for generations.

Fooled the human, and once again maintained her position among the High Folk.

He smiled. From their perspective, he had failed.
But from his, he had not.

For in the past two cycles since he had been gone,
nothing among the People had changed.

Nothing, that is, except him.

CHANGELING

John Helfers

John Helfers is a writer and editor living in
the midwest. His fiction appears in more than
thirty anthologies, including *Sol's Children*
and *The Sorcerer's Academy*. His first anthology, *Black Cats and Broken Mirrors*, was published by DAW Books in 1998 and has been
followed by several more, including *Alien Abductions*, *Star Colonies*, *Warrior Fantastic*,
Knight Fantastic, *The Mutant Files*, and *Villains Victorious*. Among his recent projects
are the third book in the first officially li-
censed *Twilight Zone* trilogy of novels and a
nonfiction history of the United States Navy.

From the very first day of his life, Trent knew this
was not his world.

Growing up he could recall being held, right after
his birth, in two gentle, delicate hands. Light, brilliant,
golden-white light was all around, obscuring the whispering faces of those clustered around him. Although
he could not comprehend what they were saying, the
voices were sibilant yet melodious, like a gentle spring
wind rippling through clusters of tinkling bells. He did

hear one word that stayed in the corners of his memory ever after, always teasing him with its insistent, echoing call:

Tren'talas

He felt a spot of wetness on his cheek, and forever after a small, pale mark remained just below his eye, which, if he grew angry or embarrassed, would stay bone white while the rest of his fair skin flushed red. As he grew up, Trent's fingers would often touch that mark, with a small part of his mind always wondering about the face it had dropped from.

From this peaceful harmony of sights, sounds and touches he was ripped without preamble or warning, taken through a portal into a lesser world, a muted world. He was passed over unceremoniously into a cradle unlike anything he had known before, a small cubicle of plastic and, to him, rough-woven cloth. The comforting, warm light and the beautiful voices receded, growing dimmer, then vanished altogether, leaving Trent swaddled in darkness.

His next memory was of harsh, blinding whiteness, cold and glaring. Two hands picked him up and carried him away, each step jarring his body, punctuated by sharp clicks that seemed to tap on his skull. This place smelled unnatural, antiseptic, enclosed. Trent always remembered that he had wanted to cry, but he was too afraid.

He was taken to another place, with a different light, not like the first warm silver gleam, but an improvement over the severe brightness of the second light. The cloth surrounding him was rough, but not totally unpleasant. The being carrying him made a noise, and was responded to by another being nearby. Trent felt himself being held out, then accepted into two other hands, brought close to another warm body.

The beings continued to make noises, and he stared into a face he did not recognize.

These were the memories he kept, often waking from the same dream in which he relived the experience, night after night. Another recurring dream—more of a brief series of individual fragmented sensations—often followed this first one. It consisted of impenetrable darkness, then searing, burning red pain, first on one side of his head, then the other. Trent always wanted to scream, to cry, to wail, but he never could. The shrieking pain continued until the darkness enfolded him again. When he had that dream, he often didn't sleep for the rest of the night.

Trent *knew* he was different. What he didn't know was how.

Growing up had not been easy. Trent had refused to nurse, and through trial and error it was discovered that he could drink only goat's milk. Disposable diapers were unusable, as the mere touch of plastic caused his skin to erupt in angry, weeping red sores. The family doctor confirmed powerful allergies to dyes, plastic, latex, metal, rubber, polyester, bleach, penicillin, practically everything manmade, even though there almost no history of existing allergies in the family.

His mother, Mona, made changes in his clothes, shoes, diet, everything that could be modified. From an early age he only wore cotton and linen clothes fastened with carved wooden buttons, tiny leather shoes, and cloth diapers, which were washed by hand in natural detergent. Everything he ate had to be as fresh as possible, nothing canned, bottled, or from a jar.

Trent also became lethargic if he was in an enclosed room for too long, complaining of headaches, and often saying, "The tips of my ears hurt." When Mona examined him, she found no inflammation. Even when Trent pointed to the top of his ear, she still saw nothing wrong. One night his mother found him sleeping underneath an open window in December, and realized the recycled air in the house was causing the problem. She made sure a window was left open for him every day, no matter how cold it was outside. Unlike the other children, two boys and a girl, Trent thrived on the outside air, even in winter. He suffered only was when he was deprived of it.

He was the same with sunlight. Every year during the middle of winter he grew irritable, snapping at his brothers, sister, and parents half the time, sleeping and barely moving the other half. Their doctor diagnosed seasonal-affective disorder, and prescribed sunlamp therapy, which helped a bit, but Mona and Trent found the best way to help was to get him outside whenever the sun came out, even if it was an hour or less. Mona often took him with her to her real estate appointments, where his calm demeanor, perfect manners, and sky-blue eyes would draw admiring glances and comments from clients.

Trent was set apart by his appearance, not only by his clothes and food, but his face as well. Where the other three children had been blond at birth, their hair turned brown as they grew up. Trent's locks remained the color of new corn, fresh and golden-white. The family's half-German, half-Native American heritage lent the other children a stocky solidity; they would be tall like their father, and dark-eyed and caramel-complected like their mother. Trent's skin was pale, to match his hair, and his eyes were that brilliant, glittering blue, like two winking sapphires embedded in wind-polished bone. Where his siblings all inherited their father's broad Germanic features, Trent's visage was tapered, almost foxlike, with angled eyes, high cheekbones, and a heart-shaped face. While growing up, his father had jokingly referred to him as "the adopted child," until Mona had stopped him. It hadn't stopped his father from loving all of their children, impartially true, but he did. He was never as close to Trent, however, as he was to the rest of the kids. Trent and his mother, however, shared a special bond.

When Trent was four, she found him in the attic one morning, the contents of a banker's box spread out around him. He was wearing the tiny cotton gloves he often used around the house, and bathed in a shaft of spring light that drifted in from the octagonal window, looked so intent on what he was doing he just about broke her heart. Sneaking back downstairs, she got a glass of milk and a plate of oatmeal cookies, then crept back upstairs. When her head cleared the top step again she found Trent regarding her as if he knew she had been there the entire time.

"What are you doing, sweetheart?" she asked, walking over to him and sitting down.

He lifted the photo album open on his lap, showing her a group of pictures.

"Is this me?" he asked.

Mona smiled as she looked at the tiny, narrow face in the picture. Unlike other newborns, Trent had lacked the baby fat most children had, but it hadn't slowed his development at all. He was ahead of all of his peers in kindergarten, and his teacher had already mentioned putting him in a gifted and talented class.

"Yes, honey, that is you, about three days after we brought you home from the hospital."

Trent stared at the picture, then grasped the page with a white-gloved hand and turned it. "What's the matter with my ears?"

Mona sighed and considered both her son and the picture, which was of a side view of Trent's head, showing a tiny, delicate ear that tapered to a distinct point at the top. "Sweetheart, sometimes, people are born . . . different from everybody else."

"Oh, like the baby we saw in the store?"

Mona smiled again. "Not exactly. The Trobers are from South Africa, an area of the world where people's skin is a different color. There are many people like them, but that's not exactly what I'm talking about.

"You've seen my ears, right?" she asked, sweeping her long hair back to reveal them. Trent looked at them again, reaching out to gently touch first the bottom, then the top of her ear. He nodded.

"And you've seen Papa's ears, and your brother Ryan's, and Jesse's, and Fiona's ears, right?"

Another nod.

"And none of them had pointed ears, right?"

Trent shook his head, his eyes straying to the picture again, then back to her.

"Well, as I said, sometimes people are born with differences. The difficulty with this is that other people don't understand, and they tease the person who's different, kind of like Jesse teases you sometimes, only they tease worse. So, before you got too big, your father and I made the decision to . . . have your ears modified slightly."

Trent took off one of his gloves and reached up to his own ear, feeling the refashioned cartilage and skin there. "So I would look like everyone else."

Mona nodded. "Yes, my dear, that's right. This way no one will tease you at school about your ears."

Trent looked back at the photo of his pointed ears again. "Like everyone else." For a moment his face darkened, then he looked up. "C'n I have a cookie?"

"Of course you can." Mona handed him the glass of milk and a cookie, and the two spent the rest of the afternoon poring over the photo albums. But from that day on, Trent began growing his hair so that it covered his ears. It was one of the few disagreements between himself and his parents, and eventually they reached a compromise where Trent could wear his hair longer than usual.

He never mentioned it again, but several months later, when Mona was in the attic again, she noticed the same photo album on top of the box where it was usually kept. When she opened it, she found the picture of Trent's ear was gone. She thought for a moment, then went to his room, shivering at the crisp fall breeze blowing in. Looking around, she went to his bed and lifted the pillow.

There, on the mattress sheet, was the picture.

Mona left it there, and never said a word to him about it.

School was a challenge every day. In its codified, cliquish environment an outsider is always looked upon askance, and no one could hold a candle to Trent for being different. His clothes, hair, aloof demeanor, and intelligence set him apart from the beginning. Whereas the other kids came to school wearing designer clothes, even in the lower grades, and eating the processed food ladled out in the school cafeteria, his clothes were styleless, through comfortable, and his lunch was always packed in a brown paper bag.

Once the other kids learned of his allergies, it became a popular game to try and spike his food with anything artificial, just to watch the reaction. Trent learned quickly not to let his food out of his sight, even for a moment, otherwise he would go hungry. It did help that he could taste the wrongness of whatever they tried to put into his lunch, but it still rankled him.

To his credit, Trent tried to make friends, but his attempts always ended in failure. Everything about him marked him as unusual, and the other kids sensed this. Even if they were able to look past his appearance, the shapeless linen clothes, the wooden buttons (even the transferred Mennonite boy made fun of him), there was something just not right about him. It went both ways. Trent saw from the beginning that he had nothing in common with the other children. Indeed, it was like he was observing a different species, a type of human, going about their lives, embroiled in their petty concerns about school and their fumbling, awkward attempts to interact with girls on the playground. Trent would often walk among them, feeling like he wasn't even there, invisible to everybody.

The only solace he found during recess was on the swingsets. Trent often whiled away the whole period, swinging higher than anyone else, oblivious to the tingling the cold metal links started in his fingers. Back and forth, back and forth, faster, higher. For when he went fast enough, he felt like he could touch the sky. He would never admit it to anyone else (and wouldn't even admit it to himself), but he secretly hoped to go fast enough to propel him back to wherever it was he had first come from, where everything was silver-white light, and that chorus of gentle voices surrounded him.

If he could just go a little faster, a little higher—he could almost *see* that place, beckoning to him—*if I can just dream hard enough—if I can just fly fast enough—*

Then the school bell would ring, and Trent would snap back to cold reality, which was sometimes so jarring that he would fall off the swing. He would look around, befuddled for a moment, then pick himself up, brush himself off, and slowly walk inside, casting one last glance at the swaying canvas swings on the deserted playground.

Maybe tomorrow, he would think to himself. *Maybe tomorrow I'll be able to.*

Trent didn't know where the place was that he wanted to go to, but he knew it existed. He had seen it in his dreams, when he wasn't dreaming about his passage over, or the bloody red painful visions. A land unlike anything he had ever seen in his young life would unfold before him, a land so verdant, so green and alive, that it made his heart ache not to be there. Gentle, rolling hills framed silent, flowing streams that meandered through the countryside, all illuminated by a shimmering golden light that was almost, but not quite like what he remembered from when he was born. And in the distance, rising like a star-filled spire toward the heavens, was a dazzling castle seemingly created out of one enormous flawless crystal, beckoning to him in his mind.

But no matter how hard he tried, whether it was on the swings or in his dreams, he could never get there. He was always on the outside looking in, seeing it through a barrier that he could not pass through. But he never stopped trying.

At times, it wasn't only the students who ignored Trent, either. Sometimes, when he didn't feel like contributing in class, he was ignored by the teachers as well. He had first discovered this ability one day during a particular boring history class, while the professor had been talking about the foggy night when General Washington had crossed the Delaware River. Trent had imagined a misty cloud oozing into the classroom that obscured him from everyone's sight. When he came out of his daydream, he was surrounded by empty desks, and the lights were off in the deserted room. Trent collected his books, then froze as the next teacher came in, turned the lights on, and began erasing the board, all without acknowledging him in any way. Picking up his backpack, Trent had slipped out of the room unnoticed. Since then he had refined the ability to become "unseen," as he called it, whenever he wished, usually to avoid conflict with the other kids.

The years passed, and Trent's problems at school worsened. Although he passed the curriculum with ease, in high school computers were becoming the preferred tool for learning. The machines were the first thing that Trent actively hated, the glowing artificial plastic monitors squatting on the desks, the whirring, clicking CPU itself, created out of silicon, worked metal, and chemicals. The soulless clack of the keys, dozens of them tapping, always tapping, reverberating inside his head until he thought he would scream. It seemed the computers shared his antipathy, for Trent always got a shock whenever he attempted to use one, even if he had grounded himself. Because of this, he stuck to books for his research, only using the computers if absolutely necessary.

One Monday afternoon his English teacher, Mr. Robertson, assigned the class a report on different mythologies of the world. He had put several scraps of paper in a hat, and the students each picked one. When it was his turn, Trent reached in and plucked a slip out with indifference, unfolding it to read:

Celtic

For some reason he couldn't describe, a strange thrill came over him when he saw the word, and something he thought had been buried long ago and almost forgotten stirred deep inside of him, the barest flicker of an emotion he hadn't felt for many years. Trent didn't hear the rest of the lecture, he just kept staring at the paper and the word on it.

In study hall he signed out to go to the library, and began looking up the school's very slim Celtic mythology selection. Bypassing the shelves crammed with Greek and Roman myth and legend, he pulled two academic tomes out. Five minutes of flipping through them made his head swim.

Returning to the shelf, he was about to put them back when he saw another book that had been shoved behind the ones he had taken. It was old, in an emerald green library binding. Trent reached back and pulled it out, blowing the fine mist of dust it had accumulated. *The Children of Danu*, he puzzled out from the near-illegible markings on the spine.

He took it to a carrel, sat down, flipped it open to a random page, and froze.

Staring back up at him from the yellowed paper was a slim being that could have been Trent's older brother. Not the sibling that he saw at home every night, this person in the painting had his hair, eyes, skin tone, face, gaze—everything the same.

For Trent, time stopped in that instant. He forgot where he was, forgot the harsh, foreign world around him. All of his attention was sucked into that page and the cool, imperious stare of the figure he was looking at. He was afraid to move, afraid to breathe, afraid to lift his eyes, fearing that if he did anything the book would disappear like it had never existed, gone to the place he could see only in his dreams. He lifted his hand, paused, then, inch by inch, reached out to touch the paper—

They do *exist.*

His trembling hand felt the dry texture of the page, his fingers skimmed over the picture of the painting. He stared at the picture until the bell rang for his next class. Silently he went to the counter, checked out the volume, and drifted through the rest of his day wrapped in a emotion he had never felt before—hope.

Trent was now a boy possessed. He began researching the Celtic pantheon, its myths and legends, learning all he could. When he had exhausted the books in the library, he reached an uneasy truce with the computer, even though using it was like being electrocuted one volt at a time.

For the first time, Trent found something that made sense to him, that felt right. He immersed himself in the tales of the Emerald Isle. The exploits of Cuchulainn, the great Celtic hero. The rise and fall of Finn, who had eaten the salmon of knowledge, and learned everything there was to know in the universe. The great and terrible gods, from Brigit, goddess of the fire and creativity, to Macha, the fearsome goddess of strife and horses, to Oenghus, the god of love. He also learned of the Tuatha de Danann, or children of the goddess Danu, the goddess who gave birth to the Celtic pantheon. The Tuatha de were fairies that live in the Otherworld, an enchanted land—

"—from which they could cross into the mortal realm on certain nights at fairy rings or mounds,"

Trent read to himself one evening. "There are many stories of persons traveling to Tir na' n-Og, or the 'Land of Youth,' but it is during the festival of Samhain, from October 31 to November 1, where the barriers between the Otherworld and the human realm disappear altogether, and both faerie and mortal can travel between the two worlds without difficulty, particularly at the dozens of *sidhe,* or fairy mounds, scattered over the landscape of Ireland."

He also read many tales from the British Isles, Scandinavia, and Germany that mentioned the changeling—a *fae* child switched at birth for a human child who caused nothing but trouble for the family he had been placed into. The majority of the folk tales always ended with the changeling being banished from the family's home, usually by suspending him over a roaring fire, which caused the changeling to flee with the smoke up the chimney.

Is that who I am? he thought while at the bathroom mirror, looking at himself in the silvered glass. *The whole idea sounds so ludicrous, and yet . . . the dreams . . . the allergies I have . . . nothing else makes sense. But it's all supposed to be a myth, and yet, there could be a way to find out . . .*

Using his family's computer, Trent struggled online and figured out the distance to Ireland. More than 3,500 miles away. With no car of his own, transportation out of Rhinelander alone would be difficult, let alone crossing the Atlantic Ocean.

But I don't have to pay for a ticket to Ireland; I can just get on board a flight in Milwaukee, if I can get there. Greyhound could do it. Trent leaned back and stared at the calendar on the wall next to the desk. *October 16, a little over two weeks.*

* * *

The next ten days passed at glacial speed. Trent's dreams grew more vivid, he could now smell the rich earth of those green fields, wreathed in early morning fog. The castle of crystal glittered in his mind's eye, the perfect spirals pointing towards the impossibly blue sky. On several nights he woke in different rooms of the house, even finding himself outside early one morning.

Trent barely ate anything, he was so focused on the trip, and just as important, his deception of the family that had raised him. While they weren't his true parents and siblings, they had raised him with all of the love and care they could give. His life here hadn't been a bad one, but he knew it simply wasn't where he belonged. His mother, sensing something was up, tried to ask him about it, but Trent hedged around the subject, telling her he was really busy in school.

On the morning of October 30, Trent got up, showered, dressed, ate, and left the house. Instead of going to school, however, he headed for the bus station, where Greyhound #5813 was leaving for Milwaukee, as it did every weekday. Trent ghosted onto the bus, right past the driver, and took a seat near the back. At 8:06 AM, the bus closed its door and pulled out of the depot, heading for Green Bay. After a brief layover at the depot on Main Street, they got on U.S. Highway 43 south to Milwaukee. Five and a half hours after they had started, the buildings of the city could be seen outside the bus windows.

After a few stops at various stations, the bus ended up at General Mitchell International Airport. When it pulled up to the terminal, Trent shouldered his backpack and got off with the rest of the passengers.

* * *

Nightfall found Trent standing at a bank of telephones. Taking a deep breath, he picked up the receiver and fed quarters into the slot. He had spent the last several hours browsing through the used bookstore in the airport and picking the edible vegetables out of a wilted salad he had bought for dinner. Now he wanted to leave a message to his adopted family before he left, close enough to his flight time that he would be away before anyone could try and stop him.

How am I going to explain this? He alternately hoped that his mother would and wouldn't answer the phone.

He heard a click, and the machine picked up. "You've reached 555-7159, please leave a message, and we'll get back to you."

"Um—hi, Mom, Dad, it's Trent. By the time you've heard this, I'll be gone. I wanted to call and let you know that I'm all right, I wasn't kidnapped or anything. Anyway, I am eighteen now, so I've made my choice—" A small part of his mind said *Quit babbling and get on with it.* "I don't know what you're going to tell the others, but—just tell them I knew I didn't belong here, and it wasn't their fault, I just—I have to find—"

"Trent, it's Mom, where are you? What's happened? Are you all right?"

For a moment he froze, startled by hearing her familiar voice. "Uh—yeah, Mom, I'm fine."

"I just got home and heard you on the machine. What are you talking about?"

"No, Mom, everything's all right, but—I'm not coming home tonight."

"What? What do you mean?"

"I don't expect you to understand this, but I had to call and let you know so you wouldn't worry. I know this isn't going to make any sense, but—I know I don't belong here, in this—world. I've known for a while now. So I'm going to find—I'm going home. To my real home."

There was nothing but silence from the other end for a long time. Then, in a voice so small it sounded like a frightened five-year-old, she said, "It never was a dream . . ."

Trent almost fell over. "What? What did you say?" he asked, pressing the plastic earpiece closer to his head, heedless of the irritation it was causing him.

"Oh, Trent, all of my life I thought it was a dream, just a side-effect of the drugs they gave me when you were born. But, deep down, so deep that I thought I'd never have to admit it, I've known—I've always known that you were—not my son."

His mother's words began coming faster, the crack in the walls of her family letting out memories in a stream that threatened to turn into a deluge. "Your ears . . . the operation . . . your allergies . . . how different you were from the other children in temperament and personality. I said nothing, for what was there to say. But that first night after the labor—*I saw them.*"

"You . . . saw . . . my real parents . . ." Trent said.

"I had thought it was only a dream until you called—" Trent heard the tears in his mother's voice. "I had crept down to the nursery—even though they told me not to—said I should rest. I saw them both in there. They were surrounded by the most beautiful silver-white light—it lit the room like daylight. The looks on their faces were heartbreaking, love, sorrow, and hope all at once. A tear from your mother dropped on your cheek. I—I must have made some noise, for they both looked up at me—and smiled. It was so serene, so peaceful, and yet they were so sad—I put my hand to the glass and watched as they took up my son and laid you down in his place. I wanted to say something, but the words just wouldn't come out.

"She—your mother—came over to me, and pressed her hand to the glass where mine was. With her other she touched her mouth, then put her hand to her breast. I just stood there, watching her. Her husband came over to her and took her hand. She was crying, but he was—stoic, I guess you'd call it, although I could see the pain in his eyes. They both bowed to me, and walked away, into the light. That's all I can remember.

"When I awoke, I was back in my hospital bed, with no memory of how I had gotten back. I woke up just in time to see you being brought in, and placed in my arms.

"For a moment I didn't know what to do, what I should say. I knew no one would believe me, and I didn't want to possibly lose my other children either. You looked enough like your brothers and sister that there would be no question as to whose child you were. And I wasn't about to have you go through a DNA test, because I was terrified of what they might find. When you were older, your blood was tested, and it appeared to be normal healthy blood, so that fear was gone. By then, for all intents and purposes, you were my son, and I already had difficulty thinking of you as anyone else's. That might have been something your parents did, to help me accept what had happened, I don't know. But just now, it has all come back to me, and I know it really happened. So I understand what you're doing, and why.

"I'm sorry I never told you. For a long time I didn't believe it, and—you have always been one of my children, no matter where you came from. Recently I'd had a feeling that something was about to happen, but I dismissed it, and now you are going." She half-chuckled, half-sobbed. "You do realize it's going to cause quite a stir around here."

"Yes, I . . . I know. Try to help the others understand, especially Fiona; she'll take it the hardest."

"Yes, honey, I will."

Now that this had been opened up to him, a thousand questions sprang up in Trent's mind, but before he could put any of them into words, he heard the last boarding call of the flight he had to get on. "I—I have to go—Mom."

"I know, son. Please be careful."

"I will. If—if I'm ever back, I will come see you."

"I'd like that. And Trent—"

"Yes?"

"If you see my son, and he is happy, please don't tell him."

"I—"

"For me, please?"

The words stuck in his throat, but he got them out. "I promise I won't tell him."

"Thank you, I knew I could count on you."

"Good-bye, Mom."

"Good-bye, my son."

At 11:30 PM Trent walked through the metal detector, which was manned by two security personnel and an armed sheriff's deputy, none of whom took any notice of him. He trotted to the gate, breezing past several boarders going through a luggage search, and headed up the walkway to the airplane, finding a seat in the middle of the coach section. Through his research he knew the stewardesses would do a head count of the checked-in passengers, so he would have to remain invisible until well into the flight.

Trent already had enough on his mind, however. The revelation from his mother had shaken him more that he'd cared to admit. Now that he had had time to digest what she had told him, he found that he wasn't angry, but more saddened than anything. The feeling of aloneness inside him intensified. Trent realized that a part of him had expected his mother here to ask him to come home, and had been disappointed when she hadn't. *But she knew who I was and where I came from long before I did. She must have felt the parting coming, even if she didn't recognize it; that was why she took it as well as she did. That must have been the reason—*

A wave of dizziness came over him, and Trent fanned himself with the magazine from the pocket ahead of him. He was also trying not to think about the stale, canned-smelling air that permeated the plane, his seat, and was infusing itself into his hair and clothes. Even to his dulled senses, the air was rank and recycled, bereft of any freshness. *It's going to be a long flight,* he thought. Having never been in a jetliner before, he was also acutely aware of every noise the vehicle made as it was prepared to fly, and, since he had no idea what each sound meant, was forced to sit and endure it, only able to relieve his frustration by gripping the armrests of his seat so hard the plastic ends flexed and creaked, which did not reassure him one bit.

The plane left the gate and taxied onto the runway right on schedule. Trent leaned back in his chair, trying to relax. He vaguely heard the flight attendant running through the safely checklist, but he was a million miles away. *I am on the right track,* he thought.

I must be, if what she said is true. Great, now I'm even rationalizing like a human, he thought, closing his eyes as the airliner shuddered through takeoff. After a minute, the vibrations decreased, and the plane lifted into the air. Trent suffered a moment of panic as the pressure swelled inside his head, but soon figured out that swallowing helped immensely. The anticipation of his journey had worn off, and, with a vague sense of surprise, despite his surroundings and the muted roar of the engines, sleep soon overtook him.

Trent awoke to the sound of the flight attendant's voice over the speakers, and jerked awake, thinking he was dreaming in his bed at home, and had just been awakened by his mother talking to him through a megaphone. Looking around, he found himself surrounded by a sea of empty seats dotted here and there with various islands of humanity, the tops of various heads poking up from the blue and green ocean of cloth.

Looking out the window, Trent saw a gold and green patchwork of fields and meadows, bordered by miles and miles of hard-packed and paved paths and roads and even more neatly-stacked stone fences parceling the countryside into a quilt as far as the eye could see. He took a deep breath, trying to taste the air, and inhaled a miasma of dead airplane atmosphere, making him double over with coughing, tears springing to his eyes.

The airplane touched down without incident, and after a few minutes Trent disembarked with the rest of the bleary-eyed passengers. The airport smelled much like the one he had left on the other side of the Atlantic, and Trent found it hard to hide his disappointment. *I would have thought the gate to the Other-world would have left a bit more of its flavor when the wall between the worlds fell each year. Ah, well . . .*

He stopped in mid-thought, concentrating. There was something in the back of his mind, calling to him, pointing him in the direction he needed to go. After exchanging what little money he had, Trent left the airport and found the bus terminal. He wandered among the buses until he found one traveling to the town of Athlone and went unseen, slipping aboard and taking a seat in the back. The bus pulled out twenty minutes later, flowing with the rest of the traffic east on the N6. Trent stared out the window at the square cement houses, boxed lawns, and old, old stacked stone fences hemming in flocks of shaggy sheep. After stops in half-a-dozen small towns and villages along the way, the bus disgorged the rest of its passengers in Athlone in the late afternoon.

The pull was stronger here, and Trent knew his final destination was nearby. He set out back along the N6 again, and after forty minutes, came to the narrow lane with a sign pointing down it that read *Castledaly Manor 3 Km.* He turned right and kept going down the narrow road.

After wending his way over several small hills, Trent came to another stone fence. Nearby was a driveway, and a wooden sign that read *Castledaly Manor.* As he looked at the sign, he felt something drawing him towards a particular area on the manor grounds. Trent took a hesitant step, not sure if he should expect something to come leaping out at him from the thick vine-choked forest concealing any buildings on the property. When nothing happened, he took another step, then another. Exhaling with relief, he kept walking down the drive.

The pull increased as he continued, becoming almost a palpable force by now. Victorian-style post lights lit the driveway every dozen yards or so, and he stopped at the third one down, tucked into an alcove in the thick foliage. There was a small break in the treeline, almost invisible just a few feet away. The pull was coming from the forest. Darkness was falling, and Trent looked around again, suddenly realizing the strange thing about where he was.

It's October, but the forest is still green, and there's absolutely no noise here, he thought. Unlike in America, where the leaves were already dropping, Trent faced an almost impenetrable wall of flora, with spindly trees growing close together interspersed with large ferns and other plants he didn't recognize at all. No birds called, nothing rustled in the underbrush, even the wind couldn't be roused here. The break in the woods beckoned him, and almost without thinking he slipped into the forest.

The trees swallowed him as if he had never existed, and he had taken no more than a dozen steps before he could barely see the opening behind him. The pull was so strong now he could almost hear it, low and insistent, coming from somewhere ahead of him.

After several twisting turns, clambering over fallen tree trunks, and trying not to twist his ankle on rocks that seemed to appear out of nowhere, Trent came to a small clearing and stopped. As the last rays of light fought through the thick cover overhead, he stared at the center of the break and what it contained.

If the forest had been quiet, the clearing was defined by the total absence of sound, with everything around him as still as if it was frozen out of time. A huge tree that, to his eye, had absolutely no business being there, didn't so much grow out of the earth as erupted from it. Compared to the other trees in the forest, all of which looked alike enough to belong, this one was as different as a palm tree in middle of a Wisconsin farm. Its roots, some as thick as his arm, sprawled out in all directions, diving into the dirt only to push back out a few yards later. Trent got the distinct impression that the tree had probably choked the life out of more than one competitor during the past few centuries. The trunk looked smooth and naked, but when he looked closer Trent saw the tree was clad in finely striated bark colored tan, chocolate, and sienna. Rough, branches poked out only a few feet from the ground, rather than clustered towards the top of the trunk. In the dim light Trent couldn't see what its leaves looked like, or if it even had any leaves at all.

He noticed that he hadn't been the first person to come here, however. Trinkets and souvenirs from previous visitors nestled in forks and hollow spaces all over the massive tree. A watch, shot glasses, empty airline liquor bottles, and coins of all kinds were wedged under peeling pieces of bark here and there, placed in every possible crook of branches, from the ones lower to the ground to those a dozen feet up. The entire place seemed ancient and eternal, as if this tree had been here when the island had first split off from the kingdom over the sea, been here when Vikings raided the small coastal fishing villages, been here during the raids, births, deaths, marriages, battles, reigns, and countless lives that had come and gone and would be here forever after.

Trent just stared at the tree for several long minutes, not moving, trying to take in everything—the tree, the clearing, the air, the approaching night—with every sense available to him. He kicked off his shoes and socks so he could stand barefoot on the rich black-brown loam, enjoying the chill as it soaked into the soles of his feet. Closing his eyes, he held out his hands, thinking he could feel the very currents of time itself flowing into and out of the tree, years, decades, centuries, millennia, and perhaps even farther back.

He didn't know how long it was, but he felt a wisp of moisture cross his face. Trent looked around and saw long tendrils of white fog encircling the clearing, shrouding the surrounding woods in a spectral haze. Trent watched as it rose and obscured the forest around him. As if lost in the depths of a distant dream, the trees bordering the clearing around him faded from sight, and he began to walk.

Encircled by the light gray mists, Trent had never felt so comfortable in his life, even though he could not see where he was going. He could, however, smell the destination waiting for him in the distance. The teasing mists brought with them a rich, earthy aroma mingled with sweet spring grasses and the crisp, cool scent of an early morning rain, the likes of which he had never experienced before. Trent took a deep breath, as if his nose had previously been two dead holes on his face, and now had just come to life, invigorated by the tantalizing smells. The memories of the harsh odors of the human world, asphalt and plastic and hairspray, were all left behind, replaced by new aromas of life and earth and wind. For the first time in his life, the lost tips of his ears didn't tingle or ache.

The mists receded around him, and Trent found himself standing in a forest of trees exactly like the one he had found in the clearing. He saw their thick branches intertwining to form a complete canopy of green, blocking out any sunlight from above. But there was light, a clean, white light that dared to enter this dark yet peaceful place. Trent reached out and placed his hand on the nearest tree trunk, exulting in the texture under his fingers; that same sense of eternity he had found in the clearing was also captured in this forest. He took a deep breath, to hold that scent and feeling somewhere inside him, and walked into the light.

Spread out before him, bathed that golden-white light that seemed to come from the entire sky, was the land he had seen only in his dreams. After years of seeing it through the dim window of sleep every night, it was a veritable feast for his senses, from the cool wind caressing his face to the bubbling river, the verdant green of the meadows and hills, and—

the castle

Several miles away rose a glittering collection of spired towers, pointing into the brilliant sky. The castle glowed with its own inner light, which reflected and refracted off a myriad of elegant arches, soaring buttresses, lofty pinnacles, and a sea of walking parapets and window-pierced gables on every spiraling, shell-like roof. The entire building came together in graceful symmetry, each tower or pinnacle or spire blending harmoniously with its neighbors. The light spilling from the windows of the castle bathed it in a glow that automatically commanded attention, as if a star had fallen to the earth and rested there, blazing gloriously for all to see.

As soon as he recognized it, Trent settled his pack on his shoulder and began walking to the castle.

Trent did not keep track of how far he walked, or how much time it took, for as soon as he took that first step he was lost in this new world, caught up in its intoxicating freshness. At the same time, he had the distinct feeling that he had been here before. When he was tired, he slept. When he was hungry, he had but to pick an apple from trees scattered throughout the fields, or scoop a handful of water from the clear river that wound its way across the fields, and he was refreshed. When he awoke each morning he would stand for a moment and look around, back at the forest which was growing smaller and smaller, and ahead at the castle, which loomed ever larger in his vision.

Occasionally he would see people in the fields, or on the neat smooth paths that crossed the land, slim, graceful, lithe people with pointed ears, angled almond-shaped eyes, and bright clothes, on their way from or to wherever they were going. He saw elegant buildings too, houses and halls, shops and other places, all inhabited by the de Danann. Trent did not approach them, but remained unseen until he passed. He did not fear them, or concern himself with their reaction, but he knew that they could not help him. Only the castle mattered now.

It may have been days, it may have been weeks, but at last he reached the huge door of the wondrous castle as the light of day faded into night. While the castle was glittering by day, at night its light was softer, muted, like bright starbeams that fell upon the lands around it, bathing the fields and towns in streams of pale silver. Trent was dwarfed by the huge edifice, which was pierced by a set of double doors that reached upward into the clouds. Yet when he approached, the doors swung open even before he touched them. Trent took a deep breath and entered.

Inside, it was as if the occupants had captured a sun and hung it from the thin rafters criss-crossing the ceiling above, channeling that light down to the floor and the hundreds of people in the main hall. The walls of the hall were transparent crystal, so that the occupants could see out, but the emanating light insured that no one could see in.

The floor was filled with de Danann, and Trent's jaw dropped as he saw among them an occasional human, escorting or being escorted by one of the Fair Folk, or at the center of a conversation, with de Danann clustered around them. Everyone was dressed in flowing silks, satins, and velvets shaded in daffodil, rose, indigo, jade, sable, and snow. The women were enrobed in gowns and the men around them were dressed in jackets and slim trousers. Some wore more outlandish costumes that either enhanced or concealed the wearer, sometimes doing both at the same time. Trent just stopped and stared at the explosion of colors and sounds, the brilliance of the entire room. Even through it all, a small part of his mind was acutely aware of his muddy leather shoes, worn wood-buttoned jeans, and his rumpled, faded, long-sleeved shirt, all as far removed from the attire here as a cockroach in a sea of butterflies.

Gradually, he became aware of the conversations nearest him stopping as people turned to look at the new arrival. Like ripples spreading from a rock thrown into a pond, the murmurings and laughter stilled as more and more people became aware of what was happening. Even as the room grew still, a path opened up in front of him, de Danann and humans moving aside, not fearful or angry, but regarding him with an expression combining surprise, wonder, and pity.

The hall seemed to stretch on forever, but as Trent began walking through the crowd, he saw a three-step dais in the distance. Atop that was a pair of beautiful high backed white thrones, which might have been carved from wood, or snow, or bone, he couldn't be sure. As he approached, he saw the woman sitting in one of them, and he stopped, unable to come any closer.

The beauty of the lady sitting in the throne could not be described in simple mortal words. She sat, arms perched on the rests, as if she had been born to it. When she inclined her head to regard him, everyone in the hall bowed to her in one single movement. Trent, however, remained as he was, staring at her though a sudden veil of tears, as if they could make her glorious countenance easier to behold. He had never seen such exquisiteness in all his days. But he did not bow, or even nod his head, he just stood in the center of the hall and looked at her.

The lady rose from her seat and descended the three steps, gliding over to where Trent stood frozen.

"Greetings and welcome, Tren'talas."

When she spoke those words, the ache that Trent had carried in his heart for seventeen years, the ache that had been gone ever since coming to this land burst forth anew inside him. His true name, spoken in that foreign yet familiar language from her lips, not the shortened, corrupted word used in the world he had come from, but the one he had carried locked up deep beneath his heart, beneath his soul, caused those tears brimming on his lashes to spill over and trickle down his cheeks. He opened his mouth, stopped, then tried again, not sure of what he was going to say even as the sounds came out.

The woman smiled and inclined her head. "I see you found the book."

"How do you know me? How is it that I understand you?"

She smiled, and Trent heard strange sounds behind him, like sacks of grain toppling to the floor. Looking around, the lady and he both saw several humans being carried into an antechamber, apparently stunned by what they had just seen.

She shook her head with amusement and regarded him again. "*I know every child of Danu, from the very first to the very last. It has been a very long time since one has crossed over into our world. You honor us with your presence.*"

She reached out with a delicate hand as if to caress his face, but Trent tilted his head back, out of her reach. She smiled, and took her hand away. "Even though you have been away from our lands all this time, some things you still carry within, things that are part of every de Danann," she said in flawless English.

Trent couldn't hold back his anger any longer. Even though there was no answer he could hear that would soothe his pain, he had to ask. "Why? Why was this—?"

Before he could finish she held a hand to his lips. "The answer you seek is best found with your family here."

"I have no family here!" Trent said, the petulance in his voice echoing throughout the hall. "Who would do such a thing and still claim to be my family?"

The lady continued as if he hadn't spoken. "I know what you seek, and I will tell you where they are. They have the answers you are looking for, but I believe that you already have an idea as to what you are going to find."

She looked around the great hall at the dozens of people there, and finally at the throne beside her own, where another human sat, resplendent in golden robes and a midnight-blue cloak. He met Trent's incredulous stare for a moment, then nodded to him.

Trent turned back to the lady before him. "You've got to be kidding."

She did not answer him, but whispered in his ear the directions to his second and final destination. When she had finished the lady stepped back and took his hands in hers. "Know that you are always welcome here, *Tren'talas*."

Trent wiped at his eyes and nodded with one stiff jerk of his head. "Thank you." He turned and stalked away, not looking to either side as he passed the length of the brilliant, beautiful great hall and out its doors into the silent night beyond.

The lady's directions were concise, and several minutes later Trent arrived at a cluster of homes that appeared to sprout from a common hill. They were all clad in similar colors, light ash and blond yew and tan oak, carved in intricate patterns, whorls, and knots. The houses were simple frames that seemed to grow out of the ground itself, with trunks forming the main and cross beams, and branches shaped into small balconies and eaves with an air of peaceful contemplation, spaces where a person could sit and watch the wondrous land around him in reflective quiet. The roofs were composed of successive layers of bark shingles, smooth with tapering ends like the point of a leaf. Every window or opening he saw was an open frame of intertwining branches and sprouting leaves that let the night air flow unimpeded in and out.

Trent felt that same light breeze nudging him toward the third house in the circle. He began walking again, trying to sort out the jumble of feelings inside him. Before he could, however, he found himself at the threshold, and he looked through the open door into the main room of the house.

Inside, a small fire flickered in a rounded stone fireplace, lighting the room with cheery winks of red and gold and orange. Next to it was a circular wooden table, with four slim chairs around it, three occupied, one empty. The de Danann ringing the table were all looking up at him, two with incredulous shock, and one with frank curiosity.

"*Tren'talas . . . my son . . . you have found your way back . . .*" the woman rose from the table, her chair tipping over in her haste, and tentatively approached him, as if he were a stag that would flee at the slightest noise. Her husband also rose, but stayed where he was, the shock on his face having given way to an unutterable sadness.

Trent put his hand on the doorframe, steadying himself, torn between going to his mother and holding her in his arms and turning his back and walking away forever. He watched her come nearer, her hand rising to touch him. Still he did not move. Her fingers came to rest on his cheek, on the one teardrop-shaped spot that even now was cool to the touch.

"*It seems we said good-bye only yesterday, and yet now you are grown, and I know that it has been half a lifetime for you,*" she said, silvered tears gleaming in her eyes.

Trent fought to keep his voice calm. "Where is the one I was traded for?"

A slap to her face would have brought the same reaction. His mother looked away, sobbing quietly. The man came from around the table. "*I will take you to him, Tren'talas.*"

Taking his wife by the shoulders, he led her back to the table and looked to his daughter, who looked to be a few years older than Trent. "*Quel'eala, please see to your mother.*"

He exited the room, motioning for Trent to follow. The two slipped into the narrow alley between the house and its neighbor and began climbing the hill behind both, leaving the lights and warmth behind.

At the top was a small bower composed of interlaced oak trees forming a loose canopy that let the luminosity from the castle drift in on lazy beams of light. In this hollow were several carved statues on a circle of stone pedestals, all facing outward, as if looking over the lands of the Otherworld. The man stopped in front of one of them, a boy who looked about Trent's age, with a serene look on his unmoving features.

"This is the memory of Joel'talas now," the man said in accented, flowing English, "and I am your father, Tyan'talas."

"I wasn't expecting—I thought everyone lived forever here," Trent said, staring up at the statue. *He looks nothing like me,* he thought.

"Not all are so fortunate, sadly," the older man replied.

"Tyan'talas," Trent said, testing the name. "And . . . and my mother? What is her name?"

"She is Sora'eala, and you saw our daughter, your sister Quel'eala," Tyan'talas said. "I imagine you must have many, many questions."

"Just one, and I'm sure you know what it is," Trent replied.

"Of course, in your shoes I would ask the same thing," his father replied. "Please, sit, for this is something that Joel'talas would know as well."

"I thought—" Trent trailed off, gesturing to the statue above them both.

"You have gone through most of your life not knowing or believing the Otherworld existed either, so please, do not presume to know that a person's spirit does not remain on this plane or another," Tyan-

'talas said. "Death, although rare, can still visit the Land of Youth. He died accidentally, in a fall, but his spirit lives on."

"Why did you two take me there?" Trent asked as if he wasn't listening. "Why was I given away for one of *them?*"

"The answers to your questions lie centuries ago, back when the de Danann walked among Men freely, in a time when human men and women believed in our existence, and would visit and trade with us, and we with them.

"In those times it was common for de Danann to visit newborn children and give them their blessing. We who held children in such esteem, not being blessed with many of our own—" Seeing the look on Trent's face, Tyan'talas held up his hand. "Hear me out, then make your judgment.

"As I was saying, since we regarded children so highly, it was a common practice to invite one of our kind to bless a newborn child for long life and health. Then as now, we were able to see whether a babe would live into adulthood. Many would, some would not, and then there was a third group that would not live past their infancy in the mortal realm.

"At the same time, the elder de Danann began to notice that our bloodlines were becoming closer and closer, mingling more and more, until there might have come a day when every de Danann would be related to every other, and to lie with one to be as lying with a member of one's own family, a repellent idea, much as it is in the human realm.

"To alleviate this, we offered a bargain to the fecund humans: we would take their weakened children to our world, where they would have a much better chance of survival. But we could not take without giving in kind. So the Queen decreed that those families who were blessed with more than one child would draw lots, and one would be chosen for an exchange, a life for a life. The mortal would receive one of our children, and we would gain new stock to refresh our blood. To your ears the practice must seem cold, but it is necessary, even today.

"The humans were wary at first, but when those children we had seen had passed away as we had predicted, later generations agreed to the exchange. The arrangement worked well for many years, with each side gaining what it desired. The humans received well-mannered, hardworking children, and in our lands the sick babes often recovered to live out healthy lives, joining with our families, keeping us strong."

Tyan'talas looked out over the hilled landscape of his homeland for a long moment before starting again. "Then a new kind of Man came to these shores, wearing metal and bringing with them strange new beliefs and rituals. Among them was the religion known as Christianity, which at its heart professed the belief in their one God. This religion spread like a plague, infecting town after town, village after village, with no way to stop it. Anyone who was different, or did not follow their ways, was suspected and feared. As you might imagine, they were against us from the start.

"That, and the human jealousy of the purity of the de Danann babes compared to the humans' own children, was enough to turn them against us. The priests denounced the idea of the exchange, saying that we were using these children, the ones that we had given another chance at life, that we had loved as our own, for some unimaginable dark purpose. de Danann children were vilified, and called 'changelings,' perverting the once-honored agreement into a mockery of what it had been. Stories were spread about our children, saying they were evil and gluttonous, existing to punish and torment the familes that had been 'deceived' into taking a de Danann infant. The religious leaders even created the ritual of 'baptism,' hoping that it would protect a newborn child from us. It didn't, of course, for how can something created by the mind of Man stop the de Danann, who have existed since time immemorial?

"And although Man has forgotten our long-ago bargain, along with much other wisdom, we have not, and kept our side to this day. Joel'thalas would not have survived past his first year in that other world, but here he was able to live and enjoy the life that would have been taken from him all too soon. To restore the balance, we had to give you in return, which was not done lightly, I assure you. Not a day goes by that we have not thought of you, where you might be, what you might be doing, whether you were alive or not. It is extremely rare that one of you finds his way back to the Otherworld. Usually growing up there lets the children forget all about us. When your mother saw you, I feared she would collapse from the shock."

"She thought she would collapse!" Trent exclaimed. "None of you have any idea of what I've gone though during the past seventeen years, how that world has changed! Every day, every hour was filled with pain and suffering, from the pollutants spewed into their world with their cars and their factories and their power plants, to even just trying to sit down, on those damned plastic or metal chairs. I was surrounded by metal, plastic, chemicals, electricity, all the time, machines coming and going, cars, trucks, buses, airplanes. I had to sit in one of those beasts to just get over here. Just trying to breathe every day was a effort."

Trent rose and stood over his father, sweeping his thick hair back from the sides of his head, showing his mutilated ears. "They cut my ears off, Father!

"The humans are destroying their world, bit by bit, and I hope they never find this place, for they would do the same to it. That was the world you put me into, whatever your best intentions were! Meanwhile, *he* was here, and I don't care how short his life was, or would have been, or whatever the reasons you did it for, it was still my life given for his!"

Trent stalked back and forth as he ranted, shaking his head with rage. Tyan'talas remained where he was, watching his son pace. "I know there isn't anything we can say or do that will make up what has been taken from you. I certainly don't expect to you understand why we did what we did. In a way—I almost wish you had acclimated over there, then you wouldn't ever have known you were missing anything. But for some the memories of our land are too strong, and they survive the passage across. Saying that we grieved for you does not bring back the years that we both have lost, we can only offer what we have now, here, for as long—or as briefly—as you wish."

Trent was silent for a long moment, his finger moving unconsciously to his cheek and the mark there. "I remember . . . I remember the crossing, and being held by my mother—then being taken from you both and given over. I spoke to her—my other mother— before I left their world and I wanted to be angry at her for not telling me. I wanted to be angry with you, all of you, for giving me up, especially now that I've seen this world, but when I look into your eyes, I see only truth there, as hard as that is for me to accept.

"But I cannot agree with the choices of you or your

people, despite how noble they were, because I had no say in them."

"But you are one of us, Tren'talas, true-named and returned to us now," Tyan'talas said, placing his hand on Trent's shoulder.

"I am, and I am not," Trent replied, tears in his eyes again. "I do not belong here, and I do not belong in the mortal realm. I'm not sure what to do. I've come all this way, and found what I thought I wanted, but it both is and isn't what I expected."

"Please, rest here, and we will try to help you," his father said. "For now, I am just happy to be able to look at my son once more, when I never thought I'd have the chance again."

"And I . . . am happy to know my true family at last," Trent replied slowly.

"Well, if you would, please come back to the house. I'm sure your mother would love to have you in our home."

As Trent followed his true father down the green hill, his mind was awash with confusion. He certainly hadn't expected to blow up at Tyan'talas, but the anger had ebbed as quickly as it had crashed over him; he had only had to take one look at his father's tear-filled eyes for it to happen. Still, the vehemence of the feelings told him that a part of him had wanted to come here for vengeance, for spite, to throw it in their faces. He had also been just as surprised when that emotion had been as hollow as his life in the human world. As he walked back to the house, Trent felt more lost than ever.

Trent stayed with his de Danann family for a time, learning about them and the Otherworld. He met other de Danann families, friends of his own, and regaled them with tales of the human world. His days were spent roaming the fields and towns of the Otherworld, and at night he would sit by the fire with his family, or visit others. He even revisited Court at the castle, dressed more suitably this time around. He saw the lady again, regal on her white throne, her consort beside; she nodded to him as he bowed, deeply this time. He was popular at the castle, as there had not been one of his kind returned to the land in decades, perhaps even centuries, so Trent was constantly plied with questions about the human world, until he ran out of stories to tell.

Everyone had been so welcoming, so friendly, his mother in particular, who often sat right next to him, her hand on his arm, as if reassuring herself that he existed. He had reconciled with her as well, telling her that he did not blame her for the decision that was made. The tears on her face when he had told her that sparkled like diamonds on her face, and Trent had gently wiped one off her cheek and put it to his lips, tasting the joy and sorrow mingled in it. With her tear still fresh on his lips, he held his mother close and kissed her cheek. That moment was the closest he had ever felt to belonging anywhere.

For although Trent did enjoy this time spent among his people, learning about this world he never knew, there was still an unsettled feeling in the back of his head, quietly chewing at him. He found himself watching the men and women of this splendid, graceful race whose blood, they claimed, flowed in his veins as well. It was as if he had come full circle, and found himself alone still, surrounded by a sea of those who would call themselves his kin. At times he felt like he was back in the schoolyard, flitting among laughing children at play, watching them, always an outsider. Even though he resembled the rest of the de Danann in his eyes, in his skin, in his bones, he still did not find the peace he was looking for.

I wonder if Joel felt the same way, Trent pondered. He began spending more time at the top of the hill, next to the statue of Joel'thalas, looking at the face of the boy who had replaced him here so many years ago. *I wish I could have known you,* he thought, *known who had been living my life here while I was living yours in your world.*

It was there that his sister Quel'eala found him one afternoon, as the light from the castle cast its golden rays across the countryside. She bounded up to him and settled by his side.

"Hello, sis," he said, grinning in spite of himself. Trent had been the youngest son in his human family, with a sister younger than him. His de Danann sibling was older by what Trent would have guessed was four or five years, the passage of time being practically unheard of in the Otherworld. She had taken to him instantly, with no jealousy or rancor, overjoyed to see her long-lost sibling.

Quel'eala leaned close to him and wrinkled her nose, albeit with a smile lighting her face. "That is one thing I don't think I'll ever get used to, Tren'talas."

"What's that?"

"Your smell."

"What do you mean?" Trent asked. "I don't smell any different."

"No, not to you, but—here, smell this." She offered a strand of her own golden brown hair.

Closing his eyes, Trent smelled the lock in his hand, and smiled, adrift in the scents of his homeland.

"Honeysuckle, clover, a hint of jasmine, dandelion, night rain, fresh cider, pear and—anise? Have you been slipping out to see Nel'lathas again?"

"Maybe I have, and maybe I haven't—I don't mean to sound cruel, brother, but your scent, it's—what was that word you used the other night?"

"Plastic?"

"No, you used it when you spoke about the human food."

"Nutrasweet?"

She giggled. "No! How they make most of their food . . . things they add to it."

"Oh . . . artificial," Trent said, nodding slowly.

"Yes . . . artificial. Oh, I hope I haven't offended you."

"No, of course not. The truth is, you're right," Trent said. "It's not like I'm not aware of it. I feel like the proverbial ugly duckling, only I'm never going to turn into that swan, am I?"

"Tren'talas, you know we do not care what you look like now, only that you are here," Quel'eala replied. "Mother thinks it is a divine blessing, your return."

"The long-lost son comes home to replace his shadow-kin . . ." Trent said, looking up at the statue. "Tell me about him."

His sister looked up at the burnished figure forever staring past the horizon. "You and he weren't very alike at all. He was, quiet, introspective, as if he had been given this great honor that he wasn't sure he could live up to. I think he had picked up enough clues about where the humans come from, and no, we don't call them changelings either."

"No, only humans persist in segregating those which they do not understand," Trent said.

"He had been betrothed when the accident happened. Mother was beside herself, not only for the family, or her son—but for you as well."

"For me . . . but how, she barely knew me," he replied.

"Oh my brother, just because a mother can only hold her own child in her arms for a few moments does not mean she does not keep those moments in her heart forever! Here our memories do not dim, or age, or fade into forgetfulness. For her the pain of your separation is as fresh now as it was for you all those years ago. But for her it was as if she had surrendered you yesterday."

"Trying to make me feel guilty, eh?" Trent said with a rueful grin.

"Not at all," she replied. "Why should I?"

"I–I don't know—" he stammered. "I mean, ever since I arrived I haven't felt . . . quite right here . . . so I thought you might have come up here to try and convince me of . . . something, I don't know."

"Tren'talas . . . at times it seems you are still living back among the humans, hiding your true self again. We are happy to have you back, but we could not keep you here, knowing what you've gone through during your life, what you've suffered—"

"But if this is where I'm supposed to belong, why don't I feel it as well?" he asked, exasperated.

"That isn't a question I can answer," Quel'eala replied. "Only you can. You've spent your entire life trying to fit somewhere that, inside, you knew you didn't belong. Now that you're free, it's time to make your own choices about where you want to be.

"It's strange—it is like you are a kind of mirror image of him, and yet not. I knew Joel'talas all his life, and yet, I feel as if I hardly knew him at all. You

I have known for such a short time, but I feel that we are closer than he and I ever were. I honor his memory every day, and yet I know you are my true brother. I sometimes think I might even miss you more if you would leave, but no one can tell you where you should be, now or ever. That is your choice, and your choice alone."

With that she slipped away down the hill, leaving Trent alone with his thoughts.

By the morning he knew, and he thought the best way was to simply let his family know as well.

"I thank you all for the warmth and love you have shown me," he said, "but even though this place does call to me, it . . . is simply not mine.

"I have spent seventeen years living a life that was not mine either, and even though I have found my true family, I am not ready to stay here either. But I will return someday, that I promise, Mother."

It seemed that she was about to protest, but was stopped by the look on his face. After a moment, she nodded "Of course I do not have the right to ask anything of you. I am grateful for the time we have spent together; that already was something I thought I would never have. But please, know this: wherever you may travel, whatever realms you may come across, our door will always be open to you."

"Thank you, Mother."

After Trent said thanks and farewell to his sister, Tyan'talas walked him to the door. "I also cannot hold your choice against you, having been denied your own course for so long. But I do hope you will return to us in time."

"I will, as I promised," Trent said. "But I need to live my own life first."

"Good-bye, *Tren'talas,* my son."
"Good-bye, Father."

Trent retraced his journey through the fields and meadows, up the foothills and into the forest. At the treeline he took one last look back at the green and yellow fields and above all the silver-white light from the castle that shone throughout the land. Trent watched it all for a long time, breathing in the pure air, listening to the sounds of the de Danann realm, and spotting, far off in the distance, his family's home, a tiny dot on the horizon.

Someday, Tren'talas will return, he thought. Then he adjusted his pack and walked into the forest without looking back once.

The trees accepted him as easily as they had released him, and the mists rose around him almost as soon as he had entered. Tren'talas stopped, waiting for the mists to obscure the deep woods, then he looked around, seeing the pale gray fog everywhere.

One way is as good as another, he thought. Turning around several times, he stopped, chose a random direction, and strode off, walking until the mists enveloped him completely.

YELLOW TIDE FOAM

Sarah A. Hoyt

Sarah A. Hoyt is the author of two critically acclaimed Shakespearean fantasies, *Ill Met By Moonlight* and *All Night Awake,* as well as the forth coming *Any Man So Daring.* She has sold more than two dozen short stories to markets such as *Absolute Magnitude, Weird Tales, Isaac Asimov's Science Fiction Magazine,* and *Analog.*

"Fairy Dust is not addictive," Skippy the Nose said. Sitting across from me at the shabby green vinyl-and-formica booth in the Athens diner, he hunched over the steaming bowl of clam chowder I'd just bought him. And he gave me a calculating look, to see if I bought his lie.

I didn't, but neither did I want to challenge it. I'd talked to Skippy long enough to know that if you stayed quiet, if you held still, he would decide you already knew everything and spill. So I looked away from him and around the diner.

It was warm and full of the smell of old frying grease and tobacco. The Athens sat in the center of Goldport, Colorado, eight blocks in either direction from the gentrification fast encroaching on the old town center. In this eight-block square, the Victorian palaces built during the gold rush looked their age, their paint scabby and graying, their windows covered in plastic against the cold of winter and numerous mailboxes on the front porch advertising the buildings' subdivided state. Here, every other warehouse sat empty, its floors rotting, its windows boarded, its interior the haven of runaways and junkies.

Here, diners and coffee houses had a look of having hit their peak in the fifties and didn't advertise any exotic brews. Cup-a-joe, served at the counter, could be had for under a buck.

Town Center was my beat. It was my home. Shabby and decayed as it was, it had nurtured my childhood and cradled my growing years. When I was fourteen, my parents, Norwegian immigrants who made good, had moved to a large home in the suburbs, leaving behind the Greek and Hispanic enclave of my childhood.

But I'd never adapted to the suburbs. It all felt too clean, too antiseptic. Unreal. I knew that, beneath that surface, crime still went on, only prettied up and therefore more revolting. I'd never felt at home in college, either, with all those kids who'd never have the nerve to walk the streets at Town Center. All those kids who thought working class meant a different species.

So I'd become a policewoman, following in my dad's footsteps—and I'd moved back to Town Center. Dad disapproved, though I was a narcotics detective and not a beat policeman, as he'd been. And sometimes I wondered if I'd made the right choice, because no one at the station understood me. The flatfoots thought I was nuts to go into that area, to walk the streets, to ask questions. And my peers just thought I was nuts.

But the people who came to the Athens were my kind of people.

Large men, with calloused hands and flattop haircuts, wearing plaid flannel shirts, hunched at the counter, with their cigarettes and their coffees. The booths were occupied by young men in workboots and stocking caps, day laborers at the nearby warehouses.

A group of flatfoots, in uniform, took up three of the booths, six crammed into each space meant for four. They had their heads together over maps and talked just above a whisper. Words like assault, proof, time of death, and domestic, emerged from their conversation. I longed to sit with them, but that would only shut them up.

And at the corner of the counter, nursing a cup of coffee and chain-smoking, sat the love of my life—or as close as I'd come to it—listening to conversations and jotting something down in his notebook now and then.

That was his job. His name was Peter Knossos. He wrote a column—"City Heart"—for the *Goldport Chronicle*. He wrote about the decaying center of our city in the way his ancestors had described the thousand ships that Helen's face launched. His column and books were widely read, very respected. And only I knew the cracks in his armor, the wistfulness beneath his competent exterior.

I let my gaze wander to his golden-skinned face, his cap of dark, curly hair. More wiry than muscular, yet he gave an impression of energy waiting to uncoil. And though I knew our relationship could never be what he wanted, looking at him sent an electric current through me.

He returned my gaze, openly, his velvety dark eyes

narrowed beneath his small round glasses, his mouth fixed in the ironic little smile that was his self-defense. He blew a tendril of smoke, in my direction and winked at me. The smoke curled, midair, convoluted and evanescent like our relationship.

I looked away. Skippy was staring at me. He looked worried. "Honest to God, Sandra. It's natural. It's all herbal."

"So is pot, Skippy," I said. I took a sip of the bitter, acidic coffee. I was so used to reheated, stewed diner coffee that the more refined brews at Starbucks tasted like alien stuff to me—nice, surely, but not real, in the same way that the too-clean, too-large McMansions in the suburbs weren't real, just facades to hide the ugliness beneath. I liked my houses shabby, my coffee acidic. I liked reality, not its counterfeit. "So is opium when it comes to that. Just because something is herbal, it doesn't mean it's not a controlled substance."

Skippy flinched, as though I'd slapped him. He rubbed the dirty sleeve of his army surplus shirt across his red and inflamed nose and tried to make his face sober and serious, to look as he had when we'd both been kids growing up in this neighborhood. "Cassandra, really. It's not like pot or opium. It's not . . . illegal."

This from the man who, after getting kicked out of the force for using, and after ten years of arrests for possession, still claimed that he'd never used an illegal substance and claimed it while rubbing his inflamed cokehead nose.

"Look here, Skippy," I said. I stubbed the cigarette down on an already-full ashtray at the table. "I just want the regular questions answered. Who is selling the stuff? Where can I find him?"

He frowned. Once upon a time, he'd looked almost cherubic, with blond hair and large, rounded blue eyes. But the street was hard on people, and though he was in his early thirties, his hair had already turned gray, growing ragged around his face like a mangy mane. His beard grew gray, too, and patchy, like weeds up the slopes of Colorado's arid mountainsides. And his eyes looked faded, as though having gazed too long on imaginary landscapes, they could no longer focus on reality.

"It's none of the usual people," he said. His voice echoed with the hint of his accustomed whine. He ate a spoonful of chowder and rubbed his nose with his sleeve again. "Not . . . There's no dope houses, no . . . None of the regular suppliers has the stuff. The . . . the Fairy Dust suppliers say they're not doing anything illegal. They just show up, like at the corner of the warehouse in the morning, in the alley in the evening. They show up . . ."

"Um . . ." I said, and just that, taking a sip of my coffee and giving Skippy the skeptical eye. Sure the dealers just showed up. "Do I have to click my heels three times and say there's no place like dope?" Truth was, Skippy was a last chance. For all I knew, it might really be like that. For all the trouble we had been having tracking the new drug in town, it might have its very own supply network.

Again Skippy gave me the wounded look, the *slurp, slurp* of the clam chowder, rub, rub, rub with the sleeve on the coke-inflamed nose. "Sandra. Why can't you believe me?"

"Because I don't see Fairy Dust in any baggies at the health food store, Skippy. Listen—" I reached across the table and grabbed hold of his wrist. It felt weird in my hand—the loose skin and bones obviously there, and yet feeling too cold for living flesh and somehow immaterial as though, at any minute, my hand might go through him. I let go and set both hands on the table, instead, bringing my head close to Skippy's, and speaking in the kind of whisper that sounds threatening, but doesn't carry too far. "Listen, Skippy. Most of the time, when there's a new drug in town we hear about it from the hospitals first. The ODs and the crashes and the withdrawals are the first sign we have of someone selling bad stuff to kids. This time? It's disappearances. We have kids missing from Town Center to Highlands Ranch. Twelve year olds, Skippy. Thirteen. Some prostitutes, some dopeheads, but also a lot of kids who were never in trouble a day in their lives. Gone without a trace. Now what I think is that this stuff is so bad, the dosage so fine that these kids are dying in some back lot, dropping dead in some warehouse, in some parking lot and no one ever finds them. Or else it's a pedophile ring, using this as some sort of knockout drug, and ferrying these kids off to Asia or the Gulf. I want to figure it out. I want to know where those kids went."

Skippy looked at me in horror, as if he'd never thought of drugs in those terms. "But it doesn't knock you out," Skippy said. "There's no crashes, either, no bad trips. You just dream, Sandra. And you wake up feeling good. And . . ."

"And it improves your muscle tone." I thought of the feel of his flesh on my fingers and made a face. The waitress refreshed my coffee and I downed it in a single gulp. Not warm enough, but I could live with it. "No doubt Olympic athletes take it."

Skippy stopped in mid-wipe of his sleeve across his nose, and blinked. "No, it doesn't . . ." Skippy looked over my shoulder into the middle distance, his eyes for once intent, not on me but on that imagined land-scape, there, beyond what I could see. "You see, it's all in the mind. It's as though it unlocks . . . It's like a gate. And then you're in another country altogether. As if . . ." He shrugged and shivered and rubbed his sleeve across his nose and blinked at me.

Right. It took you to another land altogether but it wasn't a controlled substance. Sure thing. "And you're not going to tell me where you get it?" I asked.

He shrugged. "Around. Around here. At some street corner. When you need it."

I sighed. "Right. Thanks, Skippy." For nothing. I would have to get a tail on him. But I would, damn it, find who was making the kids disappear. It was my city. I was supposed to protect it. And they were get-ting in under my guard.

I got up, took the ticket the waitress had left on the table, zipped my leather jacket tightly, and edged my way between the tables of regulars to the podium where the fiftyish, faded, blonde cashier took my change.

Behind her, the broad plate-glass window displayed the city street—dark towering warehouses, a few yel-lowish lights at the windows of converted Victorians. Cars crept down the street like blind ghosts, shrouded in the white of a fine powdery snowstorm, their head-lights fuzzy and spiderwebby with reflections. I was glad I wouldn't have to drive. My apartment was three blocks away, the upper floor of a divided Victorian.

The cashier handed me money and as I put it in my wallet, I heard the voice, just by my ear. "Hello, gorgeous. So, what are you doing tonight?"

Peter's voice always sounded smoky and low, a bed-room intimation, an invitation to romance. And his breath on my neck felt warm and intimate.

We'd come together, in a wave of physical attraction

and heady intellectual talk two years ago. It had lasted exactly two months. Peter wanted the house in the suburbs, the two and a half kids, the dog. Me? I had seen too many midnight domestic disturbances, too many lovers who broke their bond with knives and guns. I'd seen too many kids killed because they wouldn't stop crying.

Too much reality to dream. I'd turned down his proposal and broke his heart, which only made his writing more poetic and soulful. And only made me more determined to make the world as safe as it could be for the next generation.

And yet, we couldn't fully break up. We couldn't fully separate. Like planets bound by a gravitational field that allowed them to remain some distance apart, but never to escape each other's pull, we saw each other now and then. We still had each other's apartment keys.

And the tickle of his breath on my neck made my heart race. "Working," I said, without turning.

He laughed, an all-in-the-throat chuckle, and stepped around me, to open the swinging glass door with ALL YOU CAN EAT SPECIAL, SOUVLAKI AND FRIES scrawled on it in red dry-erase marker.

I stepped out into a gust of wind and snow and stopped to put my collar up.

Peter came up behind me and put his arm over my shoulders. "So, working. This late, on a stormy night."

"Crime happens on stormy nights, as well as pleasant ones," I said.

He nodded. He had managed to carry his cigarette with him, still lit, despite the snow. It only made sense if you knew Peter. That cigarette was like a part of him, as much Peter as his elongated face, his sharp Mediterranean nose, or his velvety dark eyes. Despite the weather, he wore only an unbuttoned tweed sports jacket over his trademark open-at-the-neck shirt and very tight black corduroy pants.

He smelled of cigarettes and old books, of coffee and the residual scent of the Athens. He smelled safe. He smelled of home.

"So," he said. "Do you have time for me?"

"Come on," I said. "I'm not ready to give you the story yet."

"It's not the story I want," he said, and pulled back a few strands of my blonde hair with the tip of his long, keyboard-calloused fingers.

Normally I would have said bullshit—but the snow whirled around us, white and cold, and the wind bit into my legs through my worn jeans. Peter was warm and solid.

"Yeah," I said. "Yeah, okay."

Peter leaned into me and kissed me hard. I tasted sweet Turkish cigarettes and bitter coffee in his mouth, felt the warmth of his arms around me and tried to forget the cold and the storm and Fairy Dust. For the night.

When I woke up, Peter was sitting up in bed, in my little apartment, looking at me like someone trying to figure out a puzzle. His eyes had that curious naked look that people who normally wear glasses have when going without them. The light of the morning shone on his bare back, highlighting his broad shoulders, his limber frame and burnishing his skin a deep gold, so that he looked like the idol of some lost civilization. Strangely, for just a moment, it seemed to me that light shone through him. I blinked. No. Peter was again as I remembered.

"Sandra, what you told me, yesterday . . ."

I groaned, as I realized that, in the relaxation of pillow talk, I'd told him too much—I'd told him of the disappearances, the rumors, and the tantalizing name that had reached us through our contacts in the addict grapevine. Fairy Dust. And of my frustration with the case I couldn't crack.

"Peter," I said. "I told you I wasn't ready to give you the story."

He blinked at me. "But what if it were true? What if it opened a door, took you to some place . . . I mean, there's got to be a reason it's called *Fairy Dust.*"

Yeah. Right. I resisted an impulse to run my fingers through his hair, to draw him close. His eyes were full of that dreaming look he had, the dreaming look that had separated us. I could not follow him when he wanted to go to this place where everything was nice and good and everyone redeemable.

"Whatever," I said, as I got up, dragging my sheet modestly with me, as though Peter hadn't seen all of me there was to see. "Whatever."

My mouth tasted of stale cigarettes and acidic coffee. I got into my tiny bathroom and scrubbed away the smell of smoke from my hair, the smell of Peter from my body.

When I came out, he was still sitting on the bed. He'd stopped writing and the pad sat on his knees, the pen stilled. "Hey," he said. "Hey, but what if it were true?"

I glared at him. "What?"

"The thing. Fairy Dust. It comes when you need it. It takes you to a whole other place. A better place." He grinned, a goofy, childish grin. "Fairyland. Wonder what that would be for us, eh, Sandra? A place where we could be together—"

"Right, Knossos." He'd gone around the bend. "Write the novel. I'll come to your book signing."

I left, slamming the door behind me, cursing myself for my own stupidity. What kind of an idiot was I? Peter was a dreamer. I was a realist. We shouldn't be together. I shouldn't allow it.

His fairy world was only a fantasy. A fantasy that was costing us lives. I must find out how. I must put away the scum who were stealing kids' lives.

I got a coffee to go at the Athens. The heat from it burned my fingers as I walked through the deserted morning streets to the warehouse where Skippy slept. The night before, I'd called my father's old beat partner, Joe Mayo. I'd asked him to get on Skippy's tail. Easier and more efficient than requesting some rookie from the precinct. Mayo enjoyed it too. He was retired and had very little else to do. This morning, he'd left a message in my machine, telling me Skippy was in his usual digs.

I walked past a group of men bending over the exposed motor of a parked car and past the triple-X bookshop, already doing a brisk business at this time of the day, down a quiet side street to the cul-de-sac where Skippy's place of residence stood, squarely blocking the end of the road. From it, I saw First Street where the Athens was.

Joe Mayo sat just around the corner, on the stoop of a rundown Victorian. He looked as if he were reading a cheap, X-rated comic which, at closer range, revealed itself to be the comic's cover draped over a book of poetry. Seventyish, bull-headed, with the sort of haircut that went well in this sort of place, he blended in.

"Is he in?" I asked.

He nodded. "Yeah. Hasn't come out. Do you want me to go in and visit? I do, you know, sometimes. He might talk more to me than to you."

He looked at me, his faded blue eyes strangely vulnerable beneath his bushy, lowered eyebrows, and I remembered that Mayo was widowed. His kids lived out of state. He'd known Skippy—as he'd known me and Peter—when we were children and he owned a house down the block.

"No," I said. I looked away from his gaze that mirrored a loneliness as great as my own. "I'd rather he thinks he's alone."

"Last night he came in straight from dinner," Mayo said.

I nodded and sat down next to Mayo, who got up reluctantly, as though watching Skippy was the most interesting thing he had planned for the day. And I thought that Mayo and Peter and I in our different ways were all kindred. Lost people in a world where we didn't quite fit.

Mayo made a big production of buttoning up his long overcoat and putting his book under his arm. He hesitated. "Just one thing," he said. "On his way home . . ."

"Yes?" I looked up.

"Skippy stopped and talked to a guy. . . ."

He waited this long to tell me this? "Could it be the dealer?" I asked.

Mayo shrugged. "Didn't look it. You're going to think I'm nuts, but for a moment I thought the guy was soliciting Skippy."

"Soliciting?" A prostitute, male or female, going after Skippy would have to be crazy. Skippy was so obviously broke.

Mayo shrugged. A heavy, unbecoming blush tinged

his cheeks and spread down to his neck. Men of his generation didn't talk to women about sex, particularly not deviant sex, and it made little difference to him that this woman was a police officer.

"Yeah, this guy was a pretty boy," he said. "Hair down to here." He put his hand down halfway to his knees. "But not in a hippie way. Platinum blond. Some sort of red jacket or sleeveless vest, and tight black pants. In this weather. I thought—" He stopped himself.

I looked up and nodded, encouraging him to go on.

"But they just talked for a few moments, and then Skippy came back here."

"And the other guy?"

"That's the weird thing," Mayo said. "He just . . . vanished."

Curiouser and curiouser. "Vanished, as in ran?"

"I don't know. One moment he was there, the next one gone," Mayo said.

"Uh huh. Did he give Skippy anything? Money change hands?"

"I don't think so," Mayo said.

He didn't think so, but then again with drug deals you never knew, right? You never knew. Some of these dealers on the street were better than stage magicians. A wink, a nod, a quick gesture, and it would be in the client's hand.

I sat on that stoop after Mayo left and looked through the branches of the winter-bare tree at the fire escape that was Skippy's usual entryway.

At five PM, when I was cold and hungry, I saw Peter walking down First Street, past the Athens. He saw me. I was sure of that. His head turned in my direction and for a moment he looked as though he was ready to come up to me, patch things up. The electrical feeling, the pull of his embrace called to me. I stood up. And he walked in the other direction, taking a sudden, sharp turn into an alley.

Avoiding me, I thought. Afraid I would follow him. Idiot. I wondered if he felt sorry about bringing up a stupid subject, about nattering on about some other world. Somehow I doubted it. Or perhaps only for a moment, as drunkards will regret their excesses until the hangover passes. Tomorrow he'd be romantic and poetic again.

I looked after him so long, I almost didn't notice Skippy coming down the stairs. But movement called my eyes and I turned in time to see Skippy come down the stairs. He looked . . . thinner. Not like someone who has lost weight, but like someone who is on his way to becoming transparent. I saw Skippy, in his army shirt, his dirty, grayish pants, and yet I my mind told me that I could see through him, too, see the rungs of the ladder, the rickety fire landing of his warehouse.

I remembered the unpleasant feel of his wrist in mine and shuddered. But people didn't disappear. Not by becoming immaterial.

Skippy ambled down the street, looking like a junkie in need of a fix. Wary and suspicious, his head on a swivel, looking in every direction. He shook. Okay, he was badly in need of a fix. Looking for a dealer.

I ducked behind the tree as he passed. He was talking to himself. No. Singing.

"Rivers and streams, and a place to lay my head." His voice rose reedy-thin and the melody was eerie and haunting. Folk tune, no doubt. The type of thing that should be accompanied by acoustic guitar and cymbals. No accounting for taste.

I followed him to just in front of the Athens, and

then down First Street. I realized we were headed to the same alley that Peter had ducked into before. But Peter wouldn't be there. The stupid idiot would have realized I wasn't following him. He'd have left.

Only Peter was there, in the shady, smelly space between two tall brick building. Peter and someone else. The someone else looked exactly like the description of the prostitute that Mayo had seen. Slight. Blond. Tall. Much too well-groomed and much too scantily dressed for someone who didn't have business reasons to display his body.

As I caught sight of him, he laughed, a sound like cymbals and running water. And Peter joined in, an hesitant laughter, afraid of itself.

I stopped, transfixed. Prostitutes, male or female, often solicited Peter. Despite his cultivated scruffiness, it was obvious he had a job and had used soap—my soap—in recent memory. But I'd never seen Peter do more than shrug his shoulders and walk away. Now he was talking. Talking. To this creature.

Skippy stopped at the entrance of the alley, then started shuffling his feet like a little kid waiting outside a restroom stall.

Peter nodded and turned, walking towards me, as Skippy went into the alley. Skippy went in, approached the guy. I ducked into the shadows, such as they were, in the slanting, milk-water thin sunlight of five PM in Goldport. I flattened myself into the wall, trying to look invisible.

But Peter saw me, of course. He stopped and opened his mouth. For a moment, I thought he was going to say something.

Instead, he closed his mouth, shook his head, smiled. A sad smile. And walked away.

I looked in, saw Skippy hand the man some cash. Saw the blond give Skippy a cloth parcel.

Now, the appropriate procedure for this was for me to call the precinct, ask for backup, and then go up and buy some dope from this guy and arrest him in the act.

But I remembered what Mayo had said about the guy disappearing. This was the only lead I'd got in weeks of searching for the person selling Fairy Dust. And I was sure this was Fairy Dust. I was sure Skippy was hooked on Fairy Dust.

So I grabbed my gun from the shoulder holster under my jacket, and dove into the alley, right? Scrambling madly, I stopped in classical police style. "Stop, this is the police," I said. "Stop."

The blond looked at me, his eyes wide and round. Skippy shuffled aside and gawked.

I tried to cover them both with the gun because, though Skippy should consider the pen his home away from home and though he'd never attempted to resist arrest before, you never knew. With junkies, you never knew. He clutched his cloth bundle—about the size to fit in a palm—nervously in one hand, and stared at me.

"Drop it, Skippy," I said. "You're both under arrest. You have the right—"

The blond threw his head back and laughed. The musical laughter again. "Rights? Rights, Daughter of Eve? What rights has my kind had since your kind crawled out of its caves and took over your world, and started killing our world, which is linked with it? What rights? The right to be encroached on, our sacred glades destroyed, our dancing circles paved over with concrete, our rivers bridged over with cold iron? Rights?"

"I don't know what you're talking about," I said. My heart thumped fast, because I felt I should know. There was something there. I should understand. And yet, the rational part of me told me that he was just a head case. Nothing but a head case. Head cases had their own agenda and they often sounded almost as if they made sense. "You have the right to remain silent—"

Skippy put his cloth bundle in his mouth.

I jumped toward him, forgetting the blond. "Oh, shit," I said. "Oh, shit, Skippy."

My gun went in my pocket. I tried to pry Skippy's mouth open.

Skippy fought back like the possessed, his cold, clammy hands scratching at me, with nails that seemed to have grown ten inches overnight and appeared to be ice-cold.

Skippy smelled, weirdly, of flowers and mountain air. I wondered if the cloth bundle contained detergent. Junkies had swallowed weirder things.

Over my frantic fight, I heard the blond's voice. He spoke slowly and gently, like someone in a dream. "Our population has dwindled as yours grew. But your poisonous land destroys even your children. So we're claiming them for our own. Three times. Three times of eating the fairy food is all it takes, and they become one of us. And then we'll return, stronger. We'll push back. Fairyland will be strong again."

And Skippy disappeared. One moment he was scrabbling at me, his needle-sharp nails scratching at me, and the next moment he was gone. Just gone. Like a soap bubble bursting, like a ghost vanishing into shreds of fog.

The blond laughed. "We'll take over your world this time." And, as he spoke, he disappeared, too.

I stood in the alley alone. The reek of a nearby Dumpster reached my nostrils. The freezing wind picked up and blew stray flakes of snow and yellowed newspapers around.

One of the newspapers showed Peter's column, his thin-and-dark countenance smiling at me from the stock picture next to it.

I glared at the column. Peter had been here. Peter had been with the creature. Whatever it was. I didn't for a moment believe it was an elf. Not for a moment. But it had disappeared. And Skippy had disappeared.

And the thing had talked to Peter. Could it have sold him Fairy Dust? It couldn't be Fairy Dust. It must be something toxic, something . . .

What, Sandra? Kryptonite? I shook my head. There had to be some rational explanation.

Somewhere, somehow, this all made sense. And I would find out how. But first I must find Peter. Before— I couldn't finish the thought.

I walked out of the alley. The sun vanished behind lead-colored clouds, snow danced in the howling wind.

Peter wasn't in the Athens. And he wasn't in the newspaper office, two blocks down. No one had seen him since early morning.

I walked to his apartment, in a tidy brick building two blocks from mine. I rang the bell. I knocked at the door. No answer.

I opened the door. I went in. It was an efficiency, clean to a fault. Bookshelves lined the walls, all of the shelves groaning under the weight of massed books. A huge leather chair took up a corner by the window, a narrow bed, shrouded in a white blanket, sat on the other corner. That bed was the main reason we always used my apartment and not his.

Next to the leather chair, an old, scarred oak desk

with a typewriter arranged front and center—Peter mistrusted computers—and to the side of it a box that had once housed a bottle of Jim Beam and was now filled with pens and pencils.

On the other side of the typewriter, a typed page rested. I almost walked away from it, but the first line said, clearly, "Dearest Sandra."

I approached. I read it. "Dearest Sandra," it began, primly. "Though you'll never believe that, you are my dearest, it is true. It is only your job and my job and the realities of this world that keep us apart. I feel as though you and I, and a scattering of others, maybe as many as half of the population, are revenants. Creatures that belong to another world, a vanished world, stranded in this land of computers and Internet, of tuneless music and labyrinths of concrete and glass. I couldn't tell you, but I already knew about Fairy Dust. I'd bought some the night before. It opened a door, Sandra, to another world. A world of waterfalls and green grass and trees and freedom. A world that was once part of ours, but has been pushed away by this thing we call progress. Fairy Dust takes us there and brings that world closer to ours for those who take it. Gives dreams a fighting chance. So that those of us left behind, like yellow tide foam on the shore of progress, can have a chance at happiness. Come and join me, Sandra. We'll be happy together."

The type blurred as my eyes filled with tears. I dropped the paper to the polished wood floor.

I walked out the door, slamming it behind me. I walked down the stairs and into the street, where the snow whirled, madly, in howling winds. I needed the snow and the cold. I felt as though I, too, might vanish like a soap bubble bursting.

If what Peter had said were true—and I couldn't

imagine Peter playing that kind of prank—if this were all true, then . . . Then Peter was gone forever. Gone from this world.

And yet, there was hope for me, wherever Peter was. If I followed him, this feeling of being askew to the world—this feeling of being unable to hold back the tide of evil would be gone. I would belong. And I would be with Peter. I remembered the taste of his mouth, Turkish tobacco and coffee, and I longed for his embrace with desperate hunger.

After a while, I realized steps beside mine twined them. I glanced over my shoulder at the blond. He smiled at me, and proffered a white cloth bag on an extended, well-manicured hand.

Peter had gone into that land willingly. But there were others. The kids, twelve and thirteen, who'd never had a chance to truly live in this world, never had a chance to make a real choice.

What kind of creature took advantage of children?

I looked up at the blond's face. His bright green eyes were impenetrable and cold as glass. He'd called me "Daughter of Eve" with contempt in his voice.

His kind despised us. Why would they want us in their land? Because they were using us. Using the misfits, like Peter and me, and all those kids. Using them and . . . betraying those they seduced?

I swallowed an imaginary lump that seemed to take up my whole throat.

"Come, girl," the creature—elf?—said. "You can join your lover." He threw his head back and laughed, a high, musical laughter. But his teeth, thus revealed, were small and needle sharp, the teeth of a rodent.

In fairy tales nothing good happened to the prisoners of Fairyland. They were worked to death, danced to exhaustion. I thought of Peter and rage grew in me.

I clenched my fists. I wanted to kill this trickster, this cold creature.

But my rage wouldn't solve anything. For years, I'd relied on rage and anger, on control, on punishing evildoers, and what had I done? I'd let my lover slip between my fingers. I'd refused to believe in his love, till the false promises of a glittering new life became tempting to him.

In my mind's eye I saw Peter's bewildered face, his naked, defenseless morning-look.

I'd seek out the misfits. I'd talk to them. I'd give them a reason to stay behind. I'd make our world one they could live in, so they wouldn't yield to the temptation of an illusory perfect world.

I shook my head at the elf. And, turning my back on the extended hand, the promise of Fairyland, I hugged my jacket around me and walked forth into the real world.

And it seemed to me, as the cold wind blew and the snow stung my skin, that I felt Peter's lips upon mine, the taste of his cigarettes and coffee in my mouth.

HE SAID, SIDHE SAID

Tanya Huff

Tanya Huff lives and writes in rural Ontario with her partner, four cats, and an unintentional Chihuahua. After sixteen fantasies, she's written two space operas, *Valor's Choice* and *The Better Part of Valor,* and has recently published *Smoke and Shadows,* the first in a new series affiliated with her *Blood* books. In her spare time she gardens and complains about the weather.

Last summer, they built this new skateboard park down by Carterhaugh Pond: a decent half-pipe, some good bowls, a pyramid, couple of heights of rails. Blatant attempt to keep us off the streets, to control the ride, but they put some thought into the design and I've gotta admit that sometimes I can appreciate a chance to skate without being hassled. It was October 24, early morning, and I had the place to myself. Kids were all in school and a touch of frost in the air was keeping the usual riders away.

I was grabbing some great air off the pipe and I was seriously *in* the moment, so I figured this was the time to try a backside tailslide on the lip. Yeah, yeah, there's harder tricks but for some reason, me and tailslides . . . So, I picked up some serious speed, hit the lip, held the lip, and then *WHAM!* I was ass over head and kissing concrete.

The world kind of went away for a minute or two— you know, like it does—and when I finally got my eyes open, I was staring up at this total babe. I thought, Woo! Liv Tyler! only she didn't have that whole kind of creepy "I look like the lead singer for Aerosmith" vibe.

Over the sound of the Bedrockers still jamming in my phones, she said, "Give me your hand!"

I figured she was going to help me up, so I put my hand in hers, and next thing I knew, the park was gone, the pipe was gone, hell, the whole world was gone. Good thing my other hand was locked on my board.

The land between the water and the wood has always been ours, one of the rare places where our world touches that of mortal men. The news that it had been defiled came to the High Court with a Loireag who dwelled in the pond. She was a plaintive little thing, wailing and keening as she made her way through my knights and ladies to throw herself damply before me.

The wailing and keening made it difficult to hear her complaint, but eventually she calmed enough to be understood. Great instruments of steel and sound were scraping away the earth, crushing and tearing all that was green, driving terrified creatures from their homes and into hiding.

We do not concern ourselves with the world of men, and in return we expect that which is ours to be respected. Clearly it was again time to remind them of this.

When I arrived with those of my court I trusted most, I saw that the tale of woe spun to me by the Loireag was true. A great scar had been gouged into the earth and men surrounded it. Large men. Their skins browned by the sun and made damp by their labors. Cloth of blue stretched over muscular thighs and, as I watched, one threw off a gauntlet of leather and tilted back his head to drink.

I lifted a finger and spilled a rivulet of water over his chest and down a ridged stomach until it disappeared behind . . .

"Majesty?"

I breathed deeply. "It is overly warm in the world of men," I said as a breeze sped to cool my brow at my command. "We will go and return again another day."

But our days are not the days of men. When we returned, the scar in the earth had been filled with stone sculpted into strange and impossible shapes. In stone cupped into a half-moon, a young man rode a winged board.

His hair was dark but tipped with light, his eyes the gray-green of a storm. Loose clothing hid his body from my sight but his hands were large and strong and he moved like water down a mountainside. His smile spoke of earthy joys.

I stepped forward as his head hit the stone.

"Not *again*, Majesty . . ."

Who of my court dared to voice so weary a warning I did not know, but for the sake of so enchanting a creature I disregarded it and crossed into the world of men. Admiring the broad shoulders and lean length of my fallen hero, I reached out to him.

"Take my hand," I said.

And he did.

I woke up in what I later learn is called a bower—
it was kind of like a bedroom without walls, just this
billowy curtainy stuff and I wasn't alone. The babe
who wasn't Liv Tyler was with me; we were both totally without clothes, and she was studying this major
scabbage I've got all down my right forearm.

"Screwed up a 180 out of an axle stall," I explained,
trying to sound like this sort of thing happened to me
all the time—naked with a strange babe, that is, not
the scabbage because, you know, sometimes you bail.

She touched it with one finger, all sympathetic.

I probably should have been more freaked but she
was naked and I was naked and so . . .

It was a fast ride, but no one did any complaining.

Later, we were lying all wrapped up and worn out
when this tall, skinny blonde fem wearing a lot of
swishy green just wandered in without so much as a
"Coming through!"

"Majesty, your husband has sent an emissary. Will
you receive him?"

"An emissary?" she asked.

Me, I was kind of fixating on a different word, although I totally kept my cool. "You have a husband?"

Once I had him unclothed, I was a little discon-
certed to discover that he was damaged. His shins
were an overlapping mix of purple and blue and his
right arm had been horribly disfigured.

He muttered words I did not understand but I could
feel his terror so I touched his arm to calm his fears.
His reaction to my touch was unexpected. It had been

long since a mortal man had shared my bed and I had forgotten just how impulsive they are. And how quick.

About to suggest a second attempt, my words were halted by the appearance of Niamh of the Golden Hair. "Majesty, your husband has sent an emissary. Will you receive him?"

About to ask who my husband had sent *this* time, my words were once again halted.

The mortal threw himself from the bed, hiding his manhood behind a handful of fabric. "Husband?! Oh man, you never said you had a husband!"

As he was the only man in our lands, I had no idea whom he was speaking to and would have demanded an accounting had I not caught sight of that infernal Puck hanging about at the edge of hearing. He wore his usual condescending smile that told quite clearly how he would enjoy informing my Lord Oberon of my latest dalliance.

I could hear him now, insinuating that any discontent I felt was a result of my own choices.

As I would not give him the satisfaction, I bound my mortal lover round with cobwebs and as he lay silent and unmoving said, "Tell good Robin that I will speak with him anon. I have matters here to attend to still."

Niamh raised a quizzical brow toward the mortal, but bowed and left as commanded, sweeping Puck before her.

I drew the mortal back to the bed and released his bindings. "You need not fear my husband," I told him. "The king has his own court and does not come to mine."

Now, having heard *husband,* I hadn't paid a lot of attention to the rest of what the blonde chick had said. I mean, I was cool, totally dignified, but a little stunned, you know? I couldn't think of anything to say until we were alone again and the babe was trying to explain about how they were separated and I didn't have anything to worry about.

"He's the king?"

"Yes."

"And that would make you . . . ?"

"The queen."

Of the fairies as it turns out. No, not those kinds of fairies. Real fairies. Like in fairy tales. We got dressed and she lead me out onto this balcony tree-branch thing and well, it was pretty damned clear I wasn't in Kansas anymore if you know what I mean.

I just did the Queen of the Fairies. Prime!

"What do I call you?" I asked, tearing my eyes away from a whole section of tree that would make a wild ride.

"Majesty."

I knew she was just teasing so I gave her my best *you and me, we're closer than that* smile. "Sure, but you got a name?"

She looked at me for a long moment then she smiled and I knew I had her. "I am also called *Titania*."

"Annie."

"Titania!"

"Not to me, babe." I laid my fist against my heart. "Tommy Lane. But I tag with Teal so you want to call me that, I'm cool with it. You know, TL . . . Teal."

"I think I will call you Tommy Lane," I told him. Not that it mattered; he would not be in my realm for very much longer. I would send him home the moment I had dealt with Puck.

"So while you're seeing the dude your old man sent, you mind if I ride?"

As I had no real idea of what he was talking about, I told him I did not.

He raced back into my bower and emerged with his wheeled board—it had merely seemed to have wings so quickly had it moved. Balanced on the edge of my balcony, he grinned with such joy that I felt my heart soften towards him. Then he placed the pieces of sponge upon his ears again and threw himself forward, bellowing out a most impertinent question as he raced along the branch.

"Who's your daddy!"

With any luck he would fall and break his neck and save me the walk back to the place where our lands touched.

"I can't wait for the feast!"

"What feast?" I snapped as Puck dropped down beside me. His manner of perching and appearing and making himself free of my court as though it were my husband's was most annoying.

"The feast you'll be having for your skater-boy."

Tommy Lane was no longer in sight but I could still hear the rasp of his wheels against the tree and the shriek of my ladies as he roared through bower after bower. How unfortunate that none would risk my wrath and stop his ride upon their blade. Birds took wing all around us, protesting so rude a disturbance.

"It's traditional," Puck continued, grinning insolently. "A mortal crosses over and we throw him a feast. You can't send him back without one, not unless you made a mistake bringing him here in the first place."

Oh, he would *like* to go to my husband and say I

had made a mistake. They would laugh together over it.

"Moth, Cobweb, Mustardseed!"

The sprites appeared.

"See that a feast is made ready." As they vanished, I turned to Puck and said, as graciously as I was able, "You will stay, of course."

Wise enough to recognize the command, he bowed gracefully. "I wouldn't miss it, Majesty."

After the feast, he would go to my Lord Oberon and tell my husband of the great joy and pleasure I took in my mortal companion and then my lord could feel the bite of being replaced once again.

I have no idea where the room came from. One minute I was having the wildest ride of my life and the next I'm landing an ollie on marble floors. I knew it was marble because Philly used to have this great park with marble slabs that was prime loc for street skating. Anyway, there were banners hanging from the ceiling and tables all down the middle and these little people laying out plates and stuff.

I saw my Annie up ahead, standing with some short brown dude—not a brother but brown, hard to explain—and so pushing mongo-foot, I made my way over. Just before I reached her, I decided to show off a bit and so did a quick grind along the last of the marble benches that were up against the wall. Kid's trick but she didn't ride and I could tell she was impressed.

His *board* left a black mark along the edge of the bench and only the presence of my husband's emissary kept me from freezing his blood on the spot.

*   *   *

Flashing my sharpest smile, I planted one on right on the royal lips. "Hey, babe, what up?"

I did not have the words . . .

Mostly because I hadn't understood the question but also because of his fearless stupidity. This was truly why we find mortal men so fascinating. Not content merely to die, they spend their short lives courting death in so very many ways. And, in truth, the salutation was a bit distracting.

"He wants to know what's going on," Puck said helpfully.

I ignored him and graced my unwelcome paramour with my full attention. "My people prepare a feast in your honor, my love. Rich raiment befitting one who shares my bower has been laid out for you. Go and adorn yourself in silk and velvet."

"Silk and velvet? Not my deal. I appreciate the thought but I'm cool."

"You will be warmer in the clothing that has been made ready for you."

He threw back his head and laughed and, to my horror, wrapped an arm around my waist and pulled me tightly against his side. I would have turned him into a newt then and there if not for the irritatingly superior smile on the face of Robin Goodfellow.

"Isn't my Annie the greatest?" Tommy Lane declared once he had his laughter under control.

Puck bowed deeply so that I could not see his expression. "She is indeed," he said.

The food was great. A little gay, you know, with sauces and garnishes and fancy stuff, but there was lots of it and it tasted prime. Unfortunately, the after-dinner entertainment totally sucked. One guy with

Spock-ears and a harp. I had to ask what the harp was; I thought maybe it was some kind of warped axe. Oh, and the dude was blind but he was no Stevie Wonder. I figured they were all being so nice to him because he was blind and that was cool, but the piece he was slaying went on and on and on.

I guess I wasn't too good at hiding what I thought because the little brown dude—name of Robin Good-fellow but he tagged Puck—turned to me and asked what I thought. I could've lied but he didn't look like he was having such a good time either, so I told him.

"Too bad you've got no decent tunes with you."

"I do." I tapped the player on my belt. "But I'd need a deck to plug in to."

"I could take care of that."

"Bonus!"

I handed over my player and next thing I knew, the Bedrockers were blasting out at a hundred and twenty decibels.

The queen, *my* queen, whirled around so fast it was all hair and drapery stuff for a minute. Once that settled and I got a look at her face, there was like a second where she looked totally scary. Then Puck told her it was my sound and she chilled although her smile seemed a little forced.

I spent a couple of songs teaching the crowd to move and I gotta hand it to them, for all they looked like they had a collective stick up their butts, they sure could dance.

Worn out by the exertions I would not dignify in calling dance, Tommy Lane spent the night asleep so I did not even gain the small physical pleasure I might have from his presence. When he woke he was annoyingly insistent upon eating and would not travel until he had broken his fast. Barely concealing my impatience, I had the sprites bring him bread and honey and clear water as much at this time as I would have liked him to have been fed with insects and the dregs of a swamp. Or better still, fed to insects and lost within the swamp.

Although Puck had returned to my husband's court, I did not trust his absence and resolved to keep up the pretense until the boy was gone.

With no intention of traveling to the crossing at a mortal's pace, I took his hand and we were there. Unfortunately, we were not alone.

"Sending him back so soon, Majesty?"

"Why should I not? I have wrung from him all his strength."

At that moment, the boy chose to fling himself down a sheer rock face, then up and over a bank of earth. Folding himself near in two he clutched at his board, spun about in the air, and landed with a merry whoop.

"Seems to have gotten his strength back. Your husband, my Lord Oberon, is pleased you have found amusement. How unfortunate that you find he does not suit."

I could well read the implication between his words. As much as accuse me of a foolish choice. I would not have that. Much angered, my voice sheathed in ice, I said, "Then my husband, the Lord Oberon, will be pleased to hear that I am not sending him back but rather gifting him with passage between our worlds so that he might amuse himself as he will." Masking my fury, I called Tommy Lane to my side and opened the way. "You may go once each day to the place that I found you."

"You trying to get rid of me?"

From his smile I could see that he was making fun, and for the sake of our audience, I denied it.

"Her Majesty grants you a great gift," my husband's irritating emissary declared. "Do you not, Majesty?"

"Yes," I snapped before I thought.

A fairy gift once given cannot be recalled.

For me now to be rid of Tommy Lane, the decision to leave must be his.

I had it all. A major babe, servants, and great food—after a few tries they even managed a decent burger and fries—I could ride when I wanted and some of the fairy dudes were starting to catch on.

"Finvarra, what are you doing?"

He dropped to one knee, his waist length hair wrapping around him like a silken curtain. "I believe it is called a nollie, Majesty. In essence, an ollie performed by tapping the nose of the board instead of the tail."

My lip curled, almost of its own volition, and my hand rose to teach him such a lesson as would last the length of an immortal life. Unfortunately at that moment, Tommy Lane dropped down out of the trees followed by that nuisance Puck.

"Hey Finvar! Rad move!"

"Your boy's really livening up the place," Puck announced, leaping off a board of his own. With no iron on the original, fairy magic had been able to duplicate it easily. No one knew exactly what aluminum was except that it wasn't iron. "Isn't it great?"

All three waited for my answer.

I locked my temper behind an indulgent smile. "It is."

Tommy Lane waved up toward the line of bark ripped in looping patterns from the interlocking branches of the trees. "Did you know that Disney used boards to work out how Tarzan would move?"

"No."

It seemed my husband had not yet tired of the bothersome Puck's reports.

I would have to get creative.

Riding the trees was fine but it was hard to keep it real; there were just some moves I couldn't do on bark. No matter how broad the branch. And sometimes I rolled right though living space and that was just wack. Also more danger than I needed in my life; some of those dudes had really big swords. So, every day, I went back to the skate park.

I didn't see the girl at first, I saw the flowers. Three big pink roses sprayed onto the side of the pipe. She wasn't easy to spot because she was kneeling down at the bottom of the third rose, painting in her tag. Her green jacket kind of blended in with all the foliage.

I mounted up and carved my way down to the bottom just as she stood. Her tag read Janet. Given that she was at the bottom of the pipe and couldn't get away, she stood her ground.

"Nice work," I said. "I haven't seen you around here before."

"My old man doesn't want me coming here. Says I'll meet the wrong sort." She shrugged. "I come anyway. I've seen you."

"You have?"

"Duh, you haunt this place. Yesterday afternoon, I saw that super high switch heelflip you did."

"Actually, it was switch front heelflip, switch heelflip, backside tailside and a fakie hardflip."

"Wow."

"Yeah." I was good to talk to someone who understood. She was riding an urban assault board, way bigger than most girls like at forty inches and I could see her eyeing my pro model. I have no idea what made me say it but I stepped off and pushed my board over. "Go on. You know you want to."

Her eyes widened. Letting someone else on your ride was more intimate than screwing, and I could tell from her expression, she'd never done this before. Finally, she nodded and pushed her ride toward me. "What the hell. The front trucks are a little tight."

She was right and I bailed coming out of a tailslide, trying to carve left across the bowl. Took most of the landing on my right shoulder but still buffed a strip of skin off my jaw. Late afternoon, she came off some air and into a fakie, shifted her weight wrong, hit, and rolled up, blood seeping through the knee of her cargos.

Bonded in blood. Cool.

With her leg locked up, she was finished for the day. Using her board like a crutch, she hobbled to the edge of the park and turned to stare back at me. "You want to go get some fries or something?"

Actually I did, but Annie was expecting me back, and . . .

Janet snorted. "You got a girl. I should've known."

While I was thinking of something, anything to say, she limped away.

He was bleeding when he returned to me that night and he stank of mortal company. I would have demanded to know her name but that vexatious Puck was still about and I would not have him carry tales of a mortal lover who dared to cheat on me.

Later, with the nettlesome sprite safely in sight but out of earshot, as he sought to annoy me by having

Tommy Lane teach him new tricks, I got the whole story from the Loireag.

A girl.

I would use her.

That night, as he slept, I cloaked myself in shadow and did what I had not done for many long years—I walked amid the mortal race. The girl was easy enough to find; her blood had mixed with his and his was mine.

She sat by the entrance to her dwelling. Within, raised voices discussed locking her in her room until she told them the name of the boy she was seeing.

In guise of one Tommy Lane would believe, wearing the face of my husband's emissary—which had of late become as familiar to me as my own—I sat down beside her. "They sound angry."

"Who the hell are you?"

Of old, the young were much politer. "I bring you word from Tommy Lane."

"Who?"

Thus I discovered the reason she had not told her elders the name of the boy. "You met him today at the ring of stone by Carterhaugh Pond. You rode his board and he yours."

"Yeah, so?"

"He is in grave danger. Tomorrow night the Queen of the Fairies will take his life."

"Where?"

I sighed. "She will end his life."

"Why?"

"Because a tithe to darkness must be paid and she will not sacrifice an immortal knight when a mortal man is close at hand."

"Look, I don't know what you're on, but I got troubles of my own so make like a leaf and get lost."

I drew her gaze around to mine, captured it, and held it. "Do you believe me now?" I demanded when, after many heartbeats, I released her.

She drew in a long, shuddering breath. "I guess."

As that appeared to be as good as I would get, I continued. "You must go to the park as the sun leaves the sky, and when the Queen arrives to claim him, you must snatch him from his board and hold him tight." A possible problem occurred to me. "Are you afraid of snakes?"

"No."

"Good. Do not fear although he be turned within your grasp into angry beasts or red-hot iron or burning lead or . . ."

"Does this fairy tale have a point? Because if I'm not inside in five minutes, my old man's going to come out here and kick my ass."

"If you hold tightly to young Tommy Lane, he will in time become himself again. Then you must wrap him in your mantle green."

"My what?"

"Sorry, wrap him in your green jacket and the spell will be broken."

Annie looked real pleased with herself the next morning, and when I went for a quickie before breakfast, she was so into it, it was kind of scary. I mean, I liked her enthusiasm, but man . . .

She stretched out on the bed looking all catlike, and said, "Wait at the park this evening until I come for you. I have a surprise planned."

Later, everyone I passed on the way to the park said good-bye.

I was making my third run down over Janet's roses,

when she suddenly appeared. I looked up on the lip and there she was.

I flipped up beside her. She looked pissed.

"Are you real or what?"

"What?"

"Bastard!" She punched me in the arm.

"What are you talking about?"

And then she told me this bullshit story some short brown dude told her about my Annie and sacrificing me tonight and crap.

"It's a Halloween prank," I told her.

She snorted. "I thought so. The whole thing's a friggin' lie!"

"Not all of it," I admitted. I told her my side of the story and she snorted again.

"Jeez, you are so lame! If that's true, then what makes the story I got told not true? It sounds to me like the Queen wants more than your bod. You said she looked pleased with herself. She said she has a surprise planned. Everyone said good-bye to you when you left. Duh! How many times have you bailed on your head?"

When Janet put it that way, it all began to make a horrible amount of sense. Puck. The short brown dude had to have been Puck. He liked me and he didn't seem to like my Annie much. I guess now I knew why.

I stepped onto my board. "I'm so out of here."

And that was my cue. I could not allow him to merely ride away; the power of the gift I'd given him had to be broken or I would ever live with the nagging feeling that someday he might return.

As I stepped into the mortal world, I was pleased to see the girl wrap her arms around young Tommy

Lane and drag him off his board. I wrapped myself in terrible beauty and, as she tried to stare me down, raised a hand.

First, I turned him into an adder and Janet held him close, although her language would have withered apples on the tree.

Then I turned him into a lion wild and Janet released one hand and smacked the beast upon the nose.

Then I turned him into a red hot bar of iron and Janet screamed and threw him in the pond, throwing her smoldering jacket in after him.

Close enough.

And another wailing visit from the Loireag was little enough to pay.

As I removed the glamour and he was once again Tommy Lane, I cried out, "If I had known some lady'd borrowed thee, I would have plucked out your eyes and put in the eyes of tree. And had I known of this before I came from home, I would have plucked out your heart and put in a heart of stone!"

"Possessive much?" Janet snarled from the edge of the pond.

Dragging Janet's jacket behind him, Tommy Lane wadded to the shore, shaking his head. "Babe, we are *so* over."

I had thought that was the point I was making.

When I stepped back into Fairyland, it was to find Robin Goodfellow awaiting me.

"Ah yes, the old held by mortal maid schtick." He scratched reflectively beneath one arm. "Funny thing, though, I could've sworn that tithe went out after seven years, not seven days."

Had it only been seven days? It had seemed so very much longer. "Shut up," I told him.

"Hey, rules were followed, traditions upheld, I got

nothing to say." He bowed, sweeping an imaginary hat against the ground. "If your Majesty has no further need of me."

I forbore to remind him that I never *had* need of him nor ever would. He waved in his most irritatingly jaunty manner and sped through the deepening twilight toward Lord Oberon's court, indulging in a series of kickflips as he rode out of sight.

A velvet hush settled over my court as with stately grace I moved among my knights and ladies. As I settled upon a grassy bank and allowed my ladies to twine starflowers in the midnight fall of my hair, I came to an inescapable conclusion.

It was entirely possible that I had remarkably bad taste in men.

A VERY SPECIAL RELATIVITY

Jim Fiscus

Jim Fiscus is a Portland, Oregon, writer and photojournalist. He taught military history and worked in transportation planning in Portland—fields that are clearly related to each other. He has been a freelance writer, concentrating on medicine, science, and business, for over a decade. His first fiction sale used SF to explain the theological basis of the present regime in Iran. That story let him make practical use of his master's degree in Middle East history. He is presently finishing nonfiction books on the 1956 Suez crisis and war in Afghanistan. This is his first faerie story.

Six months into the run from Tau Ceti to Centauri, I found a dead chicken outside the pilots' module. For four years, I had inspected the keel of the *Dankwart Rowtow*. I'd been aboard the *Dank* since the shipping company bought my debt, to be repaid with labor. But I'd never work it off. I paid for my food, my bunk, even for the air I breathed, and my debt grew. Soon, I knew I'd cut my losses and suck vacuum. Then I found the dead chicken.

The keel of the *Dank* is a giant pipe. It holds the ship together, linking the forward command decks with the drive engines aft. It was always the same gray tunnel filled by the clicks and whirrs of equipment. Cargo and passenger modules clamp to the keel in four rows; the wedges between the mods are packed with small cargo containers and bulk cargo that can take vacuum.

I walked through the core inspection tube, lights coming on ahead of me and dying behind me, leaving me in a moving cylinder of reality in a pearl-gray universe. I stopped every so often to check the module docking controls. Turning from inspecting the first-class module, I saw a dark spot on the gray deck at the forward edge of the light. I clicked my com. "Hey, Marengo, you dropped something when you walked the tube yesterday."

"I wasn't that far forward. I had to clean out the filters for Mod Seven before the passengers started smelling like goats."

"You're a lazy bugger, Marengo."

"Sure am, Horvath, and I'm also your boss."

I grunted a reply, walking faster as I realized that the stain was larger than I'd thought. I felt growing elation at the break in the endless monotony. As the light moved with me down the tube, the stain became a mound of brown and red feathers. "Marengo, which one of you jackers mocked up this thing?"

"Whaddya mean?"

I knelt beside the mound of feathers and prodded it with my pen. The slashed body of the bird lay as if casually tossed aside. A ragged slash had nearly severed the bird's head. "Bloody hell!"

"What're you mumbling about, Mike?"

"Get down here. It's real. We've got a dead chicken, Marengo."

Washed of blood, the feathers on the front half of the bird were dark red; the remainder of the bird was dark brown, but for a spot of white near its tail. "The *Dank* ain't even carrying frozen embryos, Horvath. Where'd this jacking chicken come from?" Marengo asked.

I tapped the mess table serving as the chicken's bier. "And that's no ordinary chicken." I poked the dead bird. "That's a fancy rooster."

"A chicken's a chicken." Marengo was short, way under two meters, blond, and pale. He talked with his teeth clenched so that his words seemed to escape from between the jail bars of his teeth. "Shouldn't be chickens on the *Dankwart*. Except to eat." He said it as if the dead bird was an affront to the laws of physics, which was absurd. The *Dank* itself was an affront to the laws of physics, flying faster than the speed of light while bypassing the relativistic time dilation. Nobody outside of the pilots' mod knew how it was done. "Com the steward in first class. He'll help you find the passenger who owned this bird."

"I checked. No security breach from the mods. Passengers didn't get out. I'm taking your keel walk tomorrow. May even knock on the pilots' door."

"The Company doesn't let anybody talk to the pilots. You'll be a dead man if you break orders." The words hissed from between his clinched teeth.

"Death isn't that much of a threat to a slave, Marengo."

The keel was over two kilometers long and fifty meters across, with the three-meter wide inspection tube running up its center. Rather than my usual moving cylinder of light, I lit the full tube. I'd started aft and walked toward the bow and the pilots' quarters. I didn't inspect the docking clamps. I was looking for blood and evidence of fowl murder.

I took three hours to reach the lock into the pilots' deck. A chicken with its neck slashed should have splattered blood all over the place if still alive, and at least dripped a bit if dead. The only blood was where I'd found the bird. Overhead, a vent screen to the outer keel-ring hung on its hinges. I saw dark blotches on the screen. I'm tall, but not tall enough to reach the hole, so I unclipped a repair ladder and moved it into place. Shoving my emergency med pack around to my back—the Company was always afraid that a passenger would find a way out of a mod and be hurt—I stuck my head into the darkness. Wedging one hand through the opening, I twisted to shine my lantern around. The deck was splattered with dark red.

"Damn, that old cock had a lot of blood in him!" The splatter made a trail leading to the bow. The vent opening was too small for me to crawl through, but the dim glow of the meter marks on the bulkhead showed the blood trail vanishing somewhere over the pilots' module.

We never saw the pilots. Flight crews boarded the *Dank* and the Company's other FTL ships in secret and never left their quarters and the bridge.

I felt a rush of adrenaline as I reached for the com beside the hatch. "Hello? Contract Engineer Horvath. I need to talk to a pilot."

I waited, the rush easing into gut-churning anxiety. Over a minute passed. I reached again for the com, jumping as a voice, smooth and calming, answered.

"Come back with the rooster, and we'll admit you."

The meaning filtered through my surprise. I'd expected denials, not an invitation into the world where time and space twisted to meet human needs. I sprinted for the mess.

We'd wrapped the chicken in a plastic bag and put it in our cooler so we could cook it later. The clear plastic fogged as soon as I pulled it from the compartment. Holding the bag—which I always seemed to end up doing—I rushed back to the keel tube, forcing myself to walk slowly as I neared the pilots' hatch so that my breathing would be normal when I spoke. I said, "I have the chicken."

The hatch slid open. I glanced around the keel tube, fearing to leave the comfort of the pale gray walls. Breathing deeply, I stepped into the pilots' module, jumping as the hatch closed behind me. I was in an airlock. The inner hatch opened, and warm light engulfed me. The air also felt much warmer and I smelled freshly cut grass and flowers. I smelled life.

I blinked against the bright light, trying to see details in the silhouetted figure waiting for me.

"Don't wait all day, Mr. Horvath. Come in." Unfiltered by the com, his voice was as deep as a Russian bass. "Bring Sigbert home." He paused, and added, "The cock. Sigbert was the cock."

I stepped out of the lock and onto a carpet of living grass. The chamber stretched forward for a hundred meters, bushes and small trees breaking the lawn. A dozen figures walked or sat in the garden.

"Our home is not what it should be, Mr. Horvath, but a bit of nature makes it bearable. I'm Senior Pilot Elford Schmidt." He lowered his head slightly, his gaze never leaving my face.

He wore no shirt, only baggy, forest green pants that looked like Thai silk. Schmidt was about my two-meter height, though with more muscles than I'd ever have. His silver-blond hair shocked my senses as it lay against his darkly tanned shoulders. I don't vector that way, but I felt an overpowering sexuality coming from Schmidt.

"I'll show you the way."

I followed him, feeling out of place in my gray coveralls. The side room was much closer in appearance to the other compartments on the *Dank*—except that it was paneled with a golden wood that I was certain was real oak. The large table in the center of the room was also wood. The woman was not. She wore a sleeveless tunic that fell in easy folds to midthigh, rich blue silk slid against light brown skin as she came around the table. Black hair cascaded over her right shoulder.

"Amaya," Schmidt called, "Sigbert is home." To me, "Second Pilot Amaya Jahan."

Amaya Jahan walked with a grace I would have believed impossible, her movements relaxed and smooth. She lowered her head slightly, as had Schmidt.

I stammered, "Pilot Jahan," as my glands—adrenal to testes—slammed into overload. I held out the chicken, "I have your pet. I'm sorry it died."

"Not really a pet, Mr. Horvath," Schmidt said, gesturing to the table.

I let go of the frozen rooster too soon, and it thunked onto the table.

"You will stay for dinner and a bit of entertainment that will explain Sigbert's death, Mr. Horvath?" Phrased as a question, Amaya Jahan's words were an order, her voice both musical and husky.

"Pilot Jahan . . ."

"Please, my name is Amaya, Michael."

"Mike. Michael Horvath was my father." I struggled

to find words that felt right, "I would be honored to stay, but my shift ends soon and I have to report back to my boss, a little Napoleon named Marengo."

"We'll manage your chief."

"Then I accept." I felt completely at ease, though far from relaxed. The sexual power of Amaya's presence ensured my full attention.

We ate around the table that had held the dead bird. Besides myself, there was Schmidt, Amaya, and two other couples pretty much like them, though all looked European without the dark beauty of Amaya. Four men sat at a separate table, rising from their own meal to serve us. They were short, chunky, and pushing into old age. Their teeth were prominent, nearly fangs, and their fingernails nearly talons. Ugliest jackers I'd seen in a decade. All wore brown coveralls and red caps. They tore chunks off of raw hunks of meat that still oozed blood. From time to time they rubbed their caps in the blood. I tried not to watch them.

Amaya saw me glancing at the four jackers. "No cause for worry, Mike. The Redcaps have poor manners, but are good pilots, more natural at it than the rest of us. They also follow orders." The tone of her voice made it impossible to believe she would be disobeyed.

Our main dish was coquilles Saint-Jacques. The bread was fresh, warm, and wonderful. I hadn't eaten so well in a decade. "Pilot Schmidt—Elford—the scallops taste fresh, perhaps frozen, but they're not the junk we get."

"We need real food, not lumps of dried molecules reconstituted with recycled piss. Our module makes up a quarter of the ship. We grow some food and carry other things frozen, lashed to the hull. And it is rightly so. Without us, interstellar commerce would die." Schmidt poured glasses of port as two of the Redcaps served fruit and cheese, the delicate china grasped awkwardly in their taloned fingers. "Mike, you said you are a contract engineer. Why did you join the crew as an inferior?"

"Not by choice. I was traveling, just to see a bit of the universe, and wandered into a casino on Jupiter Station. I was playing blackjack and holding my own. Then I started to lose. Every hand. I knew the game was rigged, and tried to stop. A big jacker moved in behind me, with his knife offering to make me a kidney donor. I figured I'd report them later and get out of the debt. I didn't get the chance. My debt was sold to the company that owns the *Dank*."

"So you work off your debt," Amaya said. "That is fair."

One of the ugly old men leaned over me, and I felt his stringy hair on my ear as he rasped, "A debt must be paid. Always."

"I'm charged for everything I eat, drink, wear, and even for the air I breathe. My debt grows with every day I spend on this ship. My only freedom is death. If I escape, the debt will transfer to my family. I don't care for them much, but I can't do that to them. My only benefit is a Company insurance policy that pays my debt if I die on duty."

The old man behind me dropped his hand on my shoulder. I felt his nails through my coveralls and nearly gagged at the stench of death that oozed from him. "Debt must be honest. Only carrion change the bargain."

"Without question, it is so. I wish we could help you, but we cannot." Schmidt pushed away from the table. "Come. Let us show you how the rooster died."

We crossed the garden to a dimly lit compartment about five meters square. Raised chairs ringed a clear area, making it look like a pit. About thirty shadowy figures waited, most arguing with other members of the audience. Schmidt led me, and Amaya, to chairs at the center of one side of the pit, then walked quickly into the shadows.

Moments later, two Redcaps entered the well-lit pit. Both of the ugly jackers held chickens.

The audience broke into loud shouting, accompanied by wild gestures. It took me an instant to realize they were betting. The last thing I expected to see in space was a cockfight, but it explained Sigbert's wounds. One of Schmidt's fellows stepped into the pit, clearly the referee. He nodded to the two Redcaps, who held their chickens firmly and knocked the bird's heads together. The contact enraged the chickens, who struggled to escape. Their handlers held the birds at arm's length, and I saw that both chickens had long, saberlike, blades attached to their legs. The blades looked five or six centimeters long and flashed razor sharp in the lights.

Amaya leaned forward, black hair swept back from her right shoulder, hands resting on the arms of her chair. "Their combat is glorious." She flashed a smile. "Sometimes, it's hard to remain dignified."

I still thought her the most beautiful woman I'd seen, but her glee at an impending chicken fight warned me to watch my back around her. And around Schmidt. I kept my words neutral. "How can you carry flocks of chickens on a spaceship?"

"We hatch a few birds at a time from fertile eggs."

The referee raised his hand. The crowd frantically placed bets as the handlers hurled their birds at each other. The cocks extended their feather ruffs, making it look as if their heads were poking through the center of tiny, red umbrellas.

That was the last clear thing I saw. Everything became a flurry of feathers, birds leaping into the air and slashing with their spurs. Blood splattered at each contact. After several attacks and counters, one bird backed away, the other leaping again to attack. The handlers rushed in and grabbed their chickens, as tokens passed between the betters. Blood pooled on the floor.

"The bird you found lost. The handlers were removing the fighting gaffs when it flapped free. It reached shelves we had against the wall and found a hole in the ventilation pipes. The hole was too small for anyone to chase him." Amaya smiled, looking into the shadows. "Now we see the real fight."

Schmidt entered from the far side of the pit, holding a large rooster in front of himself for the audience to admire. The bird's neck and upper body were golden, its body and tail dark brown. Another pilot entered from behind me, carrying a dark brown rooster with a white neck and a large spot of white at the base of its tail plume. The men passed each other. Schmidt held the cock as an assistant lashed two fighting spurs to the back of the chicken's legs, just above the feet. The sickle blades curved slightly upward. A man behind me whispered, *"Le coq d'or."*

Schmidt held the golden crested chicken high. "Korsakov's fame shall rim the sky. Five fights. Five enemies dead."

The other man held his bird aloft. "Ethelred. Five fights. Five enemies dead."

"But he is unready," Amaya whispered.

The men knelt facing the referee at the side of the pit, holding their roosters. Both birds extended their ruffs and tried to flap their wings in attempts to break free. The referee stepped to the pit. Schmidt pulled the bird toward himself, leaning to whisper to the enraged cock. The rooster kicked in a rapid running motion, perhaps trying to push away.

The fighting spurs lashed into Schmidt's groin and thigh. Schmidt froze for an instant, letting the chicken free as his hands dropped to his groin. He rolled onto his side in a tight ball. Amaya dropped to his side, yelling, "The doctor, get the doctor."

A voice answered, "He's in time lock."

Amaya ripped away Schmidt's trousers as blood spurted from a slashed artery. She reached toward the wound, hands touching one gash, then another, failing to slow the blood. She look up, her face reflecting fear and despair.

I shook off my shock and dropped to her side, hands fumbling for my emergency kit. I pushed Amaya aside. Blood gushed from a deep slash high on Schmidt's thigh. "Artery," I mumbled, pulling free an emergency bandage and a small white cylinder.

"What are you doing?" Amaya asked, grabbing his arm.

"He's bleeding out. We have to stop it." I ripped open the sealed pouch, shook out the thin fabric, and spread it on Schmidt's leg and groin. "Trauma cloth. Soaks up the blood. Also loaded with nanos." Amaya looked puzzled, so I added, "Organic machines programmed to stop hemorrhaging and seal wounds." I felt for the wound under the cloth, and thumbed the cap off of the cylinder, revealing a long needle. I plunged the needle through the cloth into the wound and pressed the top. I barely heard the hiss as it discharged. "The injection attacks the slashed artery. Nanos in the cloth heal the surface. Where's your doctor?"

"He's on as pilot, connected to the ship," Amaya said. "It will take him ten minutes to get here."

I pressed harder on the wound. The blood flow oozing between my fingers slowed.

Schmidt lay in bed, eyes closed, as I followed Amaya into a small room. She reached out and touched his cheek. "My lord, I brought the man who saved you." Her words sounded almost a ritual, not the greetings of lover for lover.

"Mike," Schmidt opened his eyes, and grinned at me. "I owe you a debt I may never be able to repay." He stopped smiling, "though I promise you I shall try."

"The nanos saved you, Elford." Something in his expression, a half smile, warned me not to absolve him of the debt. I didn't understand the feeling, but decided this was no time for modesty, and added, "though I knew how and where to apply the bandages."

Schmidt nodded, his smile fading. "Our doctor says I must stay in bed for a few hours because of my loss of blood. I could object, but it will give me a chance to read. Amaya, tell him. Show him. "

"Are you certain?" Amaya asked her question gently, not as a challenge.

"No. But the debt must be repaid."

Amaya led me into a wide passageway, turning toward the bow. As with every part of the pilots' module I had seen, wood paneling covered the walls, giving life and warmth to the cold ship. "What are you showing me?" I asked.

"We travel many times the speed of light in this ship, as do the other ships managed by the Company," Amaya said. "The laws of physics decree that if we travel for a year and return home, we should find decades or centuries have passed."

"Yep, the Company beat Einstein."

"My people beat Einstein." She stopped by a closed hatch.

I felt a chill from my soul that vanished as my excitement grew. "You're aliens, aren't you?"

"No, not really." Her hand hovered over the hatch controls. "The Company can explain what you have seen so far. For what you learn now, they will kill you."

"I am their slave, though they do not call me slave. Death would be no tragedy for me."

Amaya smiled. "But your death would be a tragedy, even if you do not believe so now." She touched the panel and the hatch slid open.

The room was gray. Bulkheads, deck, overhead, all were pearl gray. No wooden paneling, no grass underfoot, no plants. Utilitarian. Cold. Then, I saw the command couch. Raised on a meter-high wooden platform, it stood near the forward bulkhead. The reclining couch looked to be leather. One of the Redcaps lay on the couch. A golden helmet covered his head, leaving only his mouth and nose exposed. A golden haze, an aura, formed a globe around him and the couch. A second, empty, couch waited a few meters to the side. Traditional computer control consoles hugged the left bulkhead. One of Amaya's people paced before the consoles. A Redcap watched at a control station near the command couch, sucking on his blood-soaked cap.

"You control the ship from here?" I began to hope

that Amaya might lead me to freedom from the Company.

"We control time. The helmet amplifies our abilities. The computers channel the effect we create to encompass the entire ship."

"Where's the helm? How do you set our course?"

"The course is set in the computer before we're brought aboard." Amaya turned suddenly and ran toward the hatch, compelling me to follow her. I caught her in the passage. She was leaning against the bulkhead, arms crossed over her breasts. She was shivering violently. "I hate that room. Nothing is real there. All is metal and plastic. Even time is not real. I am in hell when I sit in the couch."

The desperation in her voice knifed into me. "Resign when we reach Earth on the next leg of the trip."

"We can't." She looked at me, and whispered, "I need your warmth," and stepped into my arms. Slowly, her shivering stopped. I was astounded and bewildered, and probably in mental shock. She clung to me for a time I could not count, finally backing away. "Come, there's much to tell you."

Again, I followed her, this time into the central garden. She sat, cross-legged, on the grass. I sat facing her, my back against a small tree. "We are fairies."

"I'm sorry, what did you say?"

"Fairies. Sidhe. Fey. Elves. Goblins. Those are some of the names used by the Celts and the British. My family moved from India several generations ago. I am a mix of races."

"That's absurd." I felt a flash of anger at the lie, and started to stand.

Amaya laughed. "How do ships traveling faster than light avoid the time dilation of relativity?"

I dropped back onto the grass, remembering stories I had read in childhood. "Time. Time works differently in the land of fairies." Reason told me the idea of fairies was ridiculous but everything I saw around me and everything I knew about space travel told me she was telling the truth. "Physicists always said faster than light travel was a fantasy. When engineering fails, use magic." Slowly, I accepted her words. "You're all fairies, then? What about the Redcaps?"

"Schmidt and the others like him are the highest of the fairies, the heroic Sidhe of legend, and are human in most ways. I'm proof of that. My grandmother was human. The Redcaps are fairies, but closer to goblins than men. The highest and the lowest, it seems, are best at harnessing time."

"How did you start working with the Company?"

"The Company captured a number of us. They dissected us. They scanned us. They experimented upon us, dead and alive. They discovered how we controlled time." Tears ran down her cheeks. "Once they knew that, they only had to work out the engineering and how to best enslave us. They learned how to hook us into machinery that forces us to control time as they order."

"You have told him, little Amaya, I can tell by your tears." Schmidt, limping slightly, walked toward us. A Redcap set a chair beside Amaya. Schmidt sat, and waived the jacker away. He ignored Amaya. "So, Mike, how do I repay my debt to you?"

"Take me home, for a start." I was surprised by the suddenness of my decision, and the hope of escape. Earth's law and Earth's power rejected the contract that indentured me. I would be free as soon as I reached orbit. "If you can, of course."

"Home. A wonderful dream. Home, perhaps, is always our dream and where we wish to be." He smiled. "We shall take you home. But we will need your help."

Hope and elation had me grinning instantly. Then I saw the sadness that held Amaya, and my mood sobered. "How can I help? I can't twist time."

"You can unlock the astrogation codes. That done, we will control our destination." He stared at me. "I will take you home. Do we have a bargain, Mister Horvath?"

"Mike . . ." Amaya started to talk.

Schmidt's hand slapped against his chair. "No. The answer must be his."

"I have no future here. The Company will work me till I am dead."

"Then you would be free," Schmidt said. "They control fairies, but the Company doesn't have any spooks that I know of."

I didn't look at Amaya as I said, "We have a bargain. What do you need me to do?"

"We have a chip that must plug into the main computer. Within seconds, it will destroy them. Their destruction releases the lock on the computers in our bridge. We will have total control of astrogation."

"Why haven't you done it before?"

"You saw Amaya's reaction to the bridge. She's more sensitive than most of us, but any of us would die before we reached the computers." He half smiled. "The Redcaps are nearly immune, but they don't have the wit to do the job."

"Give me the chip."

It took me twenty minutes to reach the crew's control room, my stomach tying knots like a drunken sailor the entire time. Five minutes more, and I had bypassed the hatch controls. I flipped on the light and moved to the main computer. I pried off the side panel, spotted the chip I had to replace, and took the Trojan chip out of my pocket.

"What are you trying, jacker?" Marengo's voice hissed behind me.

I turned.

Marengo's fist slammed into my stomach. I staggered back against the computer. "I warned you about the pilots," he said.

I gasped for breath, then spat my words at him. "So you're a Company snitch now?"

"Always have been, Mikeo. Always have been. You're about to fall to the bottom of the food chain. Those ugly jackers with the red caps are going to have you for dinner. Fresh food for the pilots."

I fought down my reflex to gag at the image of the Redcaps ripping human flesh with their teeth. Enraged, I kicked back against the wall and charged Marengo. I smashed him back into a table, driving my fist into his gut. He doubled over, and my knee crunched into his face. He staggered back. I snapped a kick at his groin, but he grabbed my leg and twisted. I smashed into the floor, caught my breath, and scrambled to stand.

Blood flowed from Marengo's pulped nose. A knife dropped from his sleeve into his hand and he came at me, the blade held low to gut me.

"Oh, shit," I said. Never much of a fighter, I looked for something to use as a club. I grabbed a chair and spun it toward him.

Marengo knocked the chair aside and came at me again.

I snapped a punch to his larynx. He dropped to his hands and knees, choking for breath. I grabbed the knife he had dropped and whipped the blade across his throat. You're suppose to feel sick, filled with angst, when you kill your first man. I was elated, and said to the dead man, "Better you, jacker, than me."

I turned back to the computer and plugged in the chip Schmidt had given me.

I stared out the escape shuttle's view port, but could not see Earth because of the bulk of the *Dankwart Rostow*. I'd stayed with the fairies for the months the trip had taken, not willing to risk returning to the crew compartments. I turned as the hatch opened. Amaya came in slowly, almost shyly. "Mike, you can't get away from me that quickly. You've kept your distance. Too much distance. So I'm coming with you."

"But I'm human."

"So was my grandmother, love. It may come to nothing, but we can at least have a bit of fun."

I held my hand out to her, and she sat beside me, pressing against me.

The thud of a heavy object on the deck made me look up. Schmidt stood over a large chest. "We're all coming with you, to be truthful, Mike." He moved aside as seven more of the Sidhe crowded into the shuttle.

"All of you? But no Redcaps?"

"Somebody has to pilot the *Dankwart*," Amaya said, as a fast, high, tone chimed through the shuttle. "Come on, love, strap yourself in. We'll blow off the ship in a few seconds."

I tightened my harness as the others did the same with theirs. We pounded back into our couches as the escape jets blasted us away from the *Dank*. I held Amaya's hand as the shuttle circled the ship. The blue and white globe of Earth slipped into view, filling the port. We sped closer to the planet, and I slowly realized that the continents did not match my memory of the planet. "Amaya? Where are we?"

"Earth, I thought," she answered. "But it looks wrong."

"Not Earth, Mike, but home."

"Our bargain!"

"Kept. I am taking you home. This planet is a refuge for the Sidhe and for many humans working with us. It is the place I dream of. It is my home. Now, it is your home."

Amaya reached to unfasten her harness. "Your word. Your honor, my brother. You violate the intent of the bargain. Keep your word."

"I am. In exact detail. It will be a good home to us all."

I knew I had no choice, and looking at Amaya, I didn't want one. "Looks like I'm free of the Company."

"We all are," Schmidt said.

Worry stabbed at me. "The ship, what happens when the Company finds the ship?"

"They won't. Our charming Redcap cousins will soon grow hungry, and feed, while the astrogation computer takes them on a vector toward an empty section of space. The Redcaps have to be compelled to sit in the time couch. They will quickly stop doing so. Relativity will catch up with them."

"And Einstein will win."

WITCHES'-BROOM, APPLE SOON

Jane Lindskold

This story is the first about the athanor—creatures of myth and mystery who live among us—to appear since Lindskold's novels *Changer* and *Legends Walking*. Lindskold is the author of fifty or so short stories and over a dozen novels. The most recent of these are *Through Wolf's Eyes; Wolf's Head, Wolf's Heart;* and *Dragon of Despair*. She is always writing something. You can learn more about her work at http://www.janelindskold.com.

"Don't pee on that tree," Demetrios says, pausing to cast a stern gaze upon the young coyote.

Shahrazad halts in mid-squat, cocks her head to one side, and whines inquiringly.

"At least," Demetrios amends, his large, hairy ears twitching in amusement, "not without first asking the tree's permission."

The golden-brown coyote bitch whines again before shuffling a few steps away and letting loose a long stream of pungent urine.

"Ah, you did need to go," Demetrios says, resuming his climb up the steep, forested slope. "She probably

181

would have forgiven you that, but the habit you ca-
nines have of peeing on everything in sight to mark
your territory would have really annoyed her. A dryad
is nobody's territory but her own, and let me tell you,
you don't want to get an apple tree annoyed. They've
tempers as unpredictable as cider—sometimes sweet
and refreshing, and other times hard, holding the
power to twist your mind. Remember that."

Shahrazad kicks dirt over the damp spot she's left
on the ground. She wishes everyone would stop trying
to teach her stuff. The lectures get really old, and she's
very young—some say the youngest of their immortal
kind, even as some say her father is the oldest.

But her father, the Changer, is far away now, having
decided that the best care he can give his young
daughter is to leave her in others' hands. Until recently, those hands had belonged to Frank MacDon-
ald, but Frank had received an urgent call from a cat
with too many kittens.

Though Frank had been willing to leave the uni-
corns and griffins and other creatures who dwell on
his Other Three Quarters ranch without care other
than what they themselves provide, he had not trusted
Shahrazad to manage on her own. That was why the
young coyote now finds herself under the watchful eye
of Demetrios the faun, investigating the many wooded
acres of Demetrios' isolated home.

Demetrios himself is her problem. She'd met the faun
before, and thought she knew him from the curving
horns that top his curly head to the shiny goat-hooves
on his feet. She'd thought him a fusser, a worrier,
always nervous, always anticipating trouble. She's beginning to think she was wrong.

There's something different about Demetrios here
on his own grounds. Even his scent has changed. He

smells stronger for one thing, no chemicals damping the mingled odor of goat and man, no perfume confusing the signals. And the signals are there now, clear to anyone with a nose. Demetrios smells dominant, his pheromones definitely sexually charged.

This last puzzles Shahrazad. She isn't surprised to learn that Demetrios is an alpha. Even when all he had smelled of was nerves and tension, the other fauns had deferred to his authority. Even the satyrs—bigger and stronger though they tended to be—had taken Demetrios' opinions into account.

No. It's the odor of sex that puzzles her. She herself is sexually immature, but her father radiates a similar sexuality, so it is an authority she knows and respects, even while remaining immune to its lure. But her father tends to react only when a mature female is present.

Striding through his forest, muscles tautly visible even through his shaggy brown goat pelt, Demetrios is unconsciously signaling to females of his kind. But Shahrazad has never seen a female faun, nor heard mention of one.

Do they even exist, or is Demetrios's body crying out to emptiness?

Johanna had earmarked this patch of woodland a while back as a good place in which to go foraging. From the road it had looked pretty much untouched. She'd swear there were virgin elements in there, and even the second growth forest was old.

A month ago she'd rented a small plane and made an aerial survey, but that hadn't worked too well. Gusts of unexpected turbulence had arisen, making the pilot insist that they divert away from the area. Thermal upthrusts, he'd said, but his eyes were wide with fear. There were rumors that this patch of woodland was haunted, that more than one group of hikers had seen things they would never talk about afterward. That a few who'd ventured across its borders hadn't come back at all.

Johanna hadn't bothered to try and make the pilot stay. The jolting of the plane as it tossed from thermal to thermal, the funny way the wings had bent had made her breath come fast and nearly brought her breakfast up. Anyhow, she'd seen enough—glimpses of meadows, fascinating groupings of tree species that hinted at old agriculture gone feral. She figured she could learn more from satellite maps.

The satellite maps prove disappointing, though. The images are blurred, even when Johanna does everything she can to improve the resolution. The tech she complains to says that there had probably been light cloud cover on the day the images had been downloaded. Still, there is enough information that Johanna is able to plan her day's hike with some confidence.

She'll enter near where a ravine undercuts the fencing. At other times of the year the stream that runs through the ravine would make this difficult, but this is the dry season, before snowmelt swells the current.

Cutting the fencing is out. It is all electrified, and she doesn't know what alarms an interruption of current might send to the owners. She makes note of any streams or other large obstacles that might force her to reroute into areas where she might encounter the owners of the land.

Meeting up with the owners of private property is always a problem when you are trespassing—especially when the gear you are carrying makes it clear beyond any doubt that you are trespassing with intent to steal.

*   *   *

Frank had gotten called away in late autumn, and by the time winter is putting the trees into dormancy, Shahrazad is at home on the sprawling, forested acres. Forests are a change from the scrub growth of piñon and juniper where she had been born or from the mostly evergreen stands on Frank's ranch. She likes the change, likes the sharp acrid scent of rotting leaves, likes chasing after the little creatures who live in the thick leaf mold.

As time has passed, Demetrios and his fellow fauns have become more comfortable with letting her wander unsupervised. Shahrazad senses that their assurance regarding her ability to behave herself and the dormancy of the trees have something in common.

Pleased as she is to be permitted to roam, Shahrazad remains a touch offended by the assumption that she would harm the trees—or that the trees could harm her. After all, what could a tree do? Trees just root down and grow. What are they going to do—drop leaves on her?

Grinning broadly, tongue lolling, shining young teeth sparkling white, Shahrazad bolts after a rabbit. When it dives into a burrow beneath one of the oaks Demetrios had warned her to be careful around, Shahrazad doesn't dig the rabbit out.

Kindness to her host, she thinks, not admitting she feels an element of apprehension as well. There is something about the way the oak dominates the land, a quiet power shared by other trees scattered throughout the acres the fauns tend. Even if Demetrios hadn't told Shahrazad what trees she was by no means to disturb Shahrazad would have learned to detect them on her own.

Then she catches a new scent on the wind and all thoughts of oaks flee—as forgotten as the rabbit.

*   *   *

Johanna drags the back of her hand across her fore-head. It might be winter, but without the screening canopy of foliage, she's suddenly hot. Certainly the heavy jacket she'd put on when dressing against the morning's chill is to blame. She stops to take it off, squeezing the down coat until she can fit it into a small bag that she hangs from the side of her pack frame.

When she shoulders her pack again, she reluctantly admits that more than the coat might be to blame for her exhaustion. She's let herself get out of shape—not so anyone could tell, looking from the outside. It helps to be sort of husky to start with, but from the inside she can feel the difference. She doesn't like how her heart keeps hammering even after she's stopped for a rest or how heavy the pack feels.

It's gonna get heavier if you find what you're looking for, girl, she reminds herself, and gets moving again. The going seems easier without the stifling warmth of the down jacket. Johanna inspects the surrounding growth, hoping to catch a glimpse of a thick, twiggy mass of growth nestling among the more normal limbs.

Witches'-brooms, she thinks, then smiles to herself. She likes the fanciful name, but what she is searching for is in no sense supernatural. The witches'-brooms she is looking for are natural mutations that some trees develop. There are various theories as to why they occur. Most theories favor a virus or fungus of some sort as the instigating agent. Others argue for damage to the parent tree that causes a mutation.

Johanna doesn't really care what causes witches'-brooms to form. When she is honest with herself— which she is from time to time—she'll admit that she doesn't really want to know. A neat scientific explana-tion would take some of the thrill from the search.

And would make it easier for others to do what I do, she thinks, leaning against a gnarled oak to catch her breath. The frame pack she's wearing makes her feel like she has a hunchback.

Another reason to start taking better care of myself, Johanna thinks. *Doesn't exercise help prevent osteoporosis?*

She scans the trees as she rests, thinking how ironic it would be if she makes another really good find today. Her current lack of conditioning is a direct result of her last big find, the profits from which she had invested in a partnership in one of those sprawling home garden centers. It had seemed a good decision, but it had led to her spending more time on her butt reviewing inventories and other records than getting out in the fresh air.

Several years ago Johanna had located a witches'-broom growing among the boughs of an apple tree in the remnants of an old orchard. She'd cut it away and vegetatively propagated it, tending the grafts with immense care. The best she'd hoped for had been a new variant of dwarf apple. What she'd gotten was something nursery catalogs are now calling a fairy apple.

The shining red skins of the fairy apples are delicately overlaid with pale white dappling, an accent that makes the whole apple seem to glow. A full-grown fairy apple is shaped like a Red Delicious, but grows only about as large as an apricot. Now that the first real crops are coming on, the fairy apple is the delight of haute cuisine. The young trees are selling for astronomical amounts.

But Johanna isn't coming in for any of this wealth. She'd accepted what had then seemed to her like an astonishing offer for her find—ten times what she'd ever been paid before, and she'd been offered a lot for the Blue Dust Spruce. Even better, the offer had come years before her infant trees would bear their first fruits, so she hadn't needed to spend years tending her young trees to their maturity only to discover, as she had several times before, that while she had indeed discovered a new strain it would be mostly useful as rootstock for grafting.

The man who had bought the young fairy apple trees must have been prescient. Later, when the first fairy apples were already a sensation, Johanna had gone back to the old orchard, hoping to find something that would give her a clue to how Demetrios Stangos could have known the potential of the fairy apple. The orchard was gone, a subdivision rising in its place, and no one there had the least idea what she was talking about.

But Johanna feels that Mr. Stangos owes her something, and when the garden center runs through her money without giving much back, and she has to go back to prospecting for new specimens, Johanna remembers how she'd read that Stangos is a recluse who owned vast forested acreage in several climate zones. This wasn't the first new tree variant he'd introduced to the market, but he remains remarkably secretive about his techniques, never attends any workshops or accepts speaking invitations.

Selfish old bastard, Johanna thinks, burning as she always does when she recalls those interviews. Mr. Stangos always makes clear he had not been the original finder of the fairy apple. He even names her.

Just so everyone can know how stupid I was, Johanna thinks resentfully.

After some careful reasoning, she decides that Stangos must have a technique for promoting witches'-

brooms, and that for some obscure reason he'd chosen to use his technique on the fairy apple's parent tree. Then when he'd come to collect, he'd found the witches'-broom gone and somehow found out who had taken it.

That means, Johanna thinks, *that his own acreage should have a higher than usual proportion of witches'-brooms. I'll just go there and find one or two. Then we'll be even.*

Now that she's on Stangos' land, that reasoning seems a little thin, but Johanna is nothing if not stubborn. She's come this far, and she's going to at least look. The winter days are short and if she doesn't find anything . . .

She doesn't complete that thought. All the while she's been resting, her gaze has been wandering through the lacework of naked branches. She has spotted clumps and breaks, but always a second inspection has revealed them as squirrel nests or clusters of unfallen leaves. Without letting her gaze leave the promising mass, she quests blindly with one hand for where her field glasses hang ready. They are small, efficient, high-powered things. She focuses and the tree branches race at her, so close she can see the pattern in the bark.

Perfect, she thinks, feeling her exhaustion drain from her, the pack suddenly light. Not two hundred feet away is a cluster of apple trees growing in a rough oval around a meadow knee-deep in dry grass. One of these trees, almost directly across from her, slightly to the right, cradles a witches'-broom in its boughs.

Perfect! Johanna silently exalts. An even trade, an apple tree for an apple tree.

Johanna moves forward, her tread swift in anticipation, weariness temporarily forgotten. All her attention so tightly focused on the steps she will need to take to get her prize that she doesn't realize that she is being watched.

From her first whiff, Shahrazad knew that the new scent did not belong to any of the fauns. Their scents mingle goat and human. This scent is wholly human. She doesn't think that the human scent belongs to anyone she has met.

For a moment curiosity wars with caution, and the young coyote considers going and finding Demetrios. Then she remembers that the senior faun had left the property that morning. Although she is acquainted with the other fauns, she does not accord them any authority over her—nor does she feel any great respect for them. They are skittish and shy by nature, a thing she regards as part of their essentially herbivorous nature.

Shahrazad is very young, possessed by the young's tendency to oversimplify. She likes to divide the world between predators and prey—mostly because she considers herself a very superior predator. The problem with this oversimplification is that she tends to forget that the prey can be very clever and very dangerous indeed—precisely because if they are not, then they will most certainly become not the prey, but the eaten.

So she tells no one of her discovery, but puts her nose to the wind and begins to track. It's an easy trail to follow. The human is hot, tired, and not in the best of health. By the time Shahrazad has homed in on her target and sneaked close, she doesn't need her vision to confirm that this is no human she has ever met.

The human leaning back against a twisted old oak is a full-grown female, built around square lines: big shoulders, short legs, short arms, her figure carrying just enough extra weight to fill in the curves without creating new ones. Her hair is the brown of a fallen leaf, her skin weathered, but only slightly lined. She's wearing heavy trousers and a flannel shirt. Both are in browns and grays that blend nicely in with the surrounding forest. Shahrazad, used to animal camouflage patterns, figures this is probably deliberate.

Pleased with her discovery, Shahrazad beats the golden-brown plume of her tail against the leaf mold before remembering that she doesn't want to give herself away, but the human hasn't noticed anything unusual. The woman's brown eyes are scanning the angular skeletons of the winter bare trees with a rhythmic intensity that Shahrazad recognizes. She's used a similar method herself when hunting, checking for the thing that doesn't fit the surroundings. A rabbit's brown coat doesn't hide it very well once you've spotted its heaving flanks.

Wondering what the woman is searching for, Shahrazad glances in the same direction. Nothing there but trees. Even the birds and squirrels have made themselves scarce in the face of this dual invasion by human and coyote.

What then is the stranger hunting?

Then the woman gives a start, a small, involuntary cry of pleasure breaking from her lips. She reaches for something hanging from the bundle on her back. Moments later, she puts binoculars up to her eyes.

Shahrazad knows what these are. Frank uses them a lot around the ranch. He'd explained that they allowed his human eyes to be as sharp as an eagle's. Shahrazad hadn't liked this much, especially when she realized that this meant she might be being watched when she thought she was on her own, but now she's glad for the knowledge.

Once again, she directs her gaze to where the woman is looking. This time she sees something that makes her feel very apprehensive. The tree the woman is studying through the binoculars is one of those Demetrios had warned Shahrazad about, a dryad apple tree. However, this one is special beyond even the dryad trees that grow in the surrounding grove. Demetrios had visited it several times recently, and he never passed up an opportunity to teach his young charge.

"See that clump of branches up there, pup? That's a baby dryad being formed. They don't propagate through seeds, at least they don't anymore. Stories say that they did once upon a time, but that time's long past."

Demetrios had seemed very pleased with this clump of skinny branches, and Shahrazad had caught his enthusiasm. Beating her tail on the ground she had prompted him to explain more.

He'd obliged. "Trees form those clumps naturally, and sometimes even a normal tree—if it has athanor heritage—will give birth to a dryad—but that's rare. Sometimes we can help them along, and that's a good way to expand the genetic pool."

He had seemed to remember he was talking to a young coyote, because he simplified his words.

"But this tree is a dryad, and her child has been forming for years now. Pretty soon we'll find a good place and set the little one to grow on her own, probably late this winter."

Demetrios had danced a few skipping steps, happy as could be. Shahrazad had shared his happiness without completely understanding everything he was saying. One thing she understood fully was that babies of any of the athanor types were rare and wonderful.

In some way, this tree was kin to her and this potential sapling a cousin.

Apprehensively, Shahrazad watches as the woman tucks her binoculars away, and begins to push her way through the undergrowth toward the dryad tree. Now the young coyote regrets not having called one of the fauns. She considers barking alarm, then stops.

She hasn't seen a rifle, but what if the human has a smaller gun? The human could hurt Shahrazad or the fauns. Frank had made certain Shahrazad understood how dangerous guns were, and how easily hidden.

And what if the human saw one of the fauns—really saw him? Shahrazad knows that the athanor fear discovery over almost anything else. When Demetrios had left earlier that day he'd worn trousers and boots to cover his goaty lower body, a hat to cover his curving horns.

Humans are nearly as curious as coyotes. It isn't enough to hope that the human won't believe what she's seen—and a faun coming in answer to a barked alarm wouldn't know to disguise himself. The fauns don't habitually wear human clothing here on their own lands. They find it uncomfortable and restrictive.

No. She can't bark for help. She will need to drive this human off all on her own. Shahrazad begins to close the distance between herself and the human, sniffing the air, trying to detect the scent of oil, metal, and gunpowder that goes with a handgun. She doesn't find it, but that isn't proof the woman doesn't have a gun. The human smells strongly of sweat, and if the gun hasn't been fired recently the oil and metal scents could be lost—intermingled with the smells from the other gear the woman carries.

Shahrazad decides against being perfectly quiet.

Speed is more important. She will pretend to be a dog. She will growl at the human, bark if she must and hope that the fauns take warning. An angry, defensive bark is very different from a "help me" bark. Demetrios would know this. Would his fellows?

Other than the possibility of guns and of bringing the fauns, Shahrazad likes her plan. Shahrazad knows that most humans are more afraid of dogs than they are of wild animals—for good reason. Dogs can learn caution around humans, but they aren't deep down afraid as wild things are. Humans are their masters and allies, and they defend their masters and their territories as their own.

Shahrazad prepares to leap, to interpose herself between the dryad apple tree and the human. What she doesn't count on is that the dryads might have plans of their own.

When the branches start moving, Johanna thinks a wind must be rising. Then she realizes that the sweat dampening her temples remains untouched. Given the chill of the winter day she should feel any breeze strong enough to move the trees.

But there is no breeze. The air hangs almost unnaturally still and cool. Yet the branches are moving, swaying almost lazily.

No.

Johanna makes her feet carry her forward, toward the promise of the apple tree and the cluster of twiggy growth that means her future and her fortune. She'll need to climb a few feet off the ground in order to cut the witches'-broom out, but that won't be hard. She has a rope ladder, but she shouldn't need it. Apple trees are almost the perfect climbing trees, especially well-pruned ones.

This one has been beautifully tended. Awkward crossing branches have been sawn back so they won't rub against each other and damage the bark. Old fruit has been cleared away so it won't breed infection as it rots on the ground.

Johanna concentrates on her goal. She's having more trouble reaching that tree than she had thought possible. Twiggy hands seem to be plucking at her, drawing her back. Saplings bend to interpose themselves across what she had been sure was a fairly open path. The ground is rougher than she had thought, too; roots thrusting up through the leaf mold nearly trip her several times.

Of course they can't be doing that. That's only her imagination, just like it's only her imagination that the apple tree itself is moving, that a flower garlanded woman is standing in front of the tree. She is a pregnant woman, cradling her hands protectively in front of her abdomen, those hands cupping a shining apple. The woman's expression is both frightened and resolute.

Johanna forces her foot ahead a pace. When the tree branches bend to impede her, she pulls out the two-edged cutting saw she'd brought along for cutting away underbrush. One side of the blade is serrated, but the other is smooth and sharp, like a machete or a sword. She slashes out with the sword blade at the sapling bending in front of her, feels a certain satisfaction when the slender trunk parts in two. She takes two more steps, cutting away at anything that gets in her way. If she can just get out into the open, she'll be fine. There's only some winter dried grasses there, nothing to grab or claw.

Her heart is beating a crazy, erratic tattoo, her breath is coming short, but Johanna makes her determined way forward, her gaze fixed on the promise of safety ahead. She chops through another twisting limb, watches it fall.

When she looks up, she sees a devil standing in the meadow, goat-horned and goat-hoofed, just like the illustrations in her grandmother's old Bible. The devil's eyes are pale yellow with the same weird, squared pupil goats have. He smiles, but there is nothing friendly in his expression.

This final shock is too much. Johanna forgets the grasping hands of the trees, lets the saw slide from fingers suddenly numb, screams, and turns to run.

When the trees start moving, Shahrazad forgets about her plan to impersonate a dog. She's suddenly one very frightened coyote, scenting malice as certainly as she had scented the odor of human sweat. She presses herself flat against the leaf mold, piddling in frightened submission. Her coyote brain doesn't think in words, but if it did those words would certainly be: "Don't hurt me!"

Other than where they accidentally sweep against her while straining toward the intruder, the trees seem to accept her plea. After a terrified moment, Shahrazad's natural inquisitiveness reasserts itself. She lifts her head slightly, trying to figure out what is happening, understanding all too quickly that the trees are determined to drive the human from their midst.

Shahrazad watches, ears plastered flat against her skull lest one of the thrashing branches deal them a stinging blow. She recognizes that the power granting this almost animal movement to the usually stolid trees is not their own. It is coming from the half-dozen or so dryad trees growing around the edges of the meadow. They are using the more normal trees to extend their reach, sacrificing them to protect themselves.

The coyote understands that the human is lucky the trees—both dryad and more usual—are settled into their winter dormancy. Had it been summer, when the sap runs fast and hot, the woman would have been plucked from the earth and dashed down again before she could take more than a few steps. As it is, she is offering a good fight, trying to make her way into the meadow where the cold-burned grass offers no life the dryads can awaken.

Then Shahrazad sees the faun. It is not Demetrios. She struggles to remember the human-language name by which this faun is identified. Kleon. That's it. Kleon. A sound that tells nothing, convenient, though, for those who must talk.

Scents work so much better than names, for they are always unique. By this faun's scent, Shahrazad recognizes Kleon as one of the bolder members of Demetrios's flock, one with whom Demetrios sometimes butts heads over some incomprehensible matter of policy. For example, Kleon hadn't wanted Shahrazad to stay with them. He had been among the last to offer her even grudging welcome—and that had held more the flavor of resignation than anything else.

Now Kleon stands in the center of the meadow, seeming bigger than Shahrazad remembers, but with his shaggy black and white flanks and small curling goat horns not too terribly frightening—certainly not in contrast to the tossing limbs and grasping twigs of the weirdly animated trees.

Yet the woman, who had stood her ground—even fought back—against the trees, takes one look at the faun, freezes, and screams with such pure terror that Shahrazad again flattens involuntarily into the leaf mold and squeezes her eyes shut.

When Shahrazad opens her eyes, she hears the woman crashing through the undergrowth in panicked flight, sees the faun leaping after in pursuit. Kleon is laughing, the sound cruel and harsh against the sudden quiet that comes when the trees settle into vegetable stillness once more.

Shahrazad understands what that laughter says more easily than she would have understood words. Kleon will not be content to drive the woman away. She has threatened his home, his dryads, and, perhaps worst of all, she has seen him as he is—an alien thing in the human world. For this she must die.

And Shahrazad, lectured repeatedly from puppy-hood about the dangers that come from stirring up humans, realizes that the trespasser cannot be driven to her death. Killing her would bring far more trouble than it would resolve. The faun, however, is beyond clear thought. Kleon is not Demetrios, wise and wary beyond most to the dangers offered by humankind. Kleon will be foolish, and that foolishness might well destroy the very secrets he seeks to protect.

Shahrazad forces herself to stand on trembling legs, her tail limp behind her. As she does so, she sees motion from the direction of the meadow. A woman— and yet not completely a woman, for her slender limbs are more like branches, her long hair intertwined with leaves and apple blossoms—stands before one of the trees.

"Stop the faun," the dryad says. "Please, leggy one. Stop him. We will help you if we can, but we are rooted."

Coyote pride will not let Shahrazad give into fear

in front of any plant—even one as wondrous as this dryad is proving to be. Shahrazad forces the weakness from her limbs, shakes herself, and bolts through the suddenly accommodating undergrowth in pursuit of the faun.

Johanna's flight is blind. Fingers fumbling, she unstraps her framepack and lets it thump to the ground behind her. The release of weight gives her wings, but when she spares a single panicked glance behind she sees the devil still bounding after her.

There is a wicked grin on his black-bearded face, and his lack of clothing means that nothing hides the excitement the chase has aroused. One glance is enough. Johanna presses a hand to her thudding heart and runs.

Which way is the ravine? Can she even climb down the sides without slowing too much? Yet falling would be preferable to letting the devil catch her. The cold waters of the stream would be welcoming compared to what he intends.

She is angling her steps in the direction of the ravine when something golden-brown bursts out of the undergrowth ahead of her. A dog, she thinks, or a wolf. Too small to be a wolf, too slender. A coyote?

Species identification is not important, not when the animal is rushing at her, alternately growling and barking. Johanna shies away from those sharp, white teeth. The coyote—Johanna thinks it must be a coyote—dodges behind her, swerves to run alongside. It is driving her away from the ravine, down a slope, towards, Johanna realizes, the sprawling farmhouse where Demetrios Stangos resides.

This seems like a good idea. Revealing that she had been trespassing doesn't seem all that bad now, especially when seen as an alternative to the devil chasing her. She glances back. The devil might have fallen off a few paces, but he's definitely still after her.

Even if Mr. Stangos isn't about, Johanna can certainly appeal to someone down at the house. Stangos had seemed like a steady fellow. Certainly he's married. Mrs. Stangos will protect her. They'll be glad to help her, especially when she tells them about the devil in their forests.

Meanwhile the coyote has dropped back and is directing his barking at the devil.

Maybe it isn't a devil. Maybe it's just a wildman. Johanna could have imagined the horns, couldn't she? Or maybe they were fakes, purchased from some costume store at Halloween. It's amazing the things people do with plastic these days.

Johanna's thoughts are hardly comforting—there isn't much choice between naked wildman or woods devil. What is comforting is the sight of the white-sided farmhouse set among neatly trimmed fields. Goats are grazing on the short-cropped grass, small as a child's toys at this distance. Two or three raise their heads as if hearing the crashing through the forests above their pasture.

Johanna wishes she had the breath to scream for help, but she barely has breath enough to run, and her heart is pounding wildly, its beats irregular.

I should have gotten more exercise, she thinks before her wobbly legs betray her. She trips over an exposed rock, sprawls headlong. Her own momentum carries her forward as she falls. She lifts her arms in a futile attempt to shield her head. A burst of brilliant light fills her thoughts, followed by absolute darkness.

Shahrazad's momentary thrill of triumph when she succeeds in herding the woman toward Demetrios' house dies when she sees Kleon's anger turned upon her.

"Away, little bitch," he commands in a deep, gruff voice, advancing a few steps toward the fallen woman. "Let me through and you won't get hurt."

Feeling very small and very weak, Shahrazad wants to bolt. Terror radiates from the goat-legged man, cutting into her spirit as the winter wind cuts through her coat. She runs, meaning to go only the few paces that will carry her to the human.

Beginning to run is a mistake. Once Shahrazad begins to run, she wants to keep running. Had a root not snagged her paw and slowed her headlong retreat, Shahrazad might not have stopped. As it is, she manages to dig her hindquarters into the soft ground and stop near the human.

The woman is breathing hard: short, ragged gasps. Blood is trickling from a fresh cut on her head. She smells as if she has lost control of her bladder.

The coyote stands over the unconscious figure, bares her teeth, feels her hackles raise, and growls.

"Threatening me, little dog?" The faun laughs very unkindly. "What are you going to do? Bite me? Oh, I'm so very frightened."

Shahrazad growls again, ears flat. She snaps her teeth once in Kleon's direction, doesn't step away from the human, though her every nerve is singing with raw fear.

"I'll bite you," she threatens with the fur prickling up along her back. *"It will hurt. Go away."*

The faun understands, but he sneers.

"I suppose you think I'm afraid of you," Kleon mocks. "Little dog, I'm not afraid of you. I'm not afraid of your father. I'm not afraid of Demetrios. That woman you are guarding so faithfully, little dog, she tried to steal my baby away, might have injured my wife. That human is not leaving here alive."

Shahrazad cannot believe Kleon's bravado. Anyone in his right mind would be afraid of the Changer. Demetrios is pretty formidable, too, in his fussy fashion. Demetrios is head of the herd here, isn't he? Demetrios—not Kleon.

Shahrazad has already noticed that the other fauns are keeping clear of this confrontation. That means they aren't certain Kleon is in the right. And hadn't the tree—the tree who was apparently this faun's mate—hadn't she pleaded with Shahrazad to stop Kleon?

Neither young things nor coyotes particularly like thinking things through, but faced with the consequences of failure Shahrazad thinks hard. Kleon is trying to push her into a fight. He'll probably win, too, if it comes down to that.

But he isn't coming forward. The headlong rage that had sent Kleon after the intruder is ebbing now. The incitement to panic has vanished, and Shahrazad realizes that Kleon had been causing much of her own fear.

Though unclouded eyes she looks at Kleon. She sees a strong creature, a bit small for a human, quite large for a goat. His haunches are piebald, the coarse hair clean and well-brushed. His hair is shiny black, touching his shoulders, but neatly trimmed. He wears his beard, quite naturally, in a goatee. His gaze, wholly human now with no trace of goat, holds a touch of uncertainty.

Having herself pushed acceptable limits too far numerous times, Shahrazad understands. Kleon had been genuinely furious. Had Shahrazad not intervened, had the human not run so fast, Kleon might have driven the intruder to her death. Now he has calmed somewhat, is rational enough to realize the consequences of his actions, yet he does not wish to be seen backing down. Herd creatures and pack animals are quite alike in this.

Shahrazad realizes that she knows the perfect solution to their standoff. She will do nothing. She will wait here, guarding this human. She doesn't think the woman will be waking up any time soon. Surely Demetrios will come back before long. He would not have left Shahrazad if he did not plan to return before too many hours had passed.

She will simply wait. Then Demetrios can deal with Kleon. Demetrios can figure out what to do about the trespasser.

It isn't a heroic decision, but it is a sublimely coyote one, and whatever else she is, Shahrazad, daughter of the Changer, is most certainly a coyote.

Feeling her hackles settle, Shahrazad lowers herself onto her haunches alongside the human, bends to lick the blood from the woman's head wound, and reassures herself that nothing seems smashed beyond repair.

Kleon stands staring at Shahrazad, then he grunts and turns away, trotting off into the forest. One by one, several shadows detach themselves from where they had been watching—the other fauns, joining their fellow. A few nod thanks in Shahrazad's direction. One waves a small object and shouts encouragement in which the only words Shahrazad understands are "called Demetrios."

Sometime later, Shahrazad hears the music of the panpipes, haunting and delicate, yet filled with furious energy. It is coming from direction of the distant apple orchard. Wild as the music is, it comes to her as the sound of peace.

Johanna awakens to find herself lying in a strange bed in a room hung with photographs of orchards in flower. A golden-brown dog is sleeping near her feet. When Johanna moves, the dog hops down off the bed and trots out of the room. A few moments later, she hears the sound of boots against the hallway floor and a man comes into the room. She immediately recognizes him as Demetrios Stangos.

Oddly, he is wearing a hat, though they are inside the house, a jaunty fedora that looks rather nice against his reddish-brown hair. His eyes are also brown, and though their expression mingles stern disapproval and concern, she thinks she sees kindness there as well.

"Johanna," he says. "I am Demetrios Stangos. You may recall me from some past business. How do you feel?"

"My head aches, Mr. Stangos," Johanna admits. "I ache all over."

"Please, call me Demetrios," he says. "You are a guest in my house."

Johanna colors at this, remembering how she had come to be there. Demetrios ignores her embarrassment with old-fashioned courtesy.

"You fell, several times according to the doctor. You may have had a minor heart attack."

"Doctor? Heart attack?"

"I had a doctor in to see you. He has left now, but will return with an ambulance. He would like you to come in to the hospital and be hooked into a heart monitor. However, he wanted you to rest first since you probably have a concussion."

Demetrios pauses, then goes on with the air of one

reciting a lesson. "From the concussion you should expect some lapses in memory. Do not trust what memories you do have—at least those dealing with the immediate past. Head injuries are tricky that way."

"I remember," Johanna says hesitantly. "I was in the forest, near an old orchard. I saw something that frightened me. . . . . A devil and a woman holding an apple. I was so scared I just turned and ran. The trees . . . they moved. . . ."

She hears her voice catch, the words end on a sob. Demetrios smiles at her with gentle amusement.

"Hallucination," he says, "perhaps brought on by the tales they tell about this forest. You have heard how my lands are haunted, haven't you?"

Johanna nods reluctantly. The motion makes her head throb and swim.

Demetrios pours her a glass of water from an elegantly simple stoneware pitcher.

"Drink this. The doctor left you something for the pain, but he said it was best if you used it sparingly. Concussions are tricky."

"You sound like you know personally," she says, accepting the water. It is very cold and tastes of minerals: artesian well water, no doubt.

"I've butted my head into things a few times," Demetrios admits with a wry grin. "Do you remember what brought you onto my land? I cannot believe it was by accident. There are fences, and the property is posted as private."

For a moment, Johanna thinks of pleading amnesia, but the truth comes spilling out, even to the resentment that had led to her coming here to steal.

"Why didn't you speak to me about this?" Demetrios asks when she has finished. "Had I known, I would have made an arrangement to share the proceeds with you. I did my best to make sure you received the credit. I thought it would help your business."

Johanna flushes, ashamed. Her host lets his hand drop so he can scratch the dog behind her ears. When he speaks, Johanna has to fight the odd impression that Demetrios' explanation is for both of them.

I'm still concussed, she thinks, amused and relieved, receptive to whatever Demetrios will say.

"You were right when you thought I had some idea the fairy apple might be special," Demetrios says. "I had studied the parent tree, had some hopes for the genetics if properly stimulated. When I found the witch's broom gone, I tracked down who might have taken it."

Johanna opens her mouth to ask how he'd managed, but Demetrios anticipates her.

"It really wasn't that difficult," he says. "The skills and knowledge needed to do the job are rather specialized. Then I visited your greenhouse and you pretty much told me the rest."

"That tree," Johanna says a touch defensively, "was not on your land."

"No," Demetrios agrees. "It was not, but the tree was too well established for me to move it, and I was reluctant to forgo my experiment."

"I can understand that."

"Can you?"

It strikes Johanna that Demetrios always looks slightly sad. He pauses as if considering, then goes on.

"You are interested in finding new species. You might say that I am interested in preserving the very old."

"Heirloom varieties?" she offers.

"Yes. You might call them that. The gene pool has

grown very small and very attenuated. I am always searching for traces of . . ."

Demetrios trails off. Johanna thinks that perhaps he has forgotten she is there, but he speaks before she can prompt him.

"From one point of view, the fairy apple was a success. However, from another, it was a failure. It is a new version, but definitely not an heirloom."

"And the witches'-broom I saw back there in orchard," Johanna says, "what about that one?"

Demetrios smiles.

"That one will be special," he says.

"A new variety?"

"Oh, no. One that is very, very old."

WYVERN

Wen Spencer

Wen Spencer is the winner of the 2003 John
Campbell Award for Best New Writer. A Pittsburgh native, she sets her novels in the city
she knows and loves so well. The following
story is set in the world of Tinker, which
mixes elves, oni, magic and machines for fantasy with a definite science fiction edge.

Kate wasn't sure what pissed her off most. Was it
being jerked off her first trip back to the States
in years to be shoved into an alternate dimension filled
with undocumented zoology, real magic, and snotty
elves? Or was it that her smattering of ten human
languages and knowledge of dozens of Earth's more
obscure cultures weren't worth a damn with the Elfhome natives? Or was it that this time around, her
native guide managed to always make her look
frumpy?

Crowsong came up the mountainside with all the
fluid grace of a big cat, annoyingly beautiful in the
muggy August heat. The nimble elfin bitch didn't even
pant. She paused at the edge of the kuesi's blood, and

murmured, "I told you that your 'tracer' would not work," and continued up the rock face in bounds that would impress mountain goats.

"I found this much!" Kate shouted after Crowsong.

"What an idiot could not see of the blood trail," the elf's voice came from somewhere above, "a blind man could smell."

Kate picked her way through the swimming pool's worth of viscera to rescue her tracer off of the massive kuesi skull. When she'd heard that the railway project manager for the elfin crew was a female, Kate expected to skip all the normal macho butthead stuff.

Crowsong waited on the summit beside Godzilla-sized footprints. The feet of their kuesi-snatcher mimicked the structure of birds: three digits pointed forward, one backward. The talons had gouged the granite as deep as eight inches in places. Old, weathered scratches indicated that the stone outcropping was a common perch site.

"Dragon?" Kate had checked her zoology reports last night, but they varied wildly from gigabytes of data on wargs—frost-breathing cousins of wolves—to three words on phoenixes: still believed mythical. The dragon section was nearly as scant. It stated, "While apparently dragons vary in size, they are reported to be very large, fire-breathing, and dangerous. Approach with caution." D'oh.

Crowsong shook her head. "Too small. Wyvern."

Kate tucked into an overhang and scanned the nearby mountain peaks with her binoculars. In the broad valley below them, the railroad right-of-way cut its straight raw path through the primal forest of the elfin world. Out in the vicinity of Pittsburgh—which fate chose as the human portal into this dimension—they had bulldozers, dump trucks, and earthmovers working their way east. The low-tech elves, though, working from the sparsely settled coast, only had hand tools and the kuesi. Until a connecting road was complete, trading between the two races was at an impasse. Construction had been going smoothly until the wyvern decided that the work crew was a moveable feast.

Speaking of which, Crowsong had poised herself on a rock projection like a piece of bait.

"Get down." Kate pointed to the protected ledge beside her. That only earned her a cold stare. Damn elves. "Move over here."

"I see better from here."

"The wyvern could take you from there."

The elf made a noise of understanding. "The wyvern. It sleeps. It hunts at night like a whou."

"Whou?"

Crowsong sighed at Kate's ignorance. "A night bird! It flies very quietly, and calls *whou, whou, whou.*"

Kate caught herself gritting her teeth and worked her jaw to ease the tension. What was it about Crowsong that pissed her off so much? Kate wasn't sure if it actually was the elf girl herself, or just her irritation with the general situation finding focus on the only breathing target.

Kate returned to her scanning. "These wyverns. Do they den alone or in mated pairs?"

"Mated pairs. Like falcons, females are larger. The nest will be on a peak, high up, on bare rocks with dead branches and such to keep the young in. One mate will stay on the nest and the other will hunt while there are eggs in the nest. Once the eggs are hatched, both will hunt to keep the young fed."

So they were either dealing with a solitary creature, perhaps a youngster, or two beasts—which meant that near the nest they'd have to be careful watching their backs.

"Your viceroy wasn't completely clear," Kate said. "What are we supposed to do with the wyvern?"

"Do?"

"The viceroy said this was a royal hunting preserve. On Earth, when an animal on a preserve causes a problem, we trap it and move it to another location where it's not in conflict with humans."

Crowsong shook her head. "Wyverns return to their nesting site, year in, year out. If we moved them, they would return next year."

"Zoos on Earth might take a mated pair."

Crowsong gave a musical laugh. "You might want to risk your life to trap such beasts, but not I. And no. Wyverns need magic to exist. They would die on Earth. Here on Elfhome, they nest on the strongest ley line in their range."

Native guides always believed in magic, but here it was a real, measurable force. Trying to determine reality from superstition was going to be a real bitch.

"What else about this animal can you tell me? What does it look like? Is it a bird?" Damn big bird if it was, carrying off the elfin cousin of an African elephant.

"Wyverns are a forerunner to the dragons. They have four limbs like a bird, not six, so they have no front limbs. Their bones are light but strong, as are their scales."

"Scales?"

"These are wyvern scales." Crowsong tapped the vest she was wearing. Kate had never seen the elf without the vest of overlapping glittering scales. Earlier attempts to look at it closer had been rebuffed. From the distance, the stuff looked like steel hammered into seashell shingles, and then somehow dyed blue.

"It would be nice to know what the fuck I'm dealing with here. Can I see the scales?"

Crowsong hesitated and then undid something on her left side and peeled back part of the scales. The scales were attached to a leather undergarment with a slit laced shut. The elf female undid the lacing and then wriggled a bit. If Kate had been a man, the show would have been extremely interesting.

The vest was lined with hard leather. Over it had been tacked a strong cloth, to which scales were sewn into an overlapping pattern. All in all, the vest weighed only ten pounds, but a goodly part of it would have come from the leather. The edges of the scales were sharp and slowly cutting through the leather.

"Why don't you grind down the edges?"

"It is organic carbon. There is nothing stronger that we forge that would grind it down. It can take a pistol bullet at close range without breaking. It is permitted only to the noble caste and those beholden to them."

"So this thing . . . wyvern is bulletproof?" How the hell was she supposed to kill it?

"It has points of weaknesses."

"How does it grow? Does it ever shed, like a snake?"

"No." Crowsong wriggled back into her vest and laced it back up. "The young are born with down, which is why the parents are so protective. They are vulnerable until they molt."

So she was fighting an armored attack helicopter. Oh golly joy. She wished that she'd thought to bring a missile launcher. She doubted that even her Winchester African with its .458 caliber rounds had enough stopping power for this, but she had nothing bigger

back at camp, or on this planet. Kate studied the
blood pool. If this splattering of blood and viscera on
the southern exposure was from the wyvern arriving
from their camp, then the blood trail on the northern
exposure was probably from the wyvern taking off.
She climbed up to another summit, hoping that Crowsong was right about the wyvern's sleep habits. She'd
seen falcons strike like bullets enough times to be nervous as she scanned the northern horizon.

Crowsong stood waiting as patiently as any other
native guide Kate had ever used. The wind played
with the few strands of golden hair that dared to come
out of Crowsong's thick braid down her back.

In the north lay several mountains offering possible
nesting sites. Hiking for days through virgin forest without GPS, blindly looking for something that could swallow her whole wasn't Kate's idea of smart hunting.

"You said that they nest on ley lines. That means
they're attracted to magic?"

"They will nest where it runs strongest."

"They say magic is measurable. Can you tell, from
here, which of those mountaintops has the most?"

The elf girl shot her a hard look and then, reluctantly, nodded. "Yes, of course I can."

Crowsong cleared a flat rock of twigs and dust.
From her waist pack, she produced a small, loosely
bound, hand-printed book, bundled in a layer of
suede. She flipped through the pages of complex de-
signs until she found what she wanted. Laying the
book flat, Crowsong copied the page out onto the rock
with what looked like a grease pencil, only the black
lines glittered in the sunlight, as if it contained flecks
of ground metal.

Kate frowned at the design as Crowsong carefully
rewrapped the book and tucked it away. So far it

wasn't any more impressive than Earth magic, although a hell of a lot more orderly.

"Stay back," Crowsong whispered, blocking Kate's closer inspection with an outstretched arm. "Do not get metal near it, or make any loud noises."

That annoyed Kate, although she wasn't sure why. Normally natives using magic didn't piss her off, even when it was blatantly nonsense. What Crowsong had copied out looked oddly similar to a computer circuit board design.

Taking a deep breath, Crowsong chanted a series of deep, guttural vowels. As if the mantra had thrown a switch, the black lines suddenly gleamed gold. A glowing sphere appeared over the spell, and slowly a model of the local mountain range took form. From the distinctive stone outcrop, Kate recognized that the centermost mountain was the one they stood on. Watery lines appeared in the model, of varying width and brightness, bisecting the mountains.

Crowsong peered at the model and then looked up, scanning the horizon. "There." She whispered as she pointed at a far peak. On the model, the line crossing over it was the brightest and widest. "That's the strongest ley line in spell range."

The elf extinguished the spell, and smudged out the lines on the rock with her foot.

Kate examined the distant mountain with her binoculars; it looked like the rest of the Allegheny range, an oversized rounded hill. One section of it seemed slightly bald. She unpacked her digital camera and its tripod. She had reluctantly packed these, but it seemed that they were going to come in handy. Training the telescopic lens onto the treeless area, she set the automatic capture on it, took her hands off the camera and let it capture a perfectly still image. Once the timer hit zero, she gave it another second, and then started to enhance the image.

The bald area enlarged to a wasteland of rock, strewn with broken timber.

"Well, what do you think?" Kate asked the elf girl.

Crowsong eyed the picture and then glanced out at the mountain, featureless to the naked eye. "Yes," she said flatly. "That's a nesting site."

Well, let's not jump up and down with joy. Kate packed away the camera. "What exactly are the wyvern's weak spots?"

Crowsong picked up a stone and scratched out a rough drawing on the rock. "The joints in the wingtips, here, here, and here. If you can cut this membrane," she indicated the taunt skin of the wings, "you can ground it, which will keep it from striking and flying off. Its mouth and eyes are weaknesses. Death magic works, as does light magic."

Yeah, right. "Poison? Or does it avoid poisoned bait?"

"It's an indiscriminate eater, but it takes massive amounts of poison to affect it, which we don't have."

"How big is this?"

"They are not as large as dragons, but they are considerable in size."

Considerable my ass, Kate thought, *it has to be huge.* She kept her verbal opinion to a snort. "How do your people kill these things? Or do you just pick up the scales after they die?"

Crowsong lifted up her bow in answer.

Well, that explained the declining elf population.

"It's stupid to attack it on its own grounds," Kate stated. "We'll lure it to us, and we pick the shots."

"This is not a simple animal."

"The smarter it is, the better. We give it an option.

To land in among the trees and hope for a clear take-off, or take something here on its favorite landing site."

Crowsong gazed at the blood-splattered rocks. "We will try it your way."

Baiting a trap should have been simple. Kate had done it a thousand times before, but she hadn't counted on the size of the wyvern compounding the process. Crowsong maintained that nothing smaller than one of the kuesi would do as bait. So they had to first get the beast up the steep mountainside, and then try to control it once it smelled the blood. Luckily she thought to bring her tranq pistol, although the dosage, set for a tiger, was only enough to make the massive beast groggy instead of putting it down completely.

"Well, you have some uses," Crowsong said, looking toward the setting sun. "It will not be long. It will come soon."

As a byproduct of working too long in the third world, Kate carried a computer attachment to detect incoming planes as standard equipment. She set it up, unsure if it would work on the wyvern. She liked to cover all bases.

The sun set and the sky slowly deepened into violet and then color leached out to total black. Kate had tucked herself in among the rocks, and as the sky went dark, tugged on night goggles. She could pick out Crowsong close by, silent, an arrow nocked but bowstring not drawn.

From her computer stick tucked in among the rocks, she heard the quiet pinging.

"It's coming." She called to Crowsong.

She'd made the mistake of setting it up so she couldn't

see the screen, worried only about keeping her hands free. Now, with the gentle chime indicating a closing wyvern, she didn't want to move out of her niche to check the screen for its direction.

Then she saw it, and wasn't about to leave hard cover.

She hadn't accounted for how much space the massive creature would take up on the rock ledge. She'd tucked herself into a niche that seemed a safe distance from the kuesi. She now scuttled backward along the overhang as her vision filled up with monster. Crowsong's drawing had been anatomically correct—a wedge head on a snake neck, wings of membrane like a bat's, a lizard leg redone on a falcon template—but lacked scale.

My God, that can't possibly fly. But it was flying. Or to be more precise, plummeting—rocketing down out of the night sky toward the kuesi. She planned a shot to the wyvern's vulnerable eyes; she'd expected them to be wide and round as an owl's, specialized for night hunting, done on a more massive scale. In the blur coming toward her, she couldn't see anything remotely looking like an eye.

The wyvern came out of its dive, wings unfurling with an audible crack, legs swinging forward, hooked talons longer than her arm flaring into overextension. Even drugged, the kuesi saw death and bleated. The cry cut short with an impact of bodies that she felt through the bottom of her feet. The kuesi, which had stood another head taller than her, was suddenly rabbit-small under the wyvern.

"Oh, God, oh, God," she whispered. Was Crowsong insane? Kill that? With what?

Then like an Earth-born falcon, the wyvern cocked

its head back and forth, examining its kill with its eyes. Protected by a ridge of bone, the solid pupil was a beady black target.

Kate ducked out of her niche, raised her rifle up to her shoulder, and aimed down on the eye. Breathe. Hold it. And she squeezed the trigger.

Even as the elephant rifle kicked, the wyvern jerked its head around, spotting her movement.

The bullet ricocheted off the bony ridge, making the wyvern jerk its head aside.

Reflex kicked in, and with icy calm, Kate worked the bolt—ejecting the spent round, loading another bullet, locking the action—and took aim. *Kill it, before it kills you.*

But she forgot about the massive tail until seconds before it hit her

She saw it whipping toward, knew she couldn't dodge it, and held position to get off her shot. *Kill it, before . . .*

And then darkness exploded around her, the actual contact lost in a moment of unconscious, and then she was aware of being airborne. Falling. Somewhere close by, she could hear her computer, tucked into the cliff face, pinging again.

Not off the cliff, oh, God, not off the cliff. And so the contact with solid land only a moment later actually came as a relief. She managed to tumble across the ground, lessening the impact, torn earth filling her senses.

She scrambled to her knees, trying to gain her feet, but her right leg was refusing to move. A bus-sized mouth full of teeth was coming at her—rows upon rows of sharp sharklike teeth.

She was going to die. "Goddamn it."

With a deep guttural howl, a streak of light flashed

through the air, lightning white in intensity. The light struck the wyvern in the side of the neck and sliced through the armored skin and punched through the other side of the huge neck.

What the hell? Kate didn't waste time trying to figure out. If she lived, she'd investigate closer. If the wyvern was dead, the news hadn't reached its brain yet. It came on.

She rolled to the side, whimpering in pain from her right leg. There was her rifle. The wyvern hadn't turned, and its forward motion began to look like floundering. She could still hear the pinging from her computer, though. The second one was coming.

The tumble hadn't damaged her rifle. It had been fired at some point since she last remembered holding it. She worked the bolt, reloading, and looked up.

Crowsong stood on an outcropping of rock, arrow nocked and bow drawn, sighting down on the wyvern on the ground. What was the little idiot doing? The elf released the string, and the arrow flashed toward the wyvern. Immediately the arrow howled, and light flared around it, growing in size and intensity as it leaped the span. The second arrow struck the wyvern in the back of the skull, blasting the news of its death straight into the brain this time. The wyvern collapsed into an ungainly tangle of giant limbs.

Magic arrows. The damn bitch had magic arrows.

And the damn bitch was going to get nailed from behind. The second wyvern was in a silent dive—aimed at the elf outlined against the stars. The wyvern on the ground probably was the male, because the one in the air was much bigger.

"Crowsong! Move!" Kate shouted, bringing her rifle to her shoulder.

The female wyvern was still in its power dive, wings

folded close to its body, mouth closed, its tiny eyes invisible—a great expanse of bulletproof armor. Kate held her breath, waiting for an opening.

And the chance came, as it swung forward its legs, wings spreading to brake its dive. The vulnerable joints of the wings opened up. She squeezed the trigger, and the rifle kicked hard on her shoulder. The bullet struck the joint, jerking the wyvern sidewises, and then the wing folded back at an impossible angle. The wyvern screamed and came tumbling out of the air. It struck the side of the cliff below them with an earth shaking impact.

Curling in pain on the ground, Kate reloaded the rifle's magazine. *Oh, God, please let there only be two.* Silence filled the night. Crowsong stood on her rocky lookout, staring down at the ruined mass of the female. Finally she crossed the ledge to Kate.

"I think my leg is broken." Kate didn't want to whimper, not in front of her.

Crowsong dropped down to her knees and then prostrated herself fully on the ground. "Forgiveness."

"Huh?"

"I have treated you poorly since your arrival, you who have come so far to help us. I believed myself to be superior to all humans and yet found that I was merely equal. I let it irritate me, and in spite, treated you rudely."

It was as if Crowsong held up a mirror to her soul. Kate suddenly saw her own arrogance and irritation reflected in the elf. *This is what was driving me nuts,* Kate realized, *I saw how I acted to all other natives. I didn't like what it showed of myself.*

"I wasn't at my best either." Kate muttered, dismayed by the revelation.

"We elves say 'see the beast in yourself and kill it.' I have slain my beast."

Kill the beast, before it kills you.

"Ah," Kate said, and meant every word, "how very wise of you."

A PIECE OF FLESH

Adam Stemple

Adam Stemple is an author and musician who lives in Minneapolis with his wife, Betsy, his two children, Alison and David, and a very confused tomcat named Lucy. He spends his days watching the children (and the cat), his nights playing guitar with his Irish band, The Tim Malloys, and the few hours he may once have used for sleep, writing. Adam Stemple is very tired.

I was not looking forward to another addition to our already large family. And I let my newly pregnant mother know it.

"What are we? Peasant farmers in the Middle Ages?" I asked. "Do we need a dozen children to work the fields?"

"A dozen?" my mother replied. "Vee, be reasonable. There are only four of you." She ticked them off on her fingers. "You, George, William, and little Charles. And baby here," she patted her stomach as she spoke. She wasn't showing. Yet. "Baby here makes five."

"Sure, five now. But when will it stop?" I had been

perfectly happy as an only child. For the first six years of my life I had been a pampered princess. And then, as if rubber-stamped, my three younger brothers popped out, one after another, each almost exactly a year apart. They were loud, obnoxious, and dirty, and they soon had the run of the place. There was little I could do about it: I was older and smarter, but I was badly outnumbered.

And then, completely ruining my fourteenth birthday party, I got the news that there would soon be one more little monster to make my life even more miserable.

"And I suppose you'll want me to help you take care of the new baby?" I asked.

"Want you to help? Victoria Ann, I *expect* you to help is more like it."

I stomped off to my room in a snit and locked the door behind me. I moped the rest of the day away and let my birthday party dwindle and die without me. My parents could make whatever excuses they wanted to the guests. I didn't care. I was doomed to a life of diaper changing and babysitting until I was well out of college.

Maybe the baby won't be born, I thought. *Maybe there will be a terrible accident—a miscarriage or a car accident or something.*

That night, and for many after it, I lay awake thinking up scenarios where the pregnancy was averted or the baby disappeared. But try as I might I couldn't convince myself that Mom could ever recover from the such a blow. She loved all of us so much.

I'll have to try something new then. Maybe if she knew she had other options . . .

On the first day of Mom's second trimester, I came home late from school.

"Where have you been, Vee?" asked my mother. She didn't sound angry, just tired.

"Jeanine is failing chemistry. I stayed after in lab helping her," I lied.

"Try to call next time."

"Mom, I'm fifteen minutes late! Relax!" I scampered upstairs before she could respond. I had work to do.

I slammed my bedroom door without going in. Instead, I tiptoed down the hall to my parent's bedroom. I reached under my shirt and pulled out the sheaf of adoption agency applications I had gathered after school when I was supposed to be studying with Jeanine. I stuck a few on Mom's night stand and hid a few more in her dresser drawers. In case she missed those completely, I stuck one right on her pillow.

It wasn't subtle, but I was running out of time.

At breakfast the next morning, I waited for some comment on the gifts I had left her.

Nothing. It was a typical breakfast, light on conversation and heavy on good-natured brawling between my three brothers. When my parents spoke to me it was only to ask, "Pass the toast, please," or "More eggs, Vee?"

I went to school and spent the day wondering what had happened. *Had they found the pamphlets? Had they read them?* There was still no mention of adoption when I got home. The subject wasn't brought up at dinner or when I left for swimming at Allie's house or when I returned just before dark, wet and tired. I went to bed confused.

Everything became clear when I saw what had been left on my pillow: a four-color brochure for a very private, very strict boarding school hundreds of miles from New Dresden.

Message received.

The decision to have a child had been made, and I could either live with it or . . . actually, there was no "or." I wasn't going to boarding school, so I was just going to have to live with it. No more was said about either the adoption applications or the school brochure for the rest of the pregnancy.

I woke in the pitch black one night and lay awake listening to the murmur of the television from downstairs. Mom was in her ninth month and shooting pain in her lower back woke her up every morning at three AM. She had taken to sitting in front of the tube for an hour or so with an ice pack tucked behind her before getting back into bed.

I thought about how helpless she had become and imagined how much help she would need with four children (and one young woman) to take care of. I began to think hard about children in general and my little brothers in particular. I listened to her shut off the TV, plod up the stairs, and struggle into bed. Still, I stayed awake. Thinking.

When the sun finally shone in my window hours later, I had come to a conclusion: despite their faults (and there were many!), I did love each and every one of my little brothers.

I supposed I could love one more.

I snuck downstairs and made breakfast before my mother got up: eggs, toast, sausage, and a tomato. I put it all on a tray and brought it to her in bed.

"Mom," I announced as she came blearily awake, "I'll help you with the new baby."

"In exchange for what?" She sounded doubtful of my sincerity.

"Nothing." I said. She looked like she couldn't decide whether a snort of disbelief or a heartfelt thank

you was in order. "No really, Mom. I thought about
it for a long time last night. You're going to need
someone to help around the house. The boys are too
young and Dad is . . . well . . . Dad." She nodded and
bit off the corner of her toast. "That leaves me. And
I love you and Dad and all my brothers and I will
love the new baby as well." I got the last part out in
a rush because Mom was tearing up.

"C'mere, Vee!" she said and I hugged her over her
breakfast tray, the lone tomato exploding into my
shirt. We cried and then laughed at my ruined shirt
and then cried some more.

Two weeks later, my littlest brother was born. Mom
and Dad let me hold him first. I cradled him in my
arms and looked into his watery blue eyes. My eyes
were blurry with tears as well. I was thinking about
all the terrible scenarios I had devised for him, and
now I saw his little Winston Churchill face on each of
those babies in my mind. I couldn't believe I had ever
had all those horrid thoughts and I swore to make it
up to him.

I am your second mother, I mouthed silently to him.
I will love you and protect you all the days of your life.

Mom and Dad named him Victor, after me, and we
all hugged and cried on the hospital bed until they
came and took little Victor away to the nursery.

One week after Victor was born I started fall semes-
ter. School was held a quarter mile from my home in
a squat building that was big enough to house twice
the number of students who used it. I guess New Dresden, Wisconsin, didn't get quite the population explosion it thought it was going to when the school was
built.

Nestled in a river valley inhabited mostly by Norwegians and Swedes, the immigrants who settled New Dresden had managed to carve out an almost entirely German enclave that stands to this day. Roll call at school sounded like a list of beers—Schmidt? Here! Grolsch? Here!—and lederhosen and polkas figured heavily into the community-led summer activities. There were a few non-German families in town but for the most part they kept quiet about it.

Not mine though.

My family was English. Despite the fact that our last family member to actually stand on British soil did so in the nineteenth century, and probably in direct response to the overall German-ness of the town, my family was aggressively, overbearingly, painstakingly English. We drank tea and ate mince pies. We threw big parties for the Queen's birthday and Guy Fawkes Day. On a pole in the front lawn hung a gigantic Union Jack and smaller ones adorned the bumper stickers of both family cars.

And we conveniently forgot that the Hanoverians, who have ruled England since 1714 were, originally, German.

The local school, like many small-town schools, had only enough money for one language class. Unlike the others, which usually chose French or Spanish, New Dresden High, of course, chose German. I had been forced to take German for three years now but, in keeping with family tradition, I had managed to learn only *"Ich schreibe mit einem gelben bleistift."* ("I write with a yellow pencil.") I'd also picked up a few phrases accidentally from *Nick at Nite* reruns of *Hogan's Heroes* (*"Nein, nein puddin' head!"* and *"Schnell! Schnell!"* for instance).

What bothered me was that Mrs. Arnim—whoops, *Frau* Arnim—who taught the class, was a friend of the family. She was the first of the townsfolk to visit us when we moved in and she was always coming by when any of the kids were sick to drop off some vile smelling but doubtless effective folk remedy.

But, as I said before, we were English. So, family friend or not, I resolutely slaughtered every word she had me repeat and mangled the pronunciation of every phrase on the blackboard. But when she came to our house for parties and my parents were stuffing the guests with boiled potatoes and chicken curry, I would always sneak off and cook her some nice big German sausages by way of an apology. Maybe that's why she never flunked me.

In the last period on the first day of school that fall, I sat in Frau Arnim's classroom and wished I could allow myself to wrap my mind around the language she was speaking. I knew I was close. Even if you don't do any work on it, three years of listening to a language will get you remarkably close to comprehension. But when she began stringing sentences together that I was on the edge of understanding, I just hummed "Rule Britannia" under my breath and shut the guttural sounds out completely. When class ended I shot her an apologetic smile and ran out the door and home.

It was the longest I had been away from Victor since he had been born.

The house was quiet when I arrived. This was not unusual. The three middle monsters went to a K–6 school a longish bus ride away and I easily beat them home each day. And Victor had proved himself a quiet baby for the most part, only crying when very hungry, which Mom did not allow to happen very often.

I suspected both mother and child were sleeping

and I snuck up the stairs so as not to wake anyone. The stairs creaked a little but I skipped the loudest one and peeked in the nursery. Mom was in the corner, sacked out in a gliding rocker, a paperback in one limp hand, her head back and eyes closed.

I tiptoed to the crib and peered over the side. Little Victor lay on his stomach, squinched face towards me, making soft snuffling noises as he slept. His skin seemed yellower. I would have to ask my Mom about jaundice. Two of my brothers and I had suffered from it when we were born but all I really knew about it was that it made your skin yellow. I didn't know if it was dangerous.

I did know that babies aren't supposed to sleep on their stomachs. We even had a special pillow designed to keep Victor on his side while he slept. He had pushed it aside when he rolled over. Strong boy. I extended both hands into the crib and prepared to roll him onto his side. As soon as I touched him his eyes shot open and I jumped back.

His eyes were jet black. And looking right at me. We stood frozen there for a moment, looking into each other's eyes. Week-old babies shouldn't be able to focus on anything, let alone stare directly at you. He looked at me, unblinking, for what felt like a full minute before I finally ripped myself away from his unnatural stare. Opening his mouth wide, he let out a horrible screeching wail. My mother sprung from her chair.

"What the . . ." she said, dropping her book to the floor.

"His eyes, Mom! They're black!"

She stood and took the two steps to the crib. She deftly scooped Victor up and he was already attached to a breast by the time she sat back down. She pulled his head back a little and examined his eyes, but quickly let him get back to feeding when he howled again.

"Why, so they are," she stated. "Three younger siblings before Victor and this is the first time you have noticed that babies' eyes change color, Vee?" she chided me.

"But so quickly? And so black?"

She shrugged. "They'll probably change three or four more times before we know what color they are going to be. I seem to remember *your* eyes doing that."

"Well, I can't argue with you," I said, "since I was a baby when my eyes changed."

She nodded. I was about to ask about babies staring a girl down but I realized how crazy it sounded. Deciding I had imagined it, I left the room. I forgot to ask about jaundice.

Mom nursed Victor the rest of the day and into the night. He couldn't seem to get enough. They both fell asleep at midnight but Victor awoke a half-hour later and began caterwauling until he was fed again. This continued through the night and the next day as well. When the next night was spent sleepless as well, Dad decided enough was enough and packed my mother and youngest sibling off to the doctor, leaving me to get my three other brothers ready for school.

When I came home that afternoon I found my mother sick and exhausted and my father muttering about the doctor's diagnosis.

"A colicky baby," he said, maybe to me, maybe to himself. "That's helpful. 'And what do we do for a colicky baby, Doc?' 'Why you suffer, sir.' " He used a high persnickety voice for the doctor and lowered his natural voice a little to represent himself.

"Why does this happen?" asked the Dad voice.

"Do you believe in God?" asked the doctor voice.

"Why, yes I do," replied the Dad voice.

"Then it is because God is testing you," said the doctor voice.

I decided it was time to cut in. "Do you know anything about jaundice, Dad? Victor seemed a little yellow to me. Could that cause whatever's wrong with him?"

Dad blinked and looked at me, perhaps noticing I was there for the first time. "Jaundice? I don't know much about it. Three of you kids had it when you were born and it went away the next day. None of the doctors seemed overly concerned about it." He plucked his glasses from his nose and worked at them with his shirttail. "I'll ask when we go to another doctor. Tomorrow most likely."

Over the next few weeks three more doctors gave my parents the same diagnosis. A colicky baby. Just wait it out.

The lack of sleep caused my mother to lose weight. She grew cranky and short-tempered. Her few moments of peace were spent barking at me or my brothers for any noises we made while she tried to grab a few minutes of slumber.

Meanwhile, despite the constant feedings, Victor seemed to grow skinnier and his skin became increasingly yellow and dry, stretching tight over long thin legs that should have remained short and chubby. The doctors could find nothing wrong with him physically: no jaundice, no wasting disease, no mysterious cancer. I began to wonder if they were looking at the same child I was. With his large head perched unnaturally on his skinny body and his wide black eyes staring unblinkingly—when he wasn't screaming his huge head off—he looked more freakish doll than human.

Halloween night. I volunteered to stay home with Mom and Victor while Dad took the other boys trick-or-treating.

"I'm too old for that stuff anyway, Dad." Actually, I wasn't. We were reading Greek mythology in our Lit class and my friends, Allie and Jeanine, and I had planned to go out dressed as the three Fates. We would then claim trick-or-treating as extra credit as we ate ourselves into a sugar coma.

I called them and canceled at the last minute. They weren't surprised.

"It's okay, Vee," Allie said. "We know you gotta take care of your family."

My family. My family was taking up most of my time. My schoolwork was beginning to suffer and I looked as haggard as my mother did.

"Thanks, Vee," said my father, "You've been a real life saver." He didn't look so good either. He had lost weight and hair and had dark circles under his eyes. "I'm going to make it up to you when Vic is out of this stage." But he didn't sound convinced that this "stage" would ever end. I tried to give him an encouraging smile but it died before reaching my eyes.

"Bye, Vee," sounded my three middle brothers in unison. They were all dressed as their namesakes in royal purple robes—little Charles with the addition of gigantic rubber ears—and I gave them each a pat on their crowned heads as they left.

Victor began screeching. Dad winced and scampered out the door. I leaned on the windowsill, watching them tromp down the walkway: Dad, hunched and defeated, my three younger brothers—impervious to hardship as all young children are when faced with a night full of candy and costumes—scurrying around his legs, pushing each other in good-natured combat.

"Vee!" yelled Mom. She was practically bedridden now, only shuffling downstairs occasionally to feed herself when Victor was asleep. More often, I would fix her soup or sandwiches and bring them to where she lay, exhausted.

I sighed and pushed myself away from the window. Time to get to work. I went into the kitchen and snagged a pot. I started running water into it and went to the refrigerator. Sometimes I could keep Victor quiet for a few moments with a bottle and let Mom get a little more sleep. I grabbed a bottle out of the fridge and the pot of water from the sink before lighting the stove.

Mom yelled, "Vee!" again as Victor let loose with an especially loud howl.

"One sec, Mom!" I left the pot on the stove and jogged up the stairs. I was down the hall and into Vic's room in moments but it was nearly too late. Mom was out of her room and shuffling towards us in her bathrobe when I came out, Victor, still screaming, tucked in one arm.

"Lemme try a bottle, Mom. You keep sleeping." She may have thanked me but I couldn't hear her over the inhuman din. I went downstairs.

I rocked Victor by the stove until the water was hot and juggled him from one arm to the other when I tested the temperature of the milk. Lukewarm. Time to feed. We settled into the big easy chair in the living room and he finally quieted, taking great slurps from the bottle.

The doorbell rang and I nearly dropped Victor in surprise. *Trick-or-treaters!* I thought. I had forgotten what night it was. I couldn't handle Vic, the bottle, and the candy bowl all at once.

He's a little young for it but . . . I slithered out from underneath him and left him perched, hopefully not too precariously, on the chair. He grasped the bottle easily and settled back, apparently relieved to be left to his own devices. I shook my head and went to the front door.

"Trick or Treat!" yelled the pack of witches, wizards, and superheroes on the porch.

"And *guten Abend,* Miss Victoria." said a familiar voice, its heavy accent turning my name into Veektoria.

"Good evening, Frau Arnim. Bringing your grandchildren around this year?"

"*Ja.* My son, he is so busy, he works on Halloween! He says he will send them out alone but I say, 'It is not safe. I will take them.' " She stuck her head through the door as her countless grandchildren dug greedily into the candy bowl. "Now, where is this young *Liebchen* who is giving your mother such problems?"

Before I could answer she was inside. She got to the living room and stopped cold when she could see little Victor sitting in his chair. Even I, who was growing used to Victor's odd appearance, had to admit he cut a particularly bizarre figure right then. He had managed to get his feet up on one leg of the chair and crossed his skinny legs at the ankles. His hands, long and well-formed for one his age, held the bottle easily and he rocked it back and forth rhythmically as he drank.

Frau Arnim's behavior was even stranger. She clapped one hand over her mouth but was too late to stop the loud gasp that escaped from it. Victor heard the noise and swiveled his big head to face us. He stared at her with black unblinking eyes and her hands fell limp to her sides.

"Killcrop!" she shouted. Victor started at the sound, flung his bottle away, and started screaming again. Frau Arnim backed out of the room and started shooing her grandchildren to the door. "Out! Out, children, out! *Schnell!*"

"Frau Arnim!" I yelled, grabbing her arm before she could get out the door. I was angry. "How dare you come in here and upset him like that?"

She shook me off and made sure all her grandchildren were outside. Only then did she turn back to me.

"I am sorry, Victoria," she said. "But it would take more than just me screaming to upset that *massa carnis*. I will explain tomorrow."

And before I could ask her what she meant, she left, slamming the door behind her. I watched her through the glass, herding her grandchildren to the sidewalk and down the block like a mother goose. Or *the* Mother Goose.

Vic was still screaming and now Mom was yelling for me too. I gathered him up and, knowing he couldn't be settled down by anything but Mom now, I brought him upstairs to her.

At school the next day, I was going to look for Frau Arnim right after homeroom, but she found me first, tapping me on the shoulder at my locker.

"Miss Victoria, come with me, please. I must show you something."

"But I have to get to homeroom!"

She showed me a pass and I followed her to her classroom. The room looked the same: an ordinary classroom in all aspects but on every identifiable item was a handmade sign identifying that object in German and English.

"Sit down, Miss Victoria," said Frau Arnim, perching on the edge of her desk. I sat at a desk in the front row and waited for her to continue. "I know what is wrong with your brother."

"What? Please, tell me!"

"*Ja,* I will. But you will not believe me." She ran her finger down the cover of one of the books. "I have brought some books to . . ."

"Frau Arnim!" I cried. "What is wrong with my brother?"

She pushed herself off her desk and laid an old leather-bound book on the desk where I sat. "Read the words of Martin Luther," she said.

"Martin Luther?"

"*Ja,* the founder of our church."

"Not my church. We're Church of England." Actually we weren't church of anything. But my father always said that as soon as they put a Church of England in town we would start going.

"Well then, the founder of all your friends' church."

She had me there. She opened the book to a page she had marked and pointed to a passage. It was in German.

"I can't read that," I said. She looked at me coldly.

"Well, why not, after three years of class?"

I had no answer for that except to ask why, after thirty years in this country, she still couldn't pronounce the letter *W* correctly. She stared at me openmouthed—I was not normally that rude—and I apologized quickly.

"No, no, I am sorry," she said. "None of that is important now. Let me translate." She grabbed the book from me and perched a pair of reading glasses on her nose. " 'Eight years ago at Dessau, I, Dr. Martin Luther, saw and touched a changeling,' " she read, tracing the text with her finger. " 'It did nothing but eat; in fact, it ate enough for any four peasants or threshers.' " She skipped a few lines before going on. " 'I said to the Princes of Anhalt: "If I were the prince or the ruler here, I would throw this child into the water—into the Molda that flows by Dessau. I would dare commit *homicidium* on him!" Such a changeling child is only a piece of flesh, a *massa carnis,* because it has no soul.' " She slammed the book shut with a satisfactory thump and looked at me. "You see?" she asked.

"No, Frau Arnim, I don't see." I was confused and tired. It wasn't enough that my mother and brother were sick and I was going to fail school because I couldn't ever sleep or study; now I had to listen to a crazy German woman quote another crazy German at me. "You aren't making any sense."

"Ich bün so olt as Böhmer Gold," Frau Arnim intoned, her accent subtly different.

"What does that . . ."

"Listen, Victoria," she interrupted and grabbed me by my shoulders. "Victor is not your brother. He is a changeling, a killcrop."

"That's crazy!"

She shook her head. "No, it is not crazy. It is the truth. Victor has been taken by the underground people, the *Rotkaps,* and they have left a killcrop in his place."

I wriggled free from her grip. "Let's say I believe you—which I don't—how do I get him back?"

"In the old days a woman whose child had been stolen would brew beer in eggshells where the killcrop could see it. It would be so surprised it would exclaim, *'Ich bün so olt as Böhmer Gold, doch sonn Brug'n heww ik noch nie seihn.'* Its true nature revealed, the killcrop disappears, leaving the baby in its place."

I stood from my desk. "Well." I cleared my throat. "Frau Arnim, thank you for wasting my time with this insanity. Either you believe it and need serious help, or you think it's funny to tease me and my family when we are going through such hard times." I marched to the door and spoke over my shoulder. "Either way, I don't think you should come by the house anymore."

"Victoria!" I turned and looked at her. I hadn't realized it until then, but I had grown taller than her over the summer. "The *Rotkaps* have seen enough brewing beer in eggshells by now I would think. You will have to think of something new."

I ran from the classroom.

I skipped German class for the next few days. Frau Arnim did not report me to the principal. I had trouble concentrating in the classes I actually went to.

Changelings. Killcrops. Rotkaps. It was all I could think about. Frau Arnim's story was crazy—but it did fit all the facts. I couldn't get it out of mind.

Friday, I skipped school entirely. It was Guy Fawkes day.

On November 5, 1605, a disgruntled Englishman by the name of Guy Fawkes was discovered in the basement of Parliament making ready to set off a great deal of explosives. He and his coconspirators were caught, tortured, and hanged by the neck until dead. Since then, every November 5 has been a holiday in England. And all over that country—and at a certain family's house in New Dresden, Wisconsin, as well—

parties are thrown and bonfires are lit and Guy Fawkes is burned in effigy.

My father had wanted to cancel the party for this year but my mother, fearsome in her determination even while bedridden, convinced him to put it on anyway. My twin uncles drove in from Minnesota to help out with the preparations and I, having promised to help with the food, spent the day shopping.

When I got home from the grocery store, I scooped Victor up from next to my sleeping mother and plopped him into the stroller he almost never used. When I pushed it into the kitchen he woke but, for once, he kept quiet. His big dark eyes tracked me as I worked.

I began pulling food out of the paper bags I had carried inside: leeks, tomatoes, peppers, potatoes, and some roasted chicken breasts. The potatoes I washed and put in a bowl. Two pokes with a fork each and they went into the microwave. On the butcher block counter I chopped the other ingredients into bite-size pieces. I went to the pantry and rummaged through the shelves until I found a large can of chicken stock. I opened it in the kitchen and left it to sit next to the stove.

Beep.

The potatoes were done. I slipped an oven mitt on and grabbed the hot bowl out of the microwave. I shoved the vegetables and chicken to one side before dumping the hot tubers onto the counter next to them. These too, I chopped up.

I spared a glance for my youngest brother. Though unable to sit up completely, his head had stopped lolling to one side and his eyes were fastened on me, following my every movement. He really didn't look human.

Yes, I thought, *watch carefully.*

I sauntered over to the back door and grabbed one of my father's old leather work boots. It was a tan Timberland boot, size thirteen, with hardy laces, alternating tan and dark brown. It stank.

When I returned to the stove I plunked it down on top of the closest burner and peeked at my brother out of the corner of my eye. I swore he was sitting straight up now, rapt.

Changelings. Killcrops. Rotkaps.

The can of chicken stock went into the boot first. I didn't spill a drop but it began leaking out the bottom of the shoe almost immediately. I scooped up the vegetables and meat in the bowl I had microwaved the potatoes in and dumped them into the boot as well. I shook some garlic, salt, and black pepper in and topped it off with a pinch of basil. I began stirring it with a wooden spoon.

My brother said nothing.

In for a penny, in for a pound. I turned the dial for the front burner to *light.*

Click.

It failed to light on the first try. I dug the spoon into the boot with a vengeance and thought about how big an idiot I was.

Click.

Frau Arnim was obviously insane. And apparently, so was I, since I was about to burn a perfectly good boot to a crisp in front of a colicky baby.

Click.

"What are you doing?" The speaker's voice was deep and accented and it crackled, like old leaves.

I turned to see who had spoken thinking, *Maybe my father came home early,* but knowing it was still

only me and my littlest brother. He was sitting forward
in his stroller, leaning one elbow on the tray, index
finger and thumb stroking his chin.

"Making soup," I said.

Whoosh!

The gas finally lit and blue flames shot forth. The
plastic ends of the boot laces melted and sizzled in
the first heat, dripping hot plastic onto the stove. I
smelled toxic smoke and burning hair.

Burning hair! Shoots of orange flame had run up
the laces in the initial burst and set fire to my arm
hair. I leaped backwards in surprise.

But I forgot to let go of the spoon.

The spoon was still deep in the boot and I took the
whole mess down on top of me. Plastic lava pocked
my forearms and hands while cold chicken stock and
hot potatoes splattered my face and hair.

"Ho, ho, ho. Ha, ha, ha," I heard from over me
and I looked up into deep black eyes shining with an
alien intelligence. He leaned out over his stroller to
better see me and spoke once more. "I am as old as
Bohemian gold and yet, in all my days, I have never
seen anyone making soup in a boot." He leaned back,
still chuckling. "Or failing so miserably in the attempt."

Uncooked soup dripped onto the floor and my brain
howled at me to *Move! Run! Scream!* but I sat, slack-
jawed, staring at what I had thought was my brother.

The back door flew open and my father charged in.
The changeling fell back fully into the stroller and let
his head loll to one side. A little drool leaked from
the corner of his mouth and he was every bit the infant once more.

"Your uncles are itching to light the fire, Vee. Is all

the food done?" He stopped when he saw me sitting on the floor covered in soup and boot. "What's going on here?"

I couldn't answer. What would I say? Frau Arnim was right: my brother had been stolen and this *thing* had been left in his place. She was wrong about one thing, though. Despite its true nature being revealed, the killcrop showed no signs of leaving any time soon.

I had to talk to Frau Arnim. I mumbled something about an accident to my father and told him I would clean it up in a second. Then I ran upstairs to my room and dialed Frau Arnim.

Out my window I could see the party preparations in the backyard. Lawn torches lit the area and chairs had been set up in a loose ring around the as-yet unlit bonfire. The bonfire was a man-high pyramid of wood and, once it was lit, no one could get within ten feet of it without being burned. Still, come ten o'clock, my insane uncles would risk singed eyebrows and deadly smoke inhalation to toss the straw effigy of Mr. Fawkes on to the flames.

Frau Arnim picked up on the fourth ring.

"It's a changeling," I blurted out before she could say hello. "I cooked it soup in a boot."

"Mein Gott!"

"What should I do?" I cried into the phone. "He said he was as old as Bohemian gold. I thought he was supposed to leave after that?"

"Listen, Victoria! If he has not left yet then you must beat him. Or threaten him in some way. Only if the killcrop is in danger will the *Rotkaps* bring your true brother back."

"You have to help me!" I was whining and hated the sound of my own voice. "Please, Frau Arnim."

"I am sorry, Victoria. I cannot." She sighed into the phone. "The *Rotkaps* will only deal with the family of the stolen baby. I could beat the killcrop to death and they would never come for him. And then you would lose your one hope of getting your real brother back."

There was nothing more to say. I took the phone from my ear and stood there, listening to the tinny voice of Frau Arnim repeating my name until she was replaced by the familiar recording: "Please hang up and dial again. If this is an emergency . . ."

I dropped the phone to the ground and, with a loud crash, its back flew open, sending batteries skittering across the floor.

"You okay, Vee?" called my dad from downstairs.

I didn't answer. His voice sounded small and distant. Like Frau Arnim's had when I held the phone away.

I trudged down the stairs and ignored my father's repeated, "Vee? Vee?"

The killcrop was where I had left him: drooling in his stroller, eyes shut tight. I pushed him towards the door.

"Could you get the door, Father?" I asked. He opened the door, looking at me with concern, and I pushed the stroller into the backyard. The cold hit me and I remembered we weren't wearing any coats. My father realized it at the same time.

"Coats, Vee!"

"We won't need them, Dad!" I called back, my breath frosting in the November air. I stopped next to a lawn torch. I guess the killcrop was trying not to draw more attention to himself because he hadn't started screaming yet. He wasn't strapped in and I grabbed a handful of his shirt front with my left hand

and lifted him out. "We won't need coats, will we, Victor?" I spit the last word directly into his face. He opened one dark eye to look at me.

"Why not?" he whispered in his old, cold voice.

"Because we're going on the fire!" I replied. Both his eyes shot open as I wrenched the lawn torch out of the ground with my free hand.

He began screaming then. So did I, for that matter. I ran towards the bonfire, killcrop in one hand, torch in the other, screaming at the top of my lungs. When I got three feet away, I tossed the lawn torch onto the gasoline-drenched woodpile. It exploded into flames and the ensuing fireball knocked me to the ground.

I didn't let go of the killcrop.

I stood up, the heat trying to force me further back and yelled, "He goes on the flames! Hear me now you . . . you . . . *Rotkaps!* He goes on the flames!" I could barely hear myself over the killcrop's screeching. I grabbed him with both hands as he tried to squirm out of my grasp and made as if to toss him, arms extended over my head like I was throwing a soccer ball, into the raging fire.

"Into the flames!" I screamed, louder even then before. I could smell burning hair and knew my eyebrows would soon be gone if I stayed this close to the flames.

I saw movement. Out beyond the broken ring of lawn torches, and from a direction no neighbor would approach from, I saw movement. It resolved into the figure of a short old woman with wide hips, bustling towards the firelight on stubby legs. Her face was as wrinkled as a whole box of raisins and her nose was so big it looked like it was leading her around. She wore a coarse woolen dress and had stained rags wrapped about her shoulders. On her head was a black cap.

And she carried a fat, naked, *human* baby in one arm.

"Victor," I breathed. I froze with the killcrop high over my head and watched her approach. She waddled to the other side of the bonfire, waving her free hand at me in a frantic stop! stop! motion. I could see that what I had thought was a black cap was actually dark red.

Blood red.

She stopped before coming fully into the light.

"Come over here with my brother!" I yelled to her. But she was no longer waving her hand at me. She wasn't even looking at me anymore; she was looking at something over my shoulder.

Then her mouth opened in a malevolent grin, showing three yellowing teeth. The teeth came to sharp points and bobbed up and down as she looked behind me and began to laugh, cackling in a grating tenor voice.

I tried to turn to see what she was lauging about, but it was too late. Uncle Richard plucked the killcrop from my hands just as Uncle Robert hit me in the small of the back in a perfect football tackle, bringing me to the ground. I struggled to get up, or wriggle out, or grab the killcrop from my Uncle Richard. But I was held fast. I ranted and raved at them to throw the killcrop into the fire. I screamed for them to grab the old woman.

"What old woman?" Uncle Richard asked, now a safe distance away. He handed the screaming killcrop to my father who stared at me with wide sad eyes.

I strained against Uncle Robert's weight. I scratched at his face, I tried to bite his ear. I tried every dirty trick I had ever heard about or seen on TV but he held me down easily. With my cheek pressed hard into the frozen dirt, I watched in horror as the old woman walked off into the darkness, tickling Victor's pudgy feet with her long brown fingernails.

The police eventually came and I was carted off. I was obviously insane and the prosecution refused to press criminal charges. Instead, I was moved to a juvenile facility where I got to spend the next seven months with other disturbed young people wandering the halls drooling, shaking, and mumbling to themselves.

It was enough to make you crazy—if you weren't already. But I wasn't crazy. No amount of drugs, counseling, or even ECT could change that.

My father visited yesterday. He hadn't come to see me in over a month. The last time he was here I had broken down. When I heard him talk about losing his job and Mom still being sick and the boys starting to get in trouble in school, I had begged him to destroy the killcrop—the source of all the family's bad luck. The orderlies had to drag me screaming out of the visiting room. The doctors thought that maybe my Dad's visit had triggered the relapse.

But this latest visit was a special occasion. The doctors had just told me I was to be moved to a halfway house next week. I think they arranged Dad's visit just to see if I would lose it again.

I didn't lose it.

I sat quietly and talked pleasantly and even patted my Dad on his bony knee and told him I was glad when he said that at least one person in the family was doing well: Victor. I kept my cool and when my father left the doctors were all smiles and I knew I was getting out. And if I could get to the halfway house and keep it together for a few months then they would have to send me home.

And this time, Victor goes on the fire for sure.

THE FILIAL FIDDLER

Elizabeth Ann Scarborough

Elizabeth Ann Scarborough lives in an antique
cabin on the Olympic Peninsula with four-
going-on-five cats and a lot of paints, paper-
work, and beads. She is currently working on
the sequel to *Channeling Cleopatra* and is co-
authoring the Acorna series with Anne Mc-
Caffrey.

"The new patient in ward three, bed twelve, is Mrs.
Moira O'Bannon, a ninety-three-year-old widow
admitted for pneumonia and congestive heart failure.
She's on oxygen, intake and output, and quite thor-
oughly out of it, poor dear."

"Pneumonia, the old person's friend," said Mrs.
Moran the nursing assistant, nodding to herself at the
wisdom of the old saying.

"Indeed," the evening nurse said. "As for her other
friends, well, it isn't my fault that the neighbor who
rode in the ambulance with her slipped in the hallway
while leaving the ward and broke her femur. She's in
the next bed. They took her straight to surgery to pin
it. She returned from recovery around seven. Orthope-

dics is full and we had the bed so here she is. I've medicated her once for pain."

"And she would be?" Nurse Connelly asked, checking the patient roster.

"Mrs. Sinead Finlay, age eighty-two, also a widow. Neither woman has children or anyone else as far as I can tell, but the other visitor definitely arrived at the same time."

"Well, they'll be gone by now, surely."

"Ought to be. But you know how young people are, so heedless of the rules."

Connelly raised an eyebrow. She was all of twenty-four.

"What does this person look like?"

"I'd say a girl from the hair but then it's always hard to tell and I only saw her—or him—from the back. Tall and thin, wearing blue jeans and a green sweater. She, or he as the case may be, darted behind the curtains when I started to tell them to leave and when I went to look, there was no one there. But if you see a tall young person with long blonde hair carrying a fiddle case, that would be the individual in question."

"I'm sure they'll have gone home by now," Connelly said firmly. "You run along. We'll take it from here."

"I wish you the joy of it," Kennedy replied, sounding sour, but Connelly knew she was mostly just tired. Kennedy was getting on in years for hospital nursing and her feet hurt her all the time. She had had a bone spur removed six months ago, but she still limped slightly and the wards were very long.

"Ta," Connelly said. With a sigh, she rose to make the first tour of the wards in her hourly rounds. The geriatrics ward was the most depressing in the entire hospital. True, nursing homes and the like relieved some of the pressure on the hospitals, but this wing still smelled of incontinence, illness, and old age despite the purging pong of disinfectant.

Elderly diabetics with multiple amputations; victims of fresh strokes; people who were losing their battles with tumors, heart disease, or even the advanced stages of alcoholism all were put on Connelly's floor if they were of a certain age. Most of them were suffering from one form or dementia or another. Connelly always felt any patient who could speak to her, whether sensibly or not, was uncommonly healthy for her floor.

She began the bedcheck, to make sure everyone was breathing, that all bed rails were up, and restraints, where necessary, were in place and allowed for adequate circulation to the limbs. She also checked on the flow rate of intravenous drips, and that feeding tubes, catheters, and other protruding bits of plastic were present, in working order, and had not been pulled out by the hands of confused patients.

Ward three was relatively quiet, except for the sound of labored respirations, deep coughs, and incoherent murmurs occasionally punctuated by a bit of ranting or yelling. She took her torch from bed to bed, drawing back the privacy curtains, checking the equipment and playing the light across the patient's chest, counting respirations by sight when they weren't clearly audible.

She was halfway down the ward when she heard the music, a slow air played on a fiddle. "Carrickfergus?" Was that the name of the song? No matter. Someone had obviously left on their radio, which was very much against the rules. Radios and televisions were to be turned off by ten so as not to disturb the other patients.

The music grew louder as she reached the end of the ward, near the bank of windows facing the road. But she found no radio, and all of the television screens were dark. She paused between the beds of the two new ladies. Bed twelve was next to the window. For someone with congestive failure, Mrs. O'Bannon seemed to be sleeping peacefully enough, her breathing shallow but regular, the fangs of the oxygen cannula hissing faintly into her nostrils.

In bed ten—the even beds were on one side of the ward, odd on the other—Mrs. Finlay slept with her head flung back and her mouth open. Connelly turned her onto her side and braced her back with a pillow, supported her knee with another. The patient didn't wake, since she was still sleeping off the anesthetic.

The music was very clear now and had moved to another air—something by O'Carolan, she thought, which was hardly surprising as most of the fiddle tunes seemed to be by him. Planxty someone or other, no doubt. She had been certain she'd find the radio at the bedside of one of these ladies but there was nothing of the sort.

She started to cross to beds nine and eleven on the other side of the ward, but then realized the music was coming from outside the windows. As she was on the fourth floor, it really must be rather loud. She looked out the window. Raindrops as big as teacups splattered against the window, but by the lamps outside the hospital she made out a figure standing looking up toward her, one hand raised to the neck of a violin, the elbow of the other arm crooked to allow the fingers to wield a bow. From the stance, she felt sure the fiddler was male.

It was too dark to make out much about the player,

except that light glinted off fair hair, worn long, and the musician gave a general impression of lankiness. He would also, certainly, be extremely damp.

Striding back to the nursing station, she called security and asked Mr. Fitzpatrick to have a word with the musician and move him along. Then she began pouring her medicines for the night and didn't think further about the music until it abruptly stopped.

At about one thirty, Mr. Fitzpatrick, the security guard, did his check of the wards. She offered him tea—everyone did. The poor man must be swimming in it by the end of the night. He always accepted the tea though he had only a sip or two. He'd retired from the Gardai and became the hospital's security guard after the death of his wife left him at loose ends. He had a stock of interesting stories and when he was feeling chatty, which was often, his visits helped pass the long minutes on a quiet night until shift change.

"Thank you for getting rid of that daft fiddler," Connelly told him.

"I didn't have to," Fitzpatrick said. "The road was empty when I got there and not a note of yer music did I hear. He must have seen you peering down at him and decided he'd best be elsewhere. Or perhaps," he added with a wink, "he went into the hill."

"I beg your pardon?"

"Into the hill, as I said. The hospital sits on a hill that was once thought to be a fairy knowe."

She wagged her index finger at him. "You're having me on now, you wicked man."

He shrugged and rose to continue on his way. "Indeed I am not. Simply filling you in on a bit of local history. I thought you were keen on that sort of thing."

Connelly smiled and waved dismissively at his back.

She thought little more about it until she made her rounds at four. When she came again to ward three, she stood in the doorway, looking down along the rows of beds to the bank of windows beyond. The rain had stopped, but now the glass allowed moonlight to flood the end of the room.

It outlined a silhouette against the curtain around Mrs. O'Bannon's bed. Connelly walked the length of the ward quickly but quietly in her crepe-soled nursing oxfords, but when she reached Mrs. O'Bannon's bed and drew back the curtain, no one was there but the sick old woman.

It must have been some trick of the curtain folds and the moon shadows, she decided.

The next day the nursing supervisor called her to come in early and work a double shift. Mrs. Kennedy had called in sick. Connelly was one of the youngest nurses on the staff, with the energy to work a sixteen-hour day. She was remodeling the ancient stone house she hoped to live in one day and could always use a bit of extra cash. Staffing was tight in this relatively remote rural section of the west of Ireland and the hospital did not attract many recent graduates from the teaching hospitals in Dublin, Galway, Limerick, and Cork. Connelly had come to the area to be with her boyfriend. The boyfriend was long gone, but she found country life agreed with her and stayed on.

She was something of an Irish cultural enthusiast. She enjoyed being in the Gaeltacht where Gaelic was a living language, not simply one forced upon schoolchildren. She liked the spontaneous music sessions in the pubs and the singing houses, the nosiness of the neighbors, and the old stories and songs that still survived.

And she liked feeling needed, which was why she'd become a nurse in the first place.

So she took on the earlier shift with good grace. She passed dinner trays with Mrs. O'Donovan and Mrs. Byrne, the evening nursing assistants. Then the three of them tried to get the more helpless patients who did not have feeding tubes to take something by mouth.

Mrs. Finlay was managing on her own tonight, though the sitting up was giving her enough pain that she'd be needing her injection soon. Connelly nodded to her, then raised the head of Mrs. O'Bannon's bed and tried to dribble some broth and tea into her mouth.

"It's useless, you know. She's not going to get any better," a man's gruff voice said behind her.

She jumped, spilled soup down the front of Mrs. O'Bannon's gown, mopped her with a napkin and turned to face the speaker. He was a florid faced man with a shock of white hair and watery blue eyes. Mid-sixties, she guessed.

"Excuse me, sir, but if you are this lady's doctor, you must be new to the staff as I haven't seen you before."

"Of course I'm not her doctor."

She rose and walked to his far side, saying in a low voice, "Then I'll thank you to keep your medical opinion of her condition to yourself. People hear a great deal even when they cannot respond and I won't have you upsetting my patients."

"Don't get all officious with me, young woman. I have a perfect right to be here and a perfect right to my opinion of my own mother's condition. As for upsetting her, Mother has never been a particularly sensitive woman. Now stand aside. I need something from her handbag."

Connelly said, "Then I will need some identification, sir. I was told the lady has no children and I'm sure you can understand why I can't allow just anyone to rummage about in my patients' valuables."

"No, that would make less for you, wouldn't it?" he asked nastily, but produced a wallet and identification saying he was Dennis O'Bannon of Liverpool, England.

Connelly would have liked to point out that there were many O'Bannons in Ireland and how was she to know this O'Bannon of Liverpool was actually related to Mrs. Moira O'Bannon. It wasn't that she was afraid of the row, but she did have a great deal of work to do and the food, such as it was, was getting cold. Hearty broth for dinner was bad enough but cold congealed hearty broth was enough to make anyone sick—especially her as she tried to feed it to someone.

O'Bannon jostled her slightly as he opened his alleged mother's bedside table and took out her handbag. All of the real valuables were locked up and she would take great pleasure in telling him that in order to get them, he'd have to wait until she could summon the supervisor and a security guard and produce yet more identification. However, he took something out, seemed satisfied, and strode out.

"Don't let him get away with that!" a voice suddenly croaked from the next bed. It was Mrs. Finlay.

"It's nothing," Connelly assured her automatically. "Don't distress yourself."

"It most certainly is something. It's the key to Moira's safe deposit box. The deed to her cottage, what little money she's saved, the good bits of jewelry she has are all in there. And he's got no right to them . . ." Connelly felt a moment of satisfaction that she could call Mr. Fitzpatrick to take care of the thief and impostor before Mrs. Finlay continued in a low fierce voice, ". . . that serpent's tooth who calls himself a son to her now that it might gain him something."

"Good day to you too, Mrs. Finlay, you old cow," Dennis O'Bannon called back from the door to the ward. "Why should you care? You don't think she's left you anything, do you? I'm her darling boy after all."

"Oh, prance on out of here, you bloody parasite!" Mrs. Finlay yelled and threw her pillow, then gave a little scream, followed by a moan. "Oughtn't to have done that," she said in a teary voice.

"He really is her son, though?" Connelly asked, though there was no doubt in her mind, as the entire exchange now sounded most familiarly like interfamily/neighborhood strife. She retrieved the pillow and readjusted Mrs. Finlay's position in bed.

"When it suits him. He's right about one thing. In spite of being a horrible little sod, he could always talk Moira out of anything, so she'd probably give him the key if she were able." She looked over at her neighbor and shook her head sadly. "Not as if she'll be needing it herself. It's just the principle of the thing."

"I thought she didn't have any children."

"Did he look like a child to you? I was the one who answered the questions, you know, and I didn't want him called. I suppose someone else saw the ambulance and took it upon themselves to notify him. Why I can't imagine. He probably had spies to let him know when she was gone so he could come scoop up what little she has left."

"You look as though you're in pain. Shall I get you a tablet or an injection?"

"Tablet please. I hate needles."

Connelly returned with the tablet and a fresh pitcher

of water. Pouring a glass for Mrs. Finlay, she remarked, "Mrs. O'Bannon's son doesn't look like the musical type to me. Yet I was told she had a visitor carrying a fiddle case. Do you know who that might be?"

Mrs. Finlay swallowed the tablet. "Yer man? Musical? I should say not! Not a jot of talent or wit about that one. As to who it might be, however, well, I would hardly think so after all these years. Though they said he came back when old Tom died, that was Moira's husband. He was the smart one. He never minded that Dennis was his blood son. He knew him for what he was and mourned the day he was brought back and exchanged for the other one."

"What other one? Are you speaking of an adopted child or a fosterling?"

But the pain pill was strong and worked quickly, as all of the anesthetic was not yet gone from Mrs. Finlay's system. Her mouth opened as though she were about to speak again, and then instead of words a snort and a snore emerged. Connelly took the water from her hand before it spilled all over the bed.

She tried again to feed Mrs. O'Bannon but succeeded only in smearing the broth onto the poor woman's chin and chest.

Connelly admitted two more postoperative patients that evening, which kept her and the nursing assistants very busy. Before she knew it, the shift was ending and it was time for report to the next shift. Since she was working a double shift, all she needed to do was brief Mrs. Moran on the highlights of the evening. She mentioned Dennis O'Bannon and the new admissions and then they parted, each to her own duties, and Connelly picked up her torch and began the hourly rounds.

By that time it was midnight again. She felt a moment's dismay that there was another eight hours to go. She covered the six-bed ward, the four, and the semiprivate and private rooms, then the twelve-bed one. There was no moonlight now. It was a bit stormy outside actually, but still there was light from behind the curtain at Mrs. O'Bannon's bed and a long-haired figure was outlined. Unmistakably, it lifted a fiddle to its chin.

Connelly covered the length of the ward in perhaps eight or ten seconds. As she did so, a few notes rose above the labored breathing and coughs and groans. No laments or lullabyes tonight. Those few notes were not ones she could identify but instead of walking or running to investigate them, she found she was almost dancing.

Still, she pulled the curtain aside, ready to throw the bugger out and tell him to come back during the daylight hours when he wouldn't wake the whole floor with his fiddling.

The only person there was Mrs. O'Bannon, her breathing perhaps a little easier than it had been earlier.

Mrs. Finlay, on the other hand, was wide awake once more.

"Did you see how he left?" Connelly asked her in a hushed voice. "The man who was here—the one you said was another son of Mrs. O'Bannon's—the fiddler. You must have heard the music."

"What there was of it woke me from a nasty dream," Mrs. Finlay admitted. "I suppose you could check beneath the beds and see if he ducked out that way, but I doubt it will do you any good."

"What do you mean?"

"You'd think I was senile or delirious if I told you."

"And I'll continue to think I'm hallucinating if you don't, I'm afraid. Who is that fellow and why is he too stupid to realize you don't start playing jigs after midnight in a hospital ward?"

"I don't think his kind understand about hospital wards," Mrs. Finlay said softly. "From what's said of them, they don't have sickness. I think Old Tom's death must have come as a great shock to him."

"Why would that have been and of whom are you speaking?" Connelly asked, trying not to sound as impatient as she felt. Perhaps Mrs. Finlay *was* having a strange post-anesthetic reaction but then, if she was, so was Connelly herself.

"*Him,*" Mrs. Finlay said, as though Connelly were being uncommonly thick. "Yer fiddlin' boy. He's supposed to be one of *them.*"

"Them who? Do you mean he's a Traveler?" Connelly asked, puzzled. It had crossed her mind when she was trying to think of what sort of person would show such blatant regard for hospital rules that Mrs. O'Bannon's visitor *might* be one of the Irish Traveling People, who were the same as Gypsies as far as anyone knew, only not quite so racially distinctive. The manners were the same, however, which was to say that rules made by ordinary settled people were not necessarily considered worth following by Travelers.

"No, not a Traveler, you silly girl. *Them,* one of *them.*"

"One of whom?"

Mrs. Finlay crossed her arms primly across her chest and replied, "Whatever people do in Galway and Dublin, we know better than to speak the name of them around here. The Good Folk, of course."

"I hardly think good folk would show such deliberate disregard for hospital routine and the need of the

sick to get their rest . . ." Connelly began indignantly.
The flashlight glow caught Mrs. Finlay's disgusted look
at the nurse's stupidity.

"The *Good* Folk," she said again.

This time Connelly caught her meaning but she
didn't especially want to. "Oh, come now, Mrs. Finlay.
You don't mean to be telling me he's a fa—"

Mrs. Finlay interrupted her with a "Hsst!"

"Good person," Connelly finished. "I mean, in this
day and age?"

"Moira is ninety-three years old, pet, and I am
eighty-two. Things were different back in our day.
People believed differently and acted differently. And
then there were also some who were just—different
altogether, if you take my meaning?"

"I'm afraid I don't," Connelly said briskly. She could
swallow a lot after all but really . . .

"Then run along and let an old woman sleep," Mrs.
Finlay said.

The fiddling came back that night. As it had the
previous night. And as before, when she looked out
the window, Connelly saw the long-haired fiddler outlined by the lights spilling onto the road. Again she
called Mr. Fitzpatrick, and again when he reported
back to her, it was to say that he found no one outside.

He and Mrs. Moran and Connelly sat having their
tea. Connelly sighed. She was growing very tired now
from the long shift. "That Mrs. Finlay in bed ten, Mrs.
O'Bannon's neighbor, implied that our phantom fiddler is some sort of an elf or something," she said.

"Shh," Mr. Fitzpatrick said. "You're not supposed
to be saying these things out loud."

"What things? About the fiddler?" She didn't believe he could possibly be one of the magical "little
people." For one thing what she saw of him was not

all that little. However, she felt a little thrill at the idea that not only Mrs. Finlay but Mrs. Moran and Mr. Fitzpatrick acted as if fairy folk and the superstitions surrounding them were still matters of concern in this part of Ireland. The Dublin part of her found it all so anthropological, but part of her longed for there yet to be magic and mystery at large in the world.

Both Mrs. Moran and Mr. Fitzpatrick were giving her hard stares. She was about to say something else when the fiddling began again, coming once more from the direction of Mrs. O'Bannon's ward.

She was out of her chair and halfway down the hall before she realized she was alone. Mrs. Moran had suddenly remembered her water pitchers needed to be filled before day shift arrived and Mr. Fitzpatrick strode determinedly in the direction opposite to ward three to continue his rounds. She almost called out to him, but the message his back sent to her was clear enough. Connelly was on her own.

Without slowing her stride, she walked to the doorway of the music-haunted unit. The fiddling continued as she stood in the door for a moment. She had drawn back the privacy curtains earlier, after everyone had their sleeping medication. So now the fiddler was outlined against the window instead of silhouetted by the curtain. Tonight's tune was not a familiar one to her, but it was a melodic lament, another O'Carolan, no doubt. She took a step into the ward.

Perhaps it was the change in the light from the hallway, perhaps it was that ears with a supernaturally acute sense of hearing detected her light padded footstep, or perhaps it was simply because the musician so far had only played a few bars of the tune before she interrupted: whatever the cause, the outlined fiddler was gone in an eye's blinking.

"Acushla?" a weak and querulous voice called from the end of the ward. Mrs. O'Bannon was awake and speaking for the first time on Connelly's shift. "Don't go."

"There there, Moira, don't fret. He'll be back," Mrs. Finlay whispered from the next bed.

Connelly faced them with her hands on her hips and in her sternest voice said, "Very well, ladies, who is he?"

But Mrs. O'Bannon began crying, her voice spiraling in a thin piercing squeal of misery that ended in a series of coughs. Connelly sighed, adjusted the oxygen, and gave her some cough suppressant.

"Poor thing," Mrs. Finlay said. "I wonder if she knows and if she does, what she thinks of it."

"Please, none of your riddles, Mrs. Finlay. I'm at the end of my second shift and in no mood."

"You should just let him be is what you should do," Mrs. Finlay told her sharply, her eyes glittering hard in the darkness. "He's doing no harm."

"No harm! He could wake the entire hospital!"

"With his little lullabies? Hardly! He might do everyone some good. Most of these poor souls could hardly be worse off."

"It is entirely too irregular, Mrs. Finlay. It's as much as my job's worth to let this continue."

"It won't continue long. He's only here for Moira. Not that she was ever kind to him, of course. It was her doing that he was exposed. No, he's doing it because of Tom, I'm sure. Moira had to wait until Tom was away to put him out."

"Whatever are you speaking of?"

The woman had been murmuring on as if speaking only to herself. Reminded of Connelly's presence she said, "Sit down, pet. You sound very weary."

"That I am," she said. But she pulled up the visitor's chair not because she was tired, she told herself, but because she wished to encourage Mrs. Finlay to enlighten her.

"I know you folk in Dublin think us backward here in the West. And it's true enough, I suppose, that time has been in no rush for us, at least until recently. When Moira and I were young, we could go weeks without hearing the English being spoken and many things were known—or at least remembered—for true then that are scoffed at in these scientific times."

"Such as this hospital being built on a fairy knowe?" Connelly interrupted, curious to learn if Mr. Fitzpatrick had been teasing her or simply sharing local lore.

"That was the English! Folk who grew up here never would have done such a thing. But once it was here, it was here and it served a purpose. But yes, that's the very sort of thing to which I am referring. Anyway, Moira was a youngest daughter and lived with her parents until they died, so when she married Tom, she was already a spinster of twenty-two and very set in her ways. Tom was much older than she, though, and had had his eye on her for years. He was a gentler person altogether and seemed to enjoy her bossiness and sharpness. It's like that sometimes, a good man choosing a right wagon like herself there to love, as if she could be dull for him when he was too kind-hearted to do it himself. You see it the other way around of course, too, but in this case, Moira was the one who had the say in what was what."

Mrs. O'Bannon's breathing was quick and shallow, with long gaps in its rhythm. One, two . . . three, four, five—Connelly counted under her breath while listening to Mrs. Finlay and nodding.

"When Moira became pregnant Tom was beside

himself with happiness. Although it's well known to be unlucky to make or give a present to a babe before it's born, Tom made it a little fiddle to match his own. Oh, he was in great demand at the dances and parties, was Tom. His popularity drew Moira to him. She liked having the company and admiration of someone whose company was craved by others and who was admired by others. When the baby was born, as soon as Moira was up and about, all the neighbors had a party. That wasn't particularly wise, when the child hadn't been christened yet. It must have been as he was passed from hand to hand that the exchange was made."

"Well, surely no one passed the child to someone they didn't know," Connelly said.

"If certain folk can make one child indistinguishable from another to look at, do you think they could do less for themselves if they wished to pass for local?"

"I suppose that's true enough," Connelly admitted.

"Still, even after the little one began the cryin' and the caterwaulerin' that characterize such as it was, nobody noticed the switch except Moira. When it was handed back to her she pushed it away and Tom took it up and stopped fiddling to dance it around the floor, which quieted it soon enough. Moira hastened the christening date, thinking it would never survive it. I was at the christening myself."

"If the baby was—what you have implied, wouldn't the christening have killed it?"

"Might have done, I suppose, except that Tom was taking no chances. Moira was never one to keep her suspicions to herself and though Tom swore the child was the very one she had borne from her own body, he took no chances. When he thought no one was looking, he tipped a bit from his flask into the baptismal font. He caught me watching, but I was just a little girl. I'd heard the stories too and I had seen him play with that child, sing to it, dance with it, fiddle to it, rock it. I winked at him and he winked back and you are the first I've ever told about it, from that day to this."

Connelly thought that had the sound of a tag line for a tall tale, but she only nodded.

"When the priest ducked it in, the baby squalled of course, as they all did, but in spite of the tainting, the holiness of the water seemed to make it ill for it cried and cried for weeks on end. Moira left to see her sister in Clare and left Tom to bottle-feed it. He did, and he fiddled for it and did all his tricks and eventually it did quiet down for him. But as soon as Moira returned, it commenced crying all over again. Moira was angry and hated the child. Not only did it tear at her nerves with its screaming, it kept Tom too busy to dance to *her* tune as well.

"But it grew very fast, that baby, until when it was not quite three years old it could play on the little fiddle its daddy made it."

As if on cue, the first strains of a low lament soared up through the window. Mrs. O'Bannon gave a sigh and her breathing evened out. Connelly noticed then that there was not a drop of urine in her catheter bag. "Go ahead, I'll just tend to this," she told Mrs. Finlay as she irrigated the tube, to no avail. Kidney failure it was, then. Mrs. O'Bannon was on her way out.

"Tom and Moira never fought over the child, but Tom kept him beside himself always until one day he had to go away on business of some sort. I'm not sure what it was, but it was something that was either too boring or too dangerous for a child. That was the day Moira seized her chance and took the little fellow out to the hills. I saw them go and heard her telling him they were going to meet his da. He was carrying his little fiddle with him. When she came back, she was quite alone."

"Surely that was illegal."

"It might have been, had anyone known for sure. But later on, when Tom came home, there was Moira and her boy there to meet him at the door. Tom knew at once, I'm sure. After that, Moira and the boy were always together and Tom it was who roamed the hills at all hours, him and his fiddle, as if he was calling to the boy who was the true son of his heart. Some people began to say they'd heard it said way back that there was some very old bloodline in Tom's family on his mother's side, something uncanny."

"Really?" Connelly stood and began to walk to the window but Mrs. Finlay stopped her.

"Leave him be. He's hurting no one and you see how much calmer she is with the music. I suppose she thinks it's Tom come back again."

"Or her other son? When the fiddling started before, I heard her call for someone."

Mrs. Finlay snorted, "She'd never mistake Dennis for him! Much as she lavished on that child, he was a cold and unloving sort—as distant as if he were the foreigner she always thought the other one was. He was gone as soon as he could get away, without a backward glance except to write home for money now and then. And as for Tom, he was never quite the same. When his fiddling didn't bring his own boy home, and Moira said it disturbed the boy who lived with them in his place, he stopped altogether. His fiddle was never heard again until the day he died."

"Sooo—is this his ghost then? Tom's ghost? I'm a little confused."

"Of course not. Have you not been listening to a

word I've said? The day that Tom died the fiddle disappeared from its hook on the wall. I suppose I was the only one who saw the shape at the window near Tom's bed, or saw it leave. But as that good man breathed his last, folk for miles around heard his fiddle cry and keen. It was heard at Tom's wake and when they put him in the ground, but it never more was seen."

"Until now."

"Until now," Mrs. Finlay agreed, sniffing. The sky was lightening outside, and the music grew louder, though only they three seemed to hear it. Mrs. Moran had never poked her head into the ward in all the time Mrs. Finlay spoke. "It's my belief that old Tom asked his boy to look after Moira, poor mother though she'd been to him, and to tend her as he's been doing these last two days. I know he's kept track of her. He sent her gold sometimes—she bragged about it and put it in her bank. And there was always peat for her fire when she needed it and food when she had been nowhere to fetch it. A fish, a fresh caught hare, a few turnips, and once a whole cake from the SuperQuinn. No, Tom's son has been keeping his promise."

The old lady's voice sounded choked as she spoke and ended in a cough and sniffle. Connelly thought she was weeping and reached for a tissue. But just then the fiddle broke into a raucous tearing reel.

"Well, that's all very interesting," Connelly said, "But he'll have to stop that now."

But Mrs. Finlay wasn't listening. She took in a breath and let one out, and stopped breathing altogether. Connelly rang the nurses' bell but she could hardly hear it for the screech and whine of the music which now seemed to be inside her head. She lowered the head of the bed, cleared Mrs. Finlay's airway, and began pumping at her heart in an effort to resuscitate her. The music dipped and rolled inside her head as she pumped and breathed, pumped and breathed, and then the crash cart and the code team were there and Connelly was pushed aside.

They wheeled Mrs. Finlay away to surgery again. As they did, Connelly realized the fiddle music had stopped, dawn had come, the shift was changing and Mrs. O'Bannon lingered still.

At the end of the morning report, Connelly carried her coat and purse up to the surgical ward. She was almost afraid to ask what had become of the garrulous old soul, but Mrs. O'Fallon, the head surgical nurse, saw her and waved her down. "I just wanted to say, well done, Connelly. Well done. You were certainly in the right place at the right time this morning to save that lady's life. Usually when someone throws a fat embolus like that after surgery, no one notices in time to do anything, if there's anything to be done. This time there was and—well—she is old of course, but she'll mend, thanks to you."

Connelly accepted the praise awkwardly, feeling that it better belonged elsewhere. And was it she who was the only one who heard the fiddling low and sweet as she looked in on Mrs. Finlay where she lay on the gurney in the recovery room?

"Do you hear that?" she asked Mrs. O'Fallon.

"Of course, dear, we find a little music helps soothe people. I've never heard that particular piece though."

Connelly didn't doubt it a bit. The piece never came from the CD player any more than the fiddler had been at the hospital to look after his mean mother Moira, she thought to herself.

She wasn't entirely right, however. Later that day she had to return to work for another double shift and there, at dinner time once again, was the unlovely Dennis. Mrs. O'Bannon was failing more quickly, and babbled at her son while he stood at the end of the bed. "What are you playing at, Mother?" he demanded.

"Acushla?" she asked, a whine in her voice. Perhaps she recognized him, perhaps not.

Connelly was rushing to tell him to lower his voice when he said, "I opened your bank box. You told me you had gold in there. All I found was a bunch of dead leaves."

From the surgical ward where Mrs. Finlay now rested comfortably came a fiddle's laughing lilt.

THE STOLEN CHILD

Michelle West

Michelle West is the author of several novels, including *The Sacred Hunter* duology and *The Sun Sword* series, both published by DAW Books. She reviews books for the online column *First Contacts* and less frequently for *The Magazine of Fantasy & Science Fiction*. Other short fiction by her has appeared in dozens of anthologies, including *Black Cats and Broken Mirrors*, *Elf Magic*, *Olympus*, *Alien Abductions*, *The Mutant Files*, and *Villains Victorious*.

The child who plays on the steps of the narrow building is not remarkable, except in this: she is utterly silent. Around her, other children play, and it is only by watching them for a stretch of minutes—unsafe, really, in this part of town—that one is able to discern the fact that she is all but invisible to the boisterous, colorful noisy group; children can be so unkind.

But if they are unkind, she is young enough not to be troubled; she plays with a stick and a stone, pushing

first one and then the other as if they were vehicles.
Her eyes are not remarkable, and her skin is remarkable only in the way that young skin is: it is without blemish, and seems soft in the waning day.

"What are you, stupid?" A young boy shouts, his face red. But his words pass over the girl, and after a moment, the observer is not clear whether or not they were meant for her at all; they linger in the air like ghosts, like an echo of other words. As they must be, he thinks, although he thinks again that children can be cruel.

Yet they are, in their malice, almost innocent of intent that is not immediate; it is not their goal to cause suffering, merely to take pleasure. If they do not easily see that their pleasure causes pain, it is all of an age. They are marked by the pain they have felt, and in their helplessness, they are not aware of their power except in this way: by testing.

He shakes himself, and as he does, the sun passes through the bent form of the delicate child, causing shadows to linger above her and behind her. They do not dim the light of her eyes, the pale color of her skin; it is by this that he knows he has come, at last, to the right place.

It is only by this.

He has searched the forests of the old world and the new; has crossed jungles and lingered at the long edge of deserts; he has spied the darkened skin of aboriginals in the dreaming; and he has partaken of other dreams in darkened tents thick with the sweet sweat of strangers, the lingering pockets of their silence and their old, old eyes.

He has read, and learned to read, dead languages, gaining over the stretch of focused decades the ability to judge nuance and other translations, and he has traversed the whole of civilizations in the fragments of their lost words.

But he needn't have bothered, he thinks, with just a pang at the loss of time. Because not in any of these ancient things is the ancient to be found—not the one he seeks.

And why would it? He passes hand over eyes; the stench of the sewers waft up in the muggy, summer heat, choking him. He cannot keep the distaste from his expression, and it is this expression that suddenly catches the attention of the silent child.

She looks up.

Her eyes are silver gray, a trick of the light.

But she holds his gaze a moment before she rises, stone in one hand, stick in the other, the emblems of her youth. If she throws them, he will be certain, and he finds himself waiting for a sign—but he has waited long, and in vain.

The child walks up the slender set of stairs. They are stone, but worn in the centers; they are as old as the building itself, its narrow façade trapped on either side by signs of gentrification in the heart of the city.

Like seasons, he thinks. This was once a wealthy place, and once a poor one; it rises and falls with the fortunes of the city.

She does not bend again, but instead takes the stairs one at a time. The door is covered in layers of flecked and peeling paint; gray giving way to pink, and pink to the darker edges of a red-brown that has not been entirely leached of color by long exposure to sun, exhaust, pollution.

Just this. There is no number on the door, and no sign that numbers existed here at all, although there is a nail that rides half an inch above the buckling wood, unadorned by anything it was meant to anchor. There are windows in the door, and to either side, windows as well; the curtains are drawn, and in the slowly fading day, he sees gauze and lace, a hint of faded elegance.

Yes, he thinks. Here.

But he pauses at the foot of the stairs and waits as she mounts them. There are only a handful, but it seems as he watches that she climbs a great height, dwindling in size and significance as she reaches the door itself.

Children flow past him like the currents of a moving stream; he is the rock in their center and they part and meet at his back or his chest, moving constantly, their voices a loud chitter, the angry play of squirrels.

He pauses, remembering a time when he might have joined them in their games, cruel and kind as they are cruel and kind. But he is twice their height, and age has taken him, year by year, away from the simplicity of their games; they hold interest for him—but it is, he realizes with surprise, the same interest that the texts of dead civilizations hold: he sees an echo of himself in their movements, a shadow of the knowledge he has won and lost over the years as he has been forced to examine and re-examine all of his choices.

It is no kindness, but he smiles; his hand flits a moment above the passing head of a young, burly boy, a small tank on feet. He does not touch, however.

The child is waiting.

As she did, he mounts the steps. His legs are longer, but he finds the length of the steps too short for the fall of his feet, and he is forced to walk sideways, step over step, until he reaches the door. Mute, she touches its faded panels, with first the stone and then the stick;

it swings open into the darkness of interior light, met after the brightness of the open sky.

She does not seem happy that he is there; she does not seem unhappy. But his presence has robbed her of the simplicity of the particular game she played, and her slender shoulders seem almost insubstantial as they curl in toward the ground, touched by sudden gravity.

He reaches above her head, and his hand pauses just above the panel of the door; he does not touch.

Her smile is brief and feral; there is approval and cunning in it. A test, he thinks, and he has passed it—but it is just one such test. There will be others.

He reaches into the interior pocket of his jacket, and from its hidden depths, he pulls something bright and shiny. He gives it to her: a coin, flat and old.

She recoils, and he smiles with genial approval. Not all of the tests will be theirs. She does not enter, but she does give the door a graceful shove inwards; it seems to vanish as it moves.

A voice says, "You will leave your name at the door." It is imperious, that voice, and although the language is clear and plain, it is accented and inflected in a fashion that speaks of other lands. Countless others; he will not easily find original within the pronunciation of those syllables.

But he shakes his head, and he takes instead another item from the core of his depthless pocket: a card.

"Your name," the voice says again; the darkness has not yet been lifted, his eyes have not adjusted.

"I left my name long ago," he replies, "and I would have to journey to find it before I could leave it here."

There is a momentary silence, a weighted hesitation. He is weighed, and his words are judged. At last, the voice says, "You may enter."

He nods, and bowing, removes his shoes; he leaves these in the lee of the door's frame, just to one side of the girl. He wonders if she will weight them with either stick or stone—the walking would be difficult then. But she is young, and she is not in his judgment yet willing to surrender the weighty matters of the youth she bears—not to inconvenience him.

Not yet.

He takes a step forward upon this ancient path, and the floorboards creak beneath his stranger's weight. The light fades at his back; the sounds of play and traffic recede with them, and he is left in a quiet that is almost arboreal. It is a natural silence.

There are doors.

The interior is composed of them, and they face into the hall with its creaky floors. Carpets might once have covered their surface, or runners, but they are gone now; the house seems almost empty. Spiders gather in the corner of the distant ceiling, their webs a cloudy gathering of dust and the corpses of other insects. They are small, however, as the house is small; they belong here.

He takes care when he passes beneath them, but he needn't bother; they have no power. Still, he does not touch the strands of their homes. Homes have power.

Names have power.

He shakes his head and smiles, but the smile is weary. There are three doors, and steps that climb; he knows that if he passes from the hall, he will find steps that descend. He is not yet ready for descent, however, and after a moment of hesitation, he accepts that this house, like many such houses, has a sitting room. He will wait there.

Having made his choice, the door closest to him responds; it opens, avoiding his touch. He enters.

Here, the light from the street streaming in broken beams through curtained lace, he looks. A fireplace hides behind a mantel of dark, dark wood; it boasts a mirror, and he does not approach; he is aware of what mirrors convey, and what they trap, and he has not made it all this way by being incautious.

There is a chair, meant clearly for one; its armrests are covered by the same lace that covers the window. He does not take it; instead, he chooses to stand by the window, examining the fall of his shadow. There are sliding pocket doors, wood dark as the wood of the mantel, glass opaque and cloudy. In another house, they would lead to the dining room, and from there, to the kitchen; he is not certain where they will take him from here, and he is content to be ignorant.

The room is otherwise bare; there are no shelves here, no books, no cases of glass that are filled with mementoes or history. No sign of the living.

But if there is no sign of the living, loss does not fill this house: he knows loss.

He shies away from its memory, and as he does, she comes through the pocket doors.

She is old, where the child was young, and this— this he did not expect. For a moment he wonders if he has wandered by accident into the wrong house, the wrong place. He has a map, of course, but it is not a thing of paper, with lines and words and pictograms; it is not the gift of strangers.

No, it is something he built, with care, over the passage of decades, and it is hidden in memory and covered by knowledge, shored up by the confidence that her great age has momentarily shaken. He sees the house through two sets of eyes, an odd phase distortion in which deliberate, almost mystical austerity wavers a moment, and he can see the poverty of this room so clearly he almost steps back through the open door.

But it is *not* open, and he does not touch it. The world reasserts itself.

The old woman wears black. It binds her hair, covering the whole of her body from wrist to ankle in its heavy folds. Unlike the paint on the door and the wood beneath his feet, the color is deep and perfect; time has not dimmed it, and age has not made the cloth spare. Mothballs reign a moment, their scent so strong his eyes water.

He has seen old-world widows, but not for many years; one such woman would sit upon her porch, her lines in a severe cascade as she shouted foreign words at her grandchildren from time to time—words which were, at safe distance, mostly ignored. He remembers this clearly because he was among those children at the time, and she seemed almost iconic, her words a chant or a curse deprived of the strength of homeland.

He did not expect to see it here, and it takes him a moment to gather his thoughts. When he finally does, she has taken the seat, and rested black arms so certainly across the rests that the lace is all but concealed beneath the heavy fall of her garments.

Her face is a network of lines, her lips have lost all color and blend seamlessly with the contours of the rest of her pale skin; he has no doubt that the hair bound by something wimplelike is likewise leached of color; her eyebrows are silver, and the backs of her hands are colored only by liver spots. She is, in all ways, bent by age—but her eyes are the same eyes that the child had, clear and somehow undisturbed by the whole of the world they see.

Her smile is also cold, and it is so certain, so auto-cratic, that the image of that other grandmother, de-cades past, shatters; he cannot hold it.

"You have come late," she says bitterly, and if her appearance is rustic and ancient, her voice still con-tains a measure of power and perfect grace.

"It is not yet late," he says, glancing towards the beams of unbroken light, like spokes of a slow turning wheel that shift across the bare ground.

She frowns; she is not used to being corrected. "It is twilight," she tells him. "And if you see otherwise, the doors would not have opened so easily for you. You left no name."

"I have none."

"There are few among your kin who have no name," she says.

"There are few among my kin who claim that names have power. Names are changed like clothing, and per-haps at lesser cost." He is thinking of the city, of its fashions, of the expense of going among the citizens as one of their own.

"But you have the old manners; you did not sully the path with boots that have tread upon the dimmer road. I am grateful for your courtesy." She is compel-ling. He cannot say why. But he is relieved. "Why have you come?"

"I have come," he says, bending now at the knees, stiff with the sudden weight of his request, "to ask a boon of you."

"I have no power in your world."

"You have some power yet, or you would not be among us."

Her smile is cold, but there is something about the curve of those colorless lips that speaks of regret, of the echoes of regret. "Power," she tells him softly, "is a thing you will know when you see it. What we are granted in your world is only a measure of the truth you find here." And then, as if he is stupid, she adds, "I am old, now."

He reaches again into his pockets, and from them he takes his offerings: the seed of the tree, and its fruit, leaves that are withered but not yet devoid of life. He waxed them with care, prepared them with oils. He gathered them across the face of the world, in arid desert and in humid jungle and in all the ranges in between.

She glances at them for a long moment, and then she sighs; again there is regret in her voice, in the breath that leaves her small mouth. When she bows her head, it seems that her whole neck folds, that she shrinks in on herself. He is afraid she will vanish beneath the weight.

But she lifts her head, and her chin does not tremble when she holds it up. "These would have been meager indeed in my youth," she tells him, critical, as the old are, of things that are not of their generation.

"They would not have been," he replies quietly. "For in your youth, no man could travel as I have traveled; no one would have gathered all that I have gathered."

"There is some truth in what you say. Why did you do it?"

He keeps her glance a moment, and then he sets his offerings against the bare floor and inches back along it; he does not rise. He is careful to keep the greed from his face, careful to mask need, to cultivate the expressions that hide desire.

"If I accept your gift," she says, not moving, "what gift would you have in return?"

"My child," he replies stonily.

She does not laugh, but her eyes do. "It has been many, many years since children have been taken," she tells him quietly.

"I know the old laws, and the old ways. If you accept the gift, you accept the giving as well as the taking."

"And if I do not accept the gifting?"

"I will take what I have gathered, and I will leave."

"The door will not open for you," she says. It is not a threat, although he is threatened by it. Still, he is wise enough not to speak.

She says, "You did not look into my mirror."

"No. It is said that no man can."

"It is said. But I can look into it without fear, now, so long as I am willing to accept what I see." Now she rises, and she hobbles a moment, gaining her feet; it is the first time she appears ungainly. "I have seen much," she tells him, as if she hears this unspoken criticism.

"And are you content?"

Her eyes narrow, losing their light a moment. "Are you?" But not their ability to see.

He says nothing.

"Why do you think I can help you find your child?"

But he says, "Take the leaves, lady. Listen to them."

It is her hunger he tests, and she is hungry; he can feel it, in the hollowed space, the vast emptiness of this too-small room. She lifts her wrinkled hands, and the liver spots vanish as she turns palms up toward the pale ceiling. The texture there implies stucco, something cheap and tawdry—but it moves, as he watches it, as if it were liquid. No spiders here; none in her presence.

The leaves drift upward, as if at wind, and a few come to rest in her palms.

Her eyes widen as they touch her skin. She says, "You preserved them."

"Yes, lady."

"With tallow," she tells him.

"Yes."

"There was blood in the mix."

"Yes."

"Ah." She smiles. "Your name is here."

But there is only one name he now holds, and it is a child's name. He says nothing.

"This is a gift," she tells him. The seeds rise as well, but before they reach her hands, he is in motion. He captures all save one; the one he cedes to her.

Her frown is one of displeasure, but not of surprise; she catches the one in her palm, handling it as if it was a gem, and she a jeweler of unmatched prowess. She spreads her fingers wide, and the seed tumbles slowly toward the bare, wooden planks. Those planks are worn; they have not been waxed or varnished, and the ceaseless march of careless feet are etched there, the shapes of the shoes forgotten, the damage captured.

The seed lodges in the cracks between the slats, and light takes it; sunlight, a hint of younger days. He watches, and from the seed, green sprouts.

Satisfied, almost enchanted, she watches until the shoot is half her height; she closes her palms around the rest. "Yes," she tells him. "This will be acceptable." She holds out her hand, but his has curled into a fist, and it is shaking. He slips it back into his pocket.

"Not yet, lady," he tells her.

Her smile is cold amusement, lined by age. "You have indeed read well. The leaves?"

"They are the story of the trees that will grow," he

replies. "And as in all such things, the story itself is free; take it as you will."

She laughs. "Our ghosts are contained in the stories that you call free."

"You do not die."

"We die," she replies, and her voice shifts and fades. "Come," she tells him. "You will see much beyond the walls within. Touch anything, and you will be lost to the path; I am guide, but I am not mistress."

He frowns.

"You will speak with my lord."

He walks by her side. Were she human, he would offer her his arm, for she is slow and bent. But he understands dignity and illusion; he offers no aid, and she asks for none. The doors, pocket doors, seemed so close to the chair when he first entered the room, but the walk takes hours, and she steps with care upon certain slats, avoiding others. She has done this often; he has never done it. He allows himself to be guided by her steps, although there is a risk in it.

"When did your child vanish?" She asks him as she walks.

He does not answer.

"If she is dead," she continues, "there is little that we can do."

Again, he does not answer.

She is intrigued by him; he can see the child's curiosity in the old woman's face. The child, small and delicate, the woman, bent and delicate, seem to be opposite ends of a spectrum; but while the one is possessed of a pale, fey beauty, the other is not. Why, then, is it the old woman who holds his attention?

Perhaps because she is here.

Perhaps not; he almost failed to notice the girl, with her stick and her stone and her silence.

"It is not the iron that killed," she says. She knows what he carries, and it pleases her to show him the knowledge.

"It killed some of you."

She shrugs. "It did not respond; it never has. It is the corpse of the world, and not its body, and dead have little to offer." Her glance is cast upon his profile; he is stiff with effort. "That is not so with you."

"No," he says gravely. He does not fear to lie, but he does not fear to tell the truth; he knows that she will know the one from the other. He has entered her world.

"You come late," she tells him, as she reaches the door, her hands caressing trapped wood.

"So you said," he replied. "But late and too late are not the same." He pauses; the doors do not open. "What killed your kin?"

"Nothing worthy of story," she replies.

"I'm not here to kill you."

"No, of course not. But that has been said many more times than was true in the past."

"The past is a different country."

She laughs. "You say that to me?" It is the first time she has done more than offer a cold smile, and he is shocked by the difference in the sound; it is the difference between the breeze and the gale. "Ask a different question," she tells him. A command.

"Later, lady," he replies. She has told him, in so many words, that he only has one—and although he cannot say why, he wishes to preserve it against some future need.

The doors slide open.

"Go," she says, almost bitterly.

He ignores the bitterness, as if it were something he could understand—as if it were his own—and offers her the most stately of bows. Hard, now, to imbue a simple bend with elegance or power. But he tries, and there is some reward for the attempt in the wan smile that touches her lips.

Beyond the doors, the floor stretches out for as far as the eye—his eye—can see. He was walked forests as dense as this distance; he cannot see roof or wall; he cannot see moving stream or bending stalk; he can hear the river moving someplace to the east, if he has not lost all sense of orientation.

And he can hear the cries of children; they are carried on the wind. Indistinct, they tease his ear and pierce his concentration; it is the first time that he almost missteps.

The first time, here.

He does not look back. If the old woman waits for him, she waits; if she does not, she does not. Forward momentum has carried him beyond all things time and again; he relies on it blindly. He moves, a step at a time, following the grain of wood, the flat slats and silver nails growing beneath the soft mounds of exposed feet.

His hands are in his pockets; he carries the seeds within one, and nothing within the other. The emptiness is the heavier burden. This is not his quest, but there were none left but he to undertake it.

He had a wife, once; she left him. Nor does he blame her for her absence. She is just another ghost in a forest of ghosts; the hint of her presence is undisturbed by the howl of wind on the open plain.

He walks. He feels hunger and thirst; he expected no less. They are the least of the tests he has faced, and in a distant past, they were harsh. Now, they are simply fact; they let him know that he is still alive.

One of the wooden slats has no beginning and no end; it is this one that he travels, carefully placing his heel in front of his toes, end over end. He does not count; he does not think of anything but the placement of those steps. They will take him to where he *must* be.

The court.

The court of the Faerie Queen.

As he walks, he remembers.

He would fight against these memories; he has fought them for years, for decades. They bind him, like spiders' webs; they hold him fast if he lets them.

But to fight them here is to lose: he will make no progress if he does not accept the journey's beginning. Bitter test, and bitter knowledge.

When his wife got pregnant, she was working.

The world was a different place; the vast expanse of a pretty suburbia was full of nostalgic promise. Never mind that that nostalgia belonged in the black and white boxes of televisions with rabbit-ear antennas—it was in and of itself a goal.

He had a job, then. He woke in the morning and left his home; he returned late in the evening. The evening that he returned to his wife, she was bitterly angry and not a little afraid.

"I spoke to Ernest Myers," she told him at the door, her hands pale and shaking, nails polished pink, the color already growing past the cuticles.

He shakes his head, almost in confusion.

She is dressed for work; she has not yet removed the boxed lines of a woman's business dress, and her feet are cramped by the small, pointed toes, the high arches, the pointed heels.

"What did he say?"

"He recited the rules of the company," she replied, bitterness growing. "He clearly feels that women shouldn't be allowed to work at all if they're married."

"That changed three years ago."

"He knows. But what hasn't changed is this: we're not allowed to work if we're pregnant. It's . . . unseemly. It's not part of the image the company wants to present to the rest of the business world."

He said, "You're pregnant?"

And she rolled her eyes. "I told you."

But she hadn't. It was not the way he would have chosen to find out. "I thought we—"

"Does it matter?" Weary now, her hands left the door. "I've been fired," she added, her back to his face. As if it were his fault.

He couldn't show joy at her announcement. He understood that she had given up her life and there was no way to undo it. Not then.

But she was not a woman who lived well in cages, and although the home *was* hers, even in name, it was still that; the walls were bars, and the neatness, the kept tidiness of the small life she was to inherit, was like a closed box with air holes punched carelessly in its cover.

That home was not like this one. This is endless. He walks.

When his child was born, he was not allowed to bear witness to the miracle. The doctors and nurses were quite firm in their denial; if he wished to be present he was to hire his *own* nurse. Men had a habit of fainting—or worse—in the delivery room, and once again, it was *unnatural* to want to witness the transformation of something guilty and private into something somehow less sexual. He was allowed to escort his burgeoning wife through the hospital's glass doors, and the thing he most remembers is not the smell or the flickering glare of fluorescent lights, but rather the sound of his steps, and hers, upon the endless floor. His feet, flat and heavy, and hers, still bound, clickety-clacking by his side. He feels her hand on the crook of his arm; he has carried her bags, her coat, her books and he has almost no room to carry her.

It seemed normal, then.

He almost rages at the passage of time, at the walk itself. It *seemed normal* then. Now? Now it is all different. Men are expected to be in attendance. Women are allowed to work. Lives are expected to grind on-ward, fracturing the myth—exposing the myth—of that early, tranquil existence.

She must have hated him, then. That's when it must have started. Because she was young, and she was afraid, and fear excuses no ignorance. He wanted that child, but he knew it was hers.

It was in the hospital that he met the nurse. She was young, of course; unmarried—as all women were who worked. She was not dimmed and heavy with the passage of the onerous, angry nine months, and she had the time to listen to his worries and his fretting. Although she was younger than he, it was by a handful of years—or so he then thought—and he sat by her side, when her duty ended, as if he were a child.

So little difference between a child and a man, in those days. She listened to him, as no other man could have listened, and she brought him water and solace while he waited. Hours passed.

In the end, she gave him her phone number and

she left the building, and his gaze lingered upon her as she did.

His wife was gone for a week, and during that week, he entered an odd fraternity of quietly sympathetic men. They did not offer direct comfort, but they lingered a moment when work ended, and they spoke of the days to come with oblique sympathy. They asked if his wife had sisters, or if his own sisters would be coming for the week to cook and clean for him; they offered the hospitality of their own homes when he shook his head.

Something about being a man, and alone, amused and concerned them. They laughed at his unironed shirts, his simple lunches, his lack of breakfast, and he laughed uneasily with them. He was not expected to be able to care for himself.

And he did not expect *to be able* to care for himself. How then was he to care for wife and child?

He sees it so clearly now, it is embittering.

Years and years ago, this happened.

On the third night, when the moon was full, she came. The nurse. She was pale and beautiful, slender with youth. He was grateful to see her, but he was also suddenly awkward, as he had always been awkward around women. He stood in the door of his home, and she stood outside of it waiting; he felt odd inviting her in. This was not his house.

Had she visited his office, it would have been different—*that* was his space. But she waited, and after a time, she took from behind her back a large basket. "I thought you would appreciate this," she said. She didn't smile, not exactly, but there was a peculiar cold joy in the words.

And cold comfort was better than none.

He stepped out of the way, and she passed in front of him, the scent she wore lingering in his nostrils.

He said, dumbly, "Does your family know you're here?"

And she smiled, nodding. "I told them. About you."

"And your—your husband?"

She shook her head. It was not a bitter motion, but it invited no further questions.

Yet questions were all he had; they were his defense against her sudden incursion. She walked into the house as if she owned it, and because he didn't know how to, she *did*.

His laundry was a mess, and the living room was covered in scattered papers—his work, brought home to stave off his sudden sense of uselessness. The kitchen sink was a pile of glasses and plates; the fridge was almost empty. The baby had come early enough that his wife had no time to prepare for her absence.

She did not like the carpets; she walked upon the wood. He remembers that clearly—and bitterly—as he walks the same path. His socks catch on exposed nails, but he extricates himself with care; he is not the man that he was then. If he was one, then.

She said, "I can't have children."

And he lifts his head. "How do you know that?"

"The women in my family cannot bear children."

"But you—"

"The men take wives," she replied. Just that.

"Then you won't marry."

"No." She says this as if it is not a tragedy; as if it is simple fact. And she said it then in the same way. He knows, by this conjoining of past and present, that he has almost arrived. Nothing else has changed.

"Do you like children?" He has never much trusted women who don't.

"I? Yes. I have always liked children. They are so open to possibility. They see the world differently."

"Maybe when my wife comes back from the hospital, you could come and help her. Her family is on the west coast."

"And yours?"

He says nothing.

She smiles, and her perfect teeth make him take a step back. Perfection does that. It has never been for him.

"Yes," she tells him, as she sets the basket down and makes her way to the refuse that gilds the sink, "I would like that."

And she washes the dishes, cleans the kitchen, tidies the living room, all the while humming some song that never quite reaches beyond his ears, although later it will haunt him.

Three days after that, his wife calls him from the hospital. He answers the phone, and he cradles it gently as she speaks. Her voice is shorn of strength; she sounds oddly defeated. Exhausted. She tells him that his daughter weighs seven pounds, and that she is healthy; that her eyes are blue and her face is red; that she cries too much.

The nurses take her away when she is finished feeding. It is important, they tell her, that she gets sleep. She does not sleep. She hates the hospital; it is sterile and unfriendly.

She wants to come home.

He wants her to come home.

He wants to see the child that he has only had a glimpse of through a glass wall.

* * *

The nurse is there when his wife arrives, and his wife is not pleased. But she is in pain, and the pain prevents her from being gracious. She holds the baby; he carries her bags, her things, the armor of her battle.

They have prepared a nursery for the baby; a room that is entirely made up of frills. Not pink and not blue—because they did not know what she would be— it is a work in progress. The baby's arrival hindered its completion, and it will be months yet before his wife takes up brush and paint and returns to the land of the living.

But the nurse often takes the babe.

And his wife is content, after a few days, to allow this. It buys her peace; it allows her time to pick up the pieces of her shattered life. No work, now, save the baby, and the baby is constant.

His own work becomes more difficult.

He envies his wife her time at home.

She envies him his space.

It makes them a poor couple, but they have little time for the arguments that would surely follow; the baby absorbs their time.

Even in memory he is careful; he does not speak either the name of the wife who left him, or the name of the daughter who was taken.

But he was not so careful, then, not to name the child in the presence of the nurse. He should have been. He should never have let this stranger with her exotic, pale beauty and her cold need into his house.

The babe is happy with her; his wife is resigned. He himself is moved in other directions, and they are uncomfortable ones.

When he tells him colleagues of his discomfort, they

laugh; they are men, after all, and they point out that he is as well. They ask him whether or not he's had sex with his wife since she returned.

He is too ashamed to admit that he hasn't.

But they know, and only later does he realize they know because of their own experiences. They don't judge him.

It is dark, in the faerie house.

There are no windows and no walls that he can see, but something must exist that lets in light; moonlight is streaming across the worn boards of the exposed floor. For just a moment, as he chooses his weary, careful steps, he can see that a forest stood here; its stumps are all that remain, cut and polished, smooth and flat. Loggers do less damage than was done here, and he does not know why—but he knows this: the wilderness has been confined.

He does not leave the path, not now. But he remembers when he did, and it is that regret that drives him.

By moonlight.

Cold and silver, pale and perfect, she came to him; his wife was in the guest room, with their daughter. He needed his sleep, she had said, gathering the child, weary with effort. How old was the babe?

He shakes his head; it takes effort, here.

He was not thinking of the child when the woman reached his bedside.

She did not join him there, but instead, beckoned; he rose, as if her hands were entwined, already, with his. Half-dressed, half-asleep, he followed. He can't remember how he made his way to the yard, but he remembers that she stopped beneath the drooping switches of weeping willow, veiled by the fall of yellow leaves.

He heard the music, then. He hears it now. It is the same; unchanged, unchanging, it scores his movements, underscores the oddity of his desire.

She was *so* perfect.

Did he touch her? His hands dance a moment in the air, a complicated weave, a stuttering compulsion. Memory is in the gestures. Yes, he thinks. He must have. But in the tame stretch of fenceless yard, he knows one thing: he danced.

And when the dance was over, the night had passed as well, as had the season; it was bitterly cold, and the grass was frosted white, as if with age. He stumbled to his feet, his skin blue and bruised; felt the edge of his hair across his shoulders, gnarled with the small branches and fallen leaves of the tree. He made his way to his house, and found that it was locked; that he had no key. He hovered a moment at the window's ledge, seeking some hint of what lay beneath curtains that seemed strangely colored, and the morning passed as he hunkered there, in the lee of great, square shadow.

But when he knocked on the door, he knew his first fear, his real fear: he did not recognize the woman who answered. Nor, it seems, did she recognize him, although she did not scream or run; her lips opened in a wordless expression that lay somewhere between pity and horror, and she opened the door a crack to let him in.

For one night's folly, he paid a price.

He had no job, and, it seemed, no house; he had no car, and no other information that would lead him to the two things he most valued: his wife. His child. He found his way to the police station, and after an-

swering their questions, was taken to the hospital—
the same hospital where his wife had been hidden
away for a week while a child left her body.

But in those halls, medicinal and cold, he found no
wife or child; nor did he find the strange nurse who
had haunted his last clear memory.

He thinks, as he walks, that he will find her now.
In the distance, he hears the strains of a familiar song,
and he stops. The sense of old forest has grown, and
with it, darkness, an echo of twilight. The wind across
his upturned face is cool, and it carries no scent of
city. Men do not come here, and if they do, they do
not build.

He is tired. In his youth, he might have walked this
stretch of hall forever, but his knees feel the weight
of his careful, taut steps, and his lips are cracked and
parched. The burble of a stream sounds to his right,
and to his left, he hears the thunder of a waterfall. The
thirst strengthens; hunger arrives to keep it company.
Against other hungers, these should count as trivial—
but they are never trivial. Without water, a man dies;
without food, a man dies.

And without a wife and child, he can live out the
whole of his natural life. It is both unfair and true,
and he has long since given up railing against truth;
had he not, he would not be here.

He takes, from his pocket, a single seed, and pivot-
ing carefully on the flats of his feet, he sets it to one
side of the wooden slat. It tumbles, rolls awkwardly,
and comes to a tilted stop.

When it takes root and begins to grow, he knows
that he has found the forest heart; that it, like so much
else, is hidden behind something that has become
more than façade, but remains less than real.

He watches as the slender tree becomes thicker, green gaining a coat of brown, and brown becoming cracked and textured, the color of maple bark. Sugar maple; he wounds it as it grows, and takes from its weeping cut what he needs. But he does not lift his feet; he only pivots. They are his anchor, here.

He walks until he reaches the end of the slat, and then he stops. Before him, just as behind, other slats stretch out, their surfaces worn with time, their nails dull or hidden beneath what must be stain.

He smiles.

"I have come to the court of the Queen," he says, his voice weaker than he would like. "I bear a gift and ask a boon."

The slats fall away, like scales; they are peeled back by the force of a wind that would dislodge him as well if he but moved. He waits, toes on the edge of the plank that he has chosen to follow, and as he does, as the slats are pulled up, grass and something softer spring up before his feet. On all sides, wood gives way to greenery; there are flowers that are shrouded in both mist and light, and the scent of their blossoms is thick and cloying. It is night, here.

It is always night.

The music is stronger now; his heart keeps time with its incessant beat. But he thinks that it is slower than it was when he first heard it, and he is both grateful for that, and chagrined. Has it been so long?

He stands on a single slat of wood. He waits.

Through the grass, like beautiful, curious children— but tall and slender with the grace of unselfconscious adolescence—come the Queen's courtiers.

Their eyes are wider than his could ever be, their cheekbones higher, their skin so perfect it might be soft as fur if he could but touch it. He lifts a hand,

and finds that in the doing he has dropped a second seed. He does not scramble to catch it or pick it up; it has happened, and he leaves it where it has fallen.

It too gains height, old oak. White oak, acorns beginning their buds upon the branches that are now well above his upturned face. But the trunk does not dislodge him, does not sunder the slender strip upon which he stands; instead it shores him up. He places a palm against it, and it takes some of his weight.

One of the young Sidhe frowns. Her breasts are a swell beneath diaphanous cloth; it's a wonder she wears anything at all. She turns to the girl—boy?—beside her and says, "But he's *old*."

And he is.

What the mirror did not tell him is nonetheless true.

"I have traded knowledge for time," he tells her quietly, and with some pride. "What I know now, I could not have begun to understand in my youth."

She doesn't sneer; a sneer would be unlovely. But her expression is cool and distant. She says, "The dance will kill you."

And he replies, "I have not come for the dance."

"You have no choice; you are part of the circle."

"The circle," he replies, "is broken by the path I have walked. I have not left it; you have no purchase here." He pauses, and then says, with a sharp anger, "And I have already danced your dance once; I have paid that price."

"That was—"

"Enough, Nivrene. Enough."

She comes at last.

He would recognize her anywhere. Gone is the uniform of hospital nurse, the deceit of angel of mercy; yet her skin is still luminescent, and her eyes, pale and silver, seem to see—and understand—the whole of the human condition. She is not seated; if she has a throne, it is hidden by the darkening shadows. Just as well; he has the urge to walk forward and place his head in her lap, the desire to feel those smooth and perfect fingers gently run through his hair, close his eyes.

They would never open.

Her smile is the smile of winter. Gone is the sympathy that she once offered in a suburbia that has changed shape and context; it was the vulture's mask, but he did not see it clearly, not then. He saw what he sees now: the perfection of her beauty.

He could catalog it all. Memory has failed him, veiling the truth of their first encounters. But memory has failed him in other ways, and he wills himself to be silent. If he is not young, he will *not* be prey to the traps she can set just by appearance alone.

"Why have you come?" she asks him, although she must know.

"I have come," he says quietly, "for my child."

She turns to the woman who first spoke. "You see?" she says, her voice musical. "It is as I said."

Nivrene of the pale hair is chastened, and it angers her, but the anger does not displace the delicate turn of her features. He sees it only in her eyes. Feral child, he thinks; they are all feral children. If the Queen were not strong, they would turn on her in an instant.

And if he were stronger, so would he. The anger that comes with memory is stronger than it has been for decades; knowledge does not temper it.

She says, "This is not a quest that men undertake. Ask for something else, mortal. There is much that my court can offer to one who has crossed the boundaries."

He says, again, "I want only my child."

She gestures. A mirror appears by her side, as if it

were a constant companion. "Look at it," she tells him. It is not a request, and against his will, he does as she bids.

And sees himself as he was, as he must have been, on that single night of folly so long ago; he is slender, unbowed by time, his neck unbent, his shoulders straight, his hair dark in the nighttime sky. No lines touch his lips or his eyes, no lines ring his neck, his hands are firm and strong as they lay by his side.

"Step off the path," she tells him, "and this will be yours."

"And the world, Lady?"

"You are in our world."

"Ah, no. I am still upon mine, for I chose this path, and I have not left it."

Her frown is a strange reward.

She lifts her hand, but before she can gesture, he lifts his, mirroring her. Aware, as he does, that this hand is lined and punctuated by the same liver spots, the same paleness, that marked the old woman in the salon.

"Do not offer me gold or jewels," he tells her quietly. "They are not a currency that has much value in this time and place, and even if they were, they are not what I desire."

She says, again, "This is a woman's quest. You bore no child. You cannot create life."

"That was never true," he replies.

"You were not there to see its beginning," she answers. "I was."

It is his greatest regret; the thing he most envies the young in this day. *I did what was expected of me,* he almost says. *I did what everyone did.*

But it is not an answer; it is barely an excuse. "She

did not want me there," he says. They are the weakest
words he has spoken.

"But she did," the Queen replies, with a smile that
would freeze boiling water. "She called out for you."

"I didn't know."

"No. You were not there. I was," she says it again.
"And I offered her comfort. I eased the passage."

"The child is not yours."

"How so? What did you offer?"

Money. The gold appears by her feet, and among
its scattered coins, the blood red of rubies, the cool
blue of sapphires, the warm, verdant green of emer-
alds. No diamonds, he thinks.

"I fed her. And I clothed her."

"So, too, did I. And I have done so for many, many
years, while you have wandered."

"If not for you—"

"Did I not give you what you desired?"

There is no way to lie, not here. "Yes."

"And in turn, you gave me what I desired."

"Then keep me," he says quietly. "But let my
child go."

"Your child?"

"My daughter."

"She is not yours; have I not proved this yet?"

"You did not give her what I was given."

"She has danced, little man."

"She has danced," he replies, bitter now. "But she
had no choice."

"She has one now. Will you face her, you who deserted her, and ask her what she will do?"

"Yes."

"And if she wishes to remain in my keeping, will
you abandon this quest?"

He is silent.

She laughs, and it is unkind. "You, too, would deprive her of choice."

"She was an infant—"

"She is not an infant now."

He knew this. Knew it, but refused to acknowledge it. The one thing he could not face.

"Yes," he hears himself say.

It is not the answer she expected. "I would not have come at all," she tells him, "if it were not for the unexpected nature of your questing. What have you to offer me in exchange for that which you seek to take?"

"Your children," he replies. He lifts a furled palm, a fist, fingers turned toward air and the invisible bower of unnamed leaves. "This is the life you grant."

"Come, have you not made something of value, something unique?"

"Only one thing, Lady, and it is in your keeping."

She gestures.

The mirror vanishes, and as it does, like a lifting veil, he sees the child.

The same child who stood in shadow and sunlight upon the open street, the children of the neighborhood running to either side of her as if she did not exist.

Her eyes are silver; they are not his eyes, not the eyes of the wife he barely remembers. But unlike the Queen and her coterie, there is much that is human in her expression; she is angry. She is quivering with anger.

He almost loses the game, then—for this is a game, it is always a game—because he almost steps off the path. It is the branches of oak that catch him, twining in his clothing, the back of his ancient threadbare tweeds. He braces himself against those branches, their unexpected weight; he scraps the skin off his calloused hands, and the blood there is both offered and accepted. The tree drinks.

"You left Mommy." The accusation is not the one he expected. "You left Mommy for *her*."

She carries the stick and the stone, but he sees them now as sword and shield; a trick of light, an echo of fear.

He does not name her. He does not speak for some time. Time, after all, passes slowly here, and he can take advantage of it, gathering his words with care. They are scattered. They have always been scattered.

"It was one night," he tells her. He kneels, so that he might be at her height, or so he tells himself. He is the penitent here, and he hates the whine in the words, but he cannot expunge them.

"It was more than one night."

"Not to me."

Her eyes are now blue, he thinks. They have lost the cold of silver. Blue has never been an angry color before. "If it was only *one night,* why did you do it?"

He shakes his head. "Look at her," he tells his daughter. "She says that you want to stay with her forever. Why?"

"Because she stayed *with me*."

It is not the answer he expected. Those child's eyes see nothing that his adult eyes see. "Do you not find her beautiful?"

"Her?" Her brows lift. The Queen is silent, and the playful banter of the Court itself has stopped entirely; they are transfixed, as he is, but for a different reason.

She defines beauty. She is ageless. She speaks his daughter's name as if she owns it, and his daughter looks up at her. At last she shrugs. "She's beautiful," she says, as if she were speaking of toys, of things that are common.

"Mommy was hurt."

The Queen speaks sharply, but he cannot hear what she says.

"What?"

"She was hurt. By you. She was hurt. She cried."

And the Queen speaks the name he has forgotten. She could order him off the road by the sheer force of those syllables, but she does not yet choose to do so. He sees the vast and cold amusement of her expression, and he knows that this is her game, this is her final move.

"I stayed," she tells him, laughing. "When you left, I stayed. I watched while your daughter learned to walk. I listened while she learned to talk. I helped her to understand her mother's silences, her mother's tears, her mother's helplessness.

"In all of this, you have never once spoken of your wife."

"No," he says quietly. "Never once."

"And why is that? The child was hers."

"The child was ours."

"But she was there, while you worked. She was there, while you slept. She was there, while you dallied in the willow grove."

He says, "I loved her."

"Did you? So much, then, for mortal love."

But the child steps forward, steps past the Queen, her movements so quick and so lithe the Queen bends to grab her.

And misses.

He has heard of children who come to greet their absent fathers for the first time. They are awkward with the desire to please; they are insecure and frightened, brightening that fear with a genuine happiness and uncertainty.

They are not his child. She is wild with sudden anger. She is not young. Her feet in the grass, she reaches out with her stick and her stone, and she strikes him. "*I hate you*!"

He cries out in pain, and he falls, but his training holds: his feet are planted, as if they were roots, and he does not—quite—lose his way, although the pain is more intense than he could have imagined.

She hits him again. "We waited for you!"

And again.

Each blow breaks something; that is the meaning of what she carries, and it is something that only she can do.

Were he young again, he would quail beneath the rain of her blows; he would writhe with the certain sense that they are deserved, that they are the real truth he has come all this way to face.

But he is not young, and he will never be young again. He catches her hands in his wrists, and he pulls her forward, lifting her from the grass, from the land of the Faerie Queen. When her feet clear the earth, the blows come faster and they are furious, but their fury is muted.

She is crying with rage.

He weathers her storm, knowing that it will both pass and come again. When it has passed for the first time, he carries her. She is heavier than he could have imagined; she bears the weight of decades, although they have not touched her.

This is what he came for.

Just this.

He says, although he knows it invites her anger, "I'm sorry." And he whispers a name in her ear, a baby name, a child's name.

She says, "You're old. You're too old to be my daddy." But the wildness has been depleted; the cruelty that remains he accepts.

"I'm not the same man," he tells her quietly. "I made a mistake. I will never, ever make that mistake again. Come home with me."

"I won't!"

But he says to her, "Let's go find your mother."

And she stills. "She's not here," she says, her voice suddenly cagey, her expression crafty.

"No," he says quietly, knowing. "But if I found you, I can find her. Let's go home."

The Queen comes to the edge of his plank, her hands lifted.

"I cannot bear life," he tells her. "But no more can you."

Her eyes widen.

He whispers a few words to his daughter; he is afraid she will not listen, and if she listens, will not obey.

But her arms tighten around his neck, squeezing out breath. He fumbles with her weight and the weight of the seeds he has carried, and he manages to hold them both for just long enough.

He casts the seeds at his feet, throwing them in a wide circle. "The price of my passage," he shouts, turning, the thunderous sound of trees straining for their full height and growth at his back.

He runs.

She wraps her legs around him, shouting in his ear; the words pierce him and pass, like wind, as he leaves them behind. He has lost her once. He will not do so again.

The plank that was his passage stretches out; the rest of the floor is gone. The wood, thin and old, bears the whole of his weight, and he is careful to touch nothing else with his feet—but it is hard. If he trusted her enough, he would put her down.

If he trusted himself enough.

But he is wise enough to know his own limitations; wise enough to accept them, even burdened as they are with her scorn. He thinks about love, and what love means, and he wonders if he has ever loved his child; if love is absence, if love is questing, if love is never letting go, he can profess to love her.

But if it is more, it is something he must learn—as he learned the way here—in the fullness of the scant time that remains.

You could have stayed, he tells himself, and the Queen's face shoves aside the veil of years, the weight of wisdom. *You could have stayed. Your daughter was here.*

But what could he give her here?

Nothing.

The doors of the salon rear up before him, thick and perfect, gleaming as if they were new. To either side of those doors, he sees wall, and he realizes that he has come as far as he can on his own. Beyond the plank, to left and right, he sees green, dark and placid, flat as a painting.

"They won't open," the child says, her cheek against his, water between their skin. She is looking over his back.

"They will," he tells her quietly.

"They won't. You don't know their name."

"But I do," he replies. "Give me the stick, Kaylee." She shakes her head.

He asks her again, and she shakes her head more

fiercely. She says, with a bitterness that her age can't disguise, "They're all I have."

It cuts him.

But it does not bind him. He holds her, and lifting one foot—one, with precarious balance—he kicks the doors.

They absorb the force of the blow.

"She's coming," his child whispers. "The Queen is coming."

"I know." He leans against the doors now, and pressing his lips against the crack between them, he whispers a second name, he who has none.

The doors slide open and he falls through, bending his knees and all but snapping his back in his attempt not to flatten the child he carries; he will *not* drop her.

The old woman is waiting; he sees first the black of her mourning robes. Placing one hand against the floor, he lifts himself; the room is long, but the sunlight gilds it. Dust that was not there when he walked its length the first time now shows the passage of his steps.

She is not lovely, this woman. She is not young.

"Why?" He asks her, realizing that not all of the tears are his daughter's. "Why did you not dwell within?"

And she reaches out and gently touches her daughter's face. "Because," she says, her voice old and cracked, lower than he could possibly remember, "I would have forgotten. Everything."

"What good was there to remember?"

"I remember," she tells him, as his daughter's arms grow slack. "The first time we met. I remember when we bought our house. I remember when you asked my father if you could marry me."

"You remember what I did."

Her eyes are cold for a moment, but even so, she does not turn away. "I remember that as well. That is the price of memory: good and bad."

"You would have stayed—"

"Young?"

He hangs his head.

"While I was here," she tells him, looking now toward the curtained windows, "she could leave for a time. She could play in the streets. She could almost be part of the world."

She straightens shoulders that will never be straight, and she pushes him gently aside. In the frame of those doors, the Faerie Queen now stands, her expression completely unreadable. She is, he thinks, a statue; one can touch her, can marvel at the unknown hand that created her, but one can never change her.

"So," she says softly.

The woman says little.

"I sheltered you, when he was gone. Will you now turn your back upon all that I have offered?"

"I would not have left if not for you!" he cries. It is a young man's cry. It is not worthy of him. If he could pull the words back, he would.

But his wife places a hand upon his shoulder and shakes her head.

"I have waited all this time," she tells the Queen, "as I promised. I am not the woman I was when I came to you—and he cannot be the man that he was, or he would never have returned with our child."

"Will you forgive him, then?"

"I don't know. I will try. I have made . . . the same mistake."

"He cannot leave this place without—"

"His name, yes." The old woman's smile lends texture, not color, to her expression. Turning, she touches her daughter's shoulder. His daughter's shoulder. "Kaylee," she says quietly, "can we go home?"

And the child hesitates for a profound moment before she opens her arms and jumps into her mother's. She does not relinquish the stick or the stone; they will be with her for some time yet, and it will be hard for him to find ways around them.

But to be given the chance to try . . .

His wife smiles, and if the smile is bitter, there is more than bitterness in it. She speaks a single word, and the Faerie Queen cries out in rage.

Or what should be rage: it is sorrow he hears, profound and endless.

Kaylee says quietly, "Yes, the Queen is beautiful, but she's not as beautiful as Mommy."

The wisdom, he thinks, of babes. He cannot see his wife as their daughter sees her. But he wonders what his daughter sees of him when she looks.

The doors slide shut upon the Faerie Queen's still form, and the room shrinks and dwindles until at last it is the too-small Victorian room that it at first appeared to be. The dream has passed; he will not find his way here again, and he will never try.

He turns at the sound of his name.

"There are other things," his wife says, almost pertly, "that I needed to remember. You would lose your car keys, your ties, one sock out of each pair. You'd forget your name if people weren't constantly shouting it at you."

He takes her hand. It is old; it has not changed. He wonders if it will change when they leave this place, or if it will remain as aged, as brittle, as his own.

It doesn't matter.

Age dims pain; memory cannot hold the whole of it. His wife sets their child down between them, and he offers the girl his hand. She stares at it, and then retreats into her mother's skirts, but she does not scream or shout, and this is a start.

Together, they make their way into the world, stained by their past, but no longer trapped in it.

Tad Williams

THE WAR OF THE FLOWERS

"A masterpiece of fairytale worldbuilding."
—*Locus*

"Williams's imagination is boundless."
—*Publishers Weekly*
(Starred Review)

"A great introduction to an accomplished
and ambitious fantasist."
—*San Francisco Chronicle*

"An addictive world ... masterfully plays
with the tropes and traditions of
generations of fantasy writers."
—*Salon*

"A very elaborate and fully realized setting
for adventure, intrigue, and more
than an occasional chill."
—*Science Fiction Chronicle*

0-7564-0181-X

To Order Call: 1-800-788-6262

DAW 45

MICHELLE WEST

The *Sun Sword* Novels

"Intriguing"—*Locus*
"Compelling"—*Romantic Times*

Kristen Britain

GREEN RIDER

As Karigan G'ladheon, on the run from school,
makes her way through the deep forest, a gallop-
ing horse plunges out of the brush, its rider
impaled by two black arrows. With his dying
breath, he tells her he is a Green Rider, one of the
king's special messengers. Giving her his green
coat with its symbolic brooch of office, he makes
Karigan swear to deliver the message he was carrying. Pursued by unknown assassins, following
a path only the horse seems to know, Karigan
finds herself thrust into in a world of danger and
complex magic....   0-88677-858-1

FIRST RIDER'S CALL

With evil forces once again at large in the kingdom and with the messenger service depleted
and weakened, can Karigan reach through the
walls of time to get help from the First Rider, a
woman dead for a millennium?   0-7564-0209-3

To Order Call: 1-800-788-6262